DEATH OF A BRIDE AND GROOM

A HONEYMOON FALLS MYSTERY

DEATH OF A BRIDE AND GROOM

ALLAN J. EMERSON

FIVE STAR

A part of Gale, Cengage Learning

GALE
CENGAGE Learning·

Farmington Hills, Mich • San Francisco • New York • Waterville, Maine
Meriden, Conn • Mason, Ohio • Chicago

GALE
CENGAGE Learning®

LIBRARY OF CONGRESS CATALOGING-IN-PUBLICATION DATA

Emerson, Allan J.
    Death of a bride and groom / Allan J. Emerson. — First edition.
        Pages ; cm
    ISBN 978-1-4328-3069-4 (hardcover) — ISBN 1-4328-3069-4 (hardcover) — ISBN 978-1-4328-3060-1 (ebook) — ISBN 1-4328-3060-0 (ebook)
        1. Women authors—Violence against—Fiction. 2. Police—Fiction. 3. Murder—Investigation—Fiction. I. Title.
    PR9199.4.E4676D43 2015
    813'.6—dc23   2014047844

First Edition. First Printing: May 2015
Find us on Facebook– https://www.facebook.com/FiveStarCengage
Visit our website– http://www.gale.cengage.com/fivestar/
Contact Five Star™ Publishing at FiveStar@cengage.com

Printed in the United States of America
1 2 3 4 5 6 7 19 18 17 16 15

For Diane

CHAPTER 1

Honeymoon Falls Police Chief William Halsey piloted the squad car under the painted plywood wedding bells that hung in an arch over Honeymoon Drive, turned right at the Bridal Suite Hotel onto Lovers' Lane (a major thoroughfare, in spite of the name), and began crossing the "wedding" streets—Wedding Veil, Wedding Day, Wedding Guest. After two years of exposure to them, the oddness of the names no longer registered.

Today was Parade Day—the official kickoff of the Honeymoon Falls wedding theme events. After the parade, there'd be the husband-calling contest, dancing in the park, and the bride and groom pedal-boat races, but at 7:00 A.M. the tranquility of the early June morning was undisturbed.

Halsey crested the slight rise that signaled the approach to the station and the long, brilliant blue lake that curved around the town came into view. Beyond it, the silent old-growth forest rose a thousand feet up mountains whose stony peaks were the source of the plummeting torrent that had given the town its new name.

Honeymoon Falls, for all its ridiculous wedding theme nonsense, was spectacularly beautiful, a haven from the city in which his own marriage had disintegrated. After Vivien left him for The Actor (The Actor had a name, but Halsey refused to remember it), he'd found himself in an empty apartment, drunker than he could ever recall being in his thirty-six years, pressing his service revolver against his temple hard enough to

7

Allan J. Emerson

leave welts from the muzzle. After the hangover ended, he'd refused a senior police position in Vancouver, and to the astonishment of his friends, returned to the backwater where he'd spent his youth.

It was a quiet life for most of the year: the odd drunk and disorderly logger still clinging to the vestigial remains of the forest industry, a few break-ins during the school holidays by liquor-seeking teenagers, the occasional shoplifter. Things picked up during the summer, when the town vibrated with busloads of newlyweds who patrolled the streets hand-in-hand, and were occasionally sighted by binocular-wielding hikers linked more intimately in secluded forest areas.

Halsey turned in at the station, gulping coffee to wash down the last of the doughnut holes he'd bought fresh this morning. He checked the front seat carefully for crumbs, scrunched the bag into the empty cup, and capped it. After a quick glance around, he flipped the cup into the trash can before he entered the station. The last thing his staff needed to see was their boss doing the cliché doughnut-eating cop routine.

"She's done it again," Officer John Larsen informed him as he entered, instantly putting his good mood to flight.

She was Officer Lydia Bailey, and fifty percent of the Honeymoon Falls police department loathed her. Unfortunately, the other fifty percent of the department loathed Officer Larsen: the two of them were Halsey's total staff.

"Done *what*?" Halsey'd told them both only last week that he was fed up with their childish feuds, but the lecture appeared to be having little effect.

"Arrested a cake, that's what." Larsen smothered a snicker as the expression on Halsey's face registered.

Larsen was twenty-five, but looked younger in spite of the neatly trimmed mustache he'd grown to offset his boyish wheat-colored crew cut. Halsey, a dozen years older, remembered the childhood mass of untamed blond ringlets crammed under a cap Larsen never took off, except in church, where his locks drew motherly murmurs of admiration.

"This damn well better be good," Halsey said.

"See for yourself," Larsen said, waving a hand toward the partition that divided the station's office and single cell from the front counter. "I told you she's nuts."

At the beginning of the narrow hall leading to the rear of the building, Halsey could hear Officer Bailey thumping the computer keyboard in the office. She was not a clumsy woman, but at her most delicate she seemed to be smacking the objects she touched, as if warning them she knew what they were supposed to be like, and they'd better not try being anything else. People had complained to Halsey that she was rude, overbearing, officious, and dim-witted.

"Oh, I wouldn't say she's dim-witted," he would demur.

Halsey knew from personal experience that, on occasion, she could be all of the others. Officer Bailey was forty, a bluff, strong-voiced woman with a seventeen-year-old daughter sired by a long-since vanished ex-husband. Maybe it was dealing with the daughter that explained her tendency to treat civilians as if they were teenagers who'd left the kitchen in a mess *again*.

Halsey glanced into the cell, swore, and went around the corner to the office. Bailey was concentrating fiercely on the computer monitor. Halsey looked at the heading that flashed at the top of the screen: *Outstanding Warrants*. He took a deep breath.

"Do you really expect to find any outstanding warrants for the Delbrook sisters?" he inquired, keeping his voice even.

"You can't enter a case file without running a check," she said.

"A case file? Why are you opening a case file? What did they do?"

"They put two semis in the ditch along the freeway. One of the drivers is threatening to sue. They ignored the siren when I turned it on, and they rear-ended the cruiser while I was bringing them in."

Halsey felt a familiar irritation stirring in his gut. He didn't doubt the accuracy of the details she related, but instinct told him that any mitigating context was being deliberately omitted. She was going to see that punishment was meted out come hell or high water.

He looked down at the springy mass of black curls that cloaked her skull, the color and formation both her own work, he knew—she'd been a hairdresser before graduating from a criminology course in Vancouver. Like Larsen, she was only minimally trained in police work; the town had been unable to afford anyone other than Halsey with actual experience.

"Lydia, I'm going to go talk to them," Halsey told her.

"I'm still going to file the charges," she said.

"You can't file any charges without my approval," Halsey said. "You know that—we've been over this before." He braced himself for the anger this reminder always provoked, but this time it was determination rather than fury her eyes were signaling.

"As a Honeymoon Falls police officer, I need your permission. As a citizen, I can lay a complaint with the Meadowbrook RCMP detachment. The freeway's under their jurisdiction and they'll have no choice but to investigate the complaint. You decide which you prefer." She'd obviously rehearsed the speech; it had the quality of recital.

Halsey stared at her. "Are you telling me that you would deliberately undercut the authority of your own force?"

"I don't think I'm undercutting anyone. I think I'm seeing that justice is done."

"*Justice?* Lydia, you've been watching too many TV shows

about crooked cops again. You know damn well that's not what's going on here!"

Bailey turned back to her keyboard. "I'm just telling you I'm not going to lie down on this one."

Halsey turned on his heel and stalked out, fury heating him like a furnace. She would make a decent police officer if she were ever able to perceive the rest of the world as human beings instead of two distinct species—the righteous and the erring. Her threat to embarrass him by laying a complaint in another jurisdiction showed she had relegated him to the latter category.

The Delbrook sisters were sitting side by side on the flat spring cot suspended from the wall of the cell. Both women were in their sixties: Irene, the younger and more personable sister, had been a beauty; Cora, the older, was usually described as overbearing by those who wished to be kind, and as a battle-axe by those who didn't. Halsey took the only other seat in the cell: the toilet across from the bunk.

"Good morning ladies," he said.

Cora Delbrook's cold gray eyes skewered him in place.

"There will be repercussions for this," she promised. "Council will hold you personally responsible for that woman's behavior."

That was almost certainly true, Halsey thought. Especially with Cora whipping them up to a frenzy using her position as a council member.

Irene Delbrook rested her dark eyes on him. Her married name was actually Rasmussen, but since her husband's death ten years earlier, most people had reverted to calling her by her maiden name. Halsey had arrested her son, Gary, twice.

"Chief Halsey," she said, with remote politeness.

Halsey nodded. "Would you mind telling me what happened?"

Cora glared at him. "We've already explained everything to that idiotic woman. Hasn't she told you? What kind of police

11

station are you running here?"

"I'd like to hear it from you," Halsey said, trying not to clench his teeth.

"There's nothing to hear," Cora said, each word etched in acid. "We were bringing a parade float from the old mill into town for today's Honeymoon Daze parade, and we accidentally wound up on the freeway. When we tried to get off, some trucks drove in the ditch, and that woman arrested us."

The lidless toilet rim was cutting into Halsey's rump. He shifted as subtly as possible. "You were driving a parade float?"

"I just *told* you that," Cora said.

"The details might be helpful in resolving this situation," Halsey said, his eyes narrowing and an edge appearing in his voice. Cora's face hardened, but a touch on her arm from Irene seemed to remind her where she was.

Halsey considered standing up, but felt that towering over them would only provoke Cora further. He decided to stay put and hope the story wouldn't take much longer—the toilet flushed automatically every 10 minutes. Fortunately, Cora seemed to have grudgingly accepted the need for further explanation and was addressing Halsey as if he were some particularly dense committee member at a church bake sale.

"The float is a wedding cake, of course, in keeping with the theme of the parade. It is thirty-five feet long and twenty feet high, built over a flatbed truck that used to belong to the shingle mill. There is a narrow slit about four inches high and three feet long in front of the windshield." Cora's bony fingers fiddled with one of the four brooches that decorated her tweed lapels. She always wore the same collection, each piece a clump of purplish-brown stones that, to Halsey, resembled clots of dried blood.

"Very difficult to see out of," Irene lamented, shaking her head sadly.

Cora shot her an impatient look, rose, and began to stride back and forth in the cell. Halsey observed the vacant spot on the cot with interest, but stayed put.

"The float was built by high school students near the loading dock at the mill," Cora continued. "We picked it up there this morning, and were to drive it to the parade assembly area at the park."

"I was driving," Irene said instantly, with the air of one owning up to misbehavior. "Cora was just looking after the cats, Suzie and Mr. Peepers." Irene didn't go anywhere without the cats.

"We had planned to take the old mill road along the outskirts of town to the mall." She sighed. "But we couldn't see very well."

"We could barely see out of the blasted thing at all," Cora said. Both women had graying hair in similar short bobs, Halsey noticed, but they served the sisters differently: Irene's gave her the air of a faded belle; Cora's was a Wagnerian helmet that completed the tweed armor she wore.

"Somehow we got onto a connector road that led to the freeway," Irene continued.

"The freeway." Halsey suppressed a groan.

Irene faced him squarely. "I'm afraid so. We realized almost instantly that we were heading the wrong way—"

This time Halsey did groan.

Cora gave him an irritated glance. "We immediately tried to back up to where we'd entered, but no viewing slits had been created at the rear of the float, so that was impossible. There was nothing for it but to attempt a U-turn."

"A U-turn," Halsey echoed despairingly. "On the freeway."

"You try backing up a thirty-five-foot cake," Cora said. "What else could we do?"

Irene soldiered dutifully on. "We'd nearly completed the turn when a moving van shot out of nowhere behind us and blasted its air horn. It went right through me, that sound," Irene said, fluttering her hands in front of her face. She'd chewed off all her lipstick, reminding Halsey of the way some animals will gnaw their leg off to escape from a trap.

"It startled Irene," Cora confirmed, giving her sister a concerned look. "She veered into the other lane. The sudden movement frightened Mr. Peepers. He leapt out of my lap and into Irene's."

"That's when I lost control," Irene said. "Mr. Peepers sank his claws into my—um—chest."

Halsey forced himself not to look at the injured area. "And then?" he asked, wishing he didn't sound quite so much like a twelve-year-old listening to a ghost story around a campfire.

"And then the other semi appeared," Irene said. "So now there was one in each lane behind us."

"Both blasting that awful loud noise," Cora said. "Ignorant pigs. Acted like they owned the road. You'd think they'd never seen a parade float before. Doesn't every driver have a responsibility to be prepared for the unexpected?"

"I suppose," Halsey conceded. "But if they'd been on the road for ten or twelve hours, a U-turning wedding cake on the freeway must have seemed like a hallucination to them."

Irene rested her hands gingerly on the areas Mr. Peepers had despoiled. "Perhaps that's why they both drove in the ditch."

"Then we heard the siren," Cora said.

Halsey recognized the cue for the wicked witch's entrance. "Officer Bailey."

"Yes," Cora said. "The ridiculous woman wouldn't listen to a word we said."

"And those truck drivers used such foul language," Irene continued. "Officer Bailey ordered us to follow her, but she didn't seem to understand that we could only proceed very slowly. She kept stopping to wave us on to go faster."

"And of course, at one point we didn't realize she'd stopped, and we tapped the bumper of her car." Cora's eyes narrowed. "She lectured us while we were still on the freeway, and when I insisted we postpone the discussion until we were out of the danger area—"

"She said not to try that high-and-mighty attitude with her just because we're on the town council," Irene burst out indignantly. "We never *thought* of such a thing. We just wanted to get away from those awful men."

You might not have considered using the council connection, Halsey thought, *but I'll bet Cora made it clear.*

Halsey's brain was reeling under the onslaught of images the sisters' words provoked. "Well, look ladies, I'm sure this can be sorted out—we'll have to get some statements from you and the truck drivers, of course—I'll speak to Officer Bailey—"

As if the mention of her name had conjured her up, Bailey swung the door back on its hinges. Irene looked at Halsey imploringly; Cora and Bailey traded basilisk stares.

"Well, Officer," Halsey said, assuming the most commanding voice possible given his seating arrangement, "what charges are you prepared to lay?"

"Murder," Bailey said, as the toilet flushed with a Niagara-like roar.

CHAPTER 2

"Have you taken leave of your senses?" Irene inquired, the exquisite courtesy of her tone suggesting it was the only reasonable explanation, and by far the kindest one, that could explain such a bizarre accusation.

"Don't play the hoity-toity lady of the manor with me," Bailey warned.

Halsey wasn't sure if it was his imagination or not, but the air seemed full of the sound of steel ringing against steel. Cora was bloated with fury, her face almost the same shade of mauve as her suit.

"Officer!" he said. "Are you telling me that you've found outstanding murder warrants for these women?"

"Nnnoo," Bailey said, sliding the word out as though unsheathing a blade. Her eyes were shiny as a cat's with a mouse in its claws. "No, there's nothing in *Outstanding Warrants* for either of them."

"Of course there isn't!" Cora said. "Irene's right—you must be demented."

"Chief Halsey, you may wish to discuss this privately," Bailey said, with a peremptory tone that suggested that he would regret doing otherwise. Halsey, too, had had enough of the public display of animosity between himself and his staff.

"I'm sure this can be cleared up shortly," he assured the sisters as he followed Bailey out of the cell.

"Don't be *too* sure," Bailey cautioned. In the last glimpse

Halsey had of the sisters, they were sitting side by side on the cot again, their eyes projecting twin laser beams at Bailey's retreating spine.

"This better be good," Halsey warned when they were in the passageway outside the cell. "Those women are on the council, and they've lived here forever. If it comes to a showdown, and you're wrong, you'll be out of a job."

"Don't worry. I'm not expecting any support from you," Bailey said. "I know you're not going to do anything to risk your paycheck." She charged down the hall to the station's back door with Halsey in furious pursuit.

Her behavior was clearly insubordinate and insulting, but Halsey was astonished at the strength of his response—he was barely able to prevent himself from grabbing her and slamming her against the wall, something he would not even have contemplated with anyone else. She seemed able to awaken in him the instincts of a thug—he could feel the desire rising in him to punch her insulting words down her throat. Instead, his feelings erupted from his own.

"Officer Bailey!" he roared, in the command voice that had paralyzed recruits on the parade ground during his RCMP drill instructor days. *"Get back here!"*

The voice still worked, he was relieved to see. In fact, it appeared to have broken through the odd frenzy that was animating her. She froze in place and turned slowly to face him, although she did not move from where she stood.

Halsey closed the distance between them and stood looking down at her. "You will not ever speak to me like that again," he informed her with freezing finality. "I am your superior, and I will fire you if you do."

Her face reflected a series of emotions in rapid succession: fury, embarrassment, excitement, apology. And something else—panic? Even horror? Halsey was close enough to see that her

17

pupils were dilated, and the color in her face fluctuated unevenly. Her lips were trembling, and when she raised one broad hand against them, it was shaking. Halsey knew she took medication for an arthritic condition and wondered if she was feeling unexpected side effects from it—he'd never seen her like this before. Her manner was in astonishing contrast to the arrogance she'd been displaying only a moment before.

"I'm sorry," she whispered from behind her fingers. "I'm sorry, Will. I didn't mean to say those things."

Her use of his Christian name had a peculiar effect—it diluted his anger, where the apology would not have. Although he called both members of his staff by their first names, usually only Larsen reciprocated. Bailey had always seemed uncomfortable calling him anything other than Chief, and her resort to the more personal mode of address was a clear signal something was wrong. He thought perhaps she was in shock—he'd seen the expression she wore on the faces of accident victims.

"What is it, Lydia?" he asked.

"They're—*dead*," she said, the last word coming out in a whimper.

Halsey felt as if he'd been slammed in the midriff with a battering ram. There was something here that it was not going to be possible to put right. His mind raced after the plural pronoun she'd employed. *They?* To whom could she be referring? Certainly not the Delbrook sisters. The only other *they* involved, so far as he knew, were the two truck drivers, and at least one of them was certainly alive, since he was threatening a lawsuit. *They?* Had the Delbrooks run over people too?

"Dead? Who is dead?" Halsey asked finally.

Bailey's sturdy body was suddenly racked by shudders. "Oh, God—all I could think about was making the arrest—I didn't even care that someone had died. The first thought in my head was that I'd finally beaten everyone else—beaten them and

18

won, once and for all."

"Who is dead, Lydia?" Halsey asked, reaching out to steady her.

Bailey made a feeble gesture behind her at the door into the parking lot. Her mouth opened to speak, then she swayed toward him, and he caught her as her knees buckled.

CHAPTER 3

The small parking lot behind the police station was almost completely filled by the parade float. The giant wedding cake Cora Delbrook had described was made of graduated plywood layers painted white and festooned with flowers constructed from hubcaps and plant pots spray-painted pink. At the top edges of each layer, a thick plaster piping had been applied in pendant green loops. The smell of new lumber and fresh paint hung in the air.

To the right of the viewing slit in front of the bottom layer of the cake, there was a small door hanging ajar. Halsey leaned inside and saw the door led to the cab of the flatbed truck that served as the base for the float. The truck door on the driver's side was open as well; the two open doors apparently marked the Delbrook sisters' exit route when they'd arrived at the station.

Halsey felt his scalp prickling as he began to move around to the rear of the float. He felt there was something terribly obvious wrong, something he couldn't see because he was too close and the float was so large. He tried to back off far enough to take in the whole structure, but kept coming up against the station wall or the parking lot fence before he could achieve an overall view. Something white fluttered at the summit of the float, tossed teasingly over the edge of the top layer and then drawn quickly back.

There was another door at the rear of the float. A piece of

white plastic sheeting designed to hide it was drawn aside; Bailey must have searched the interior. Was this where she'd seen whatever it was she'd seen? Halsey had bellowed for Larsen when Bailey fainted, and the two of them lowered her to the floor. The young officer's face was a study in astonishment, and Halsey realized Larsen thought Bailey's unconsciousness was the culmination of the shouting match the two of them had been having.

"She fainted," Halsey said. "There's something wrong out back. Stay with her till she comes to." He'd sprinted for the back door, leaving Larsen kneeling behind Bailey, awkwardly supporting her against his chest while her head lolled back on his shoulder.

Halsey now pulled the door open and found himself looking at the rear wheels of the 5-ton truck, a few feet inside the structure. He stepped through the opening and immediately realized it was too dark inside to see anything clearly. He'd have to go back into the station to get a flashlight. As he turned to go, the breeze caught the plastic sheet and dropped it down over the place he'd entered. Just as the space around him was plunged into darkness, his peripheral vision caught the merest flicker of movement far back along the flatbed deck, near the cab.

He yanked the sheet aside and stepped out. He looked back inside the float as far as he could see, but the shadows remained still.

"Come out of there," Halsey demanded. Nothing moved. He debated going back into the station for a flashlight. If there was somebody in the float, leaving it unattended even briefly might allow an escape. On the other hand, he wasn't about to fumble around the innards of the structure without being able to see, especially if there was someone inside.

Halsey slipped his shoes off and ran silently back to the sta-

tion door. His feet sliding on the hallway linoleum, he leapt over
Bailey and Larsen, retrieved the powerful emergency lamp from
the wall rack in the office, and seconds later skidded past the
duo again.

Halsey ripped the plastic flap off the opening at the rear of
the float and shone the searchlight beam into the darkness. The
truck deck was bare except for a set of portable steps leading up
into the second layer of the cake. Halsey squatted and shone
the light under the vehicle. The beam penetrated to the far end
of the truck, under the cab. Nothing there either. Still, he had a
feeling. . . .

"Come out of there!" he demanded again. There was no
response.

Halsey swung himself up onto the truck deck. The bottom of
the layer overhead was only five feet above the deck, and Halsey
had to lean sideways to move forward to the steps. He swept the
space around him with the light as he continued his crab-like
progress, but saw nothing.

He paused at the steps and shone the light up into the hole
that led to the second layer. He could see nothing through the
opening but the bottom of the topmost layer. He realized that
for anyone hanging back out of sight above, he'd make a perfect
target as his head and shoulders passed through the opening.

"I know you're there," he said. "You'd better come out." Had
something shifted position overhead?

Halsey drew his gun and started up the steps. His shoulders
no sooner cleared the bottom of the hole than he was bunted
from behind and almost knocked off the steps. Halsey yelled,
his adrenaline pumping furiously, and swung the heavy
searchlight in an arc toward the source of the blow. There was a
frantic scrabbling in the darkness, and Halsey tracked the sound,
gun and light swinging through the darkness in tandem. There
was no one behind him. He jerked through a 360-degree turn

on his precarious perch, the top of his head aching with the expectation of a skull-crushing blow. He could hear nothing except his own hoarse breathing.

Halsey climbed another two steps up. The space around the hole was empty.

"I'm going to put a bullet in you if you don't come out," he warned.

Halsey swung the light around him, gun at the ready. In a dark corner, he sensed rather than saw a presence. He turned the light on it and let his breath escape in a gusty sigh.

"Mr. Peepers, I presume," he said. The cat stayed in its corner, yellow eyes gleaming in the light, tail lashing. After having its affectionate overture so brutally rebuffed, it was taking no chances.

"Where's the other one—waiting to jump on me too, I suppose?" Halsey muttered.

He waited for his heart rate to slow, and then climbed the rest of the way into the second layer. The ceiling here was slightly higher than Halsey's six-two, and he was able to stand upright. He swung the searchlight toward the back of the float, and there, pinned in the beam, was the back of a woman's blonde head. He inhaled abruptly, and let the light travel along the rest of her body, which lay in an oddly humped, unnatural position under a long white gown. There appeared to be a man's arm flung over her from the far side, as though the two were lying in an embrace. Both had the stillness of inanimate objects.

And that was because they were, Halsey discovered, after cautiously navigating the remaining distance between him and them, gun at the ready. He reached out with his toe, flipped the blonde over, and looked into her painted plastic face. Her partner's bare arm clattered to the floor, and his body rocked face down against the floor, drumming hollowly against the plywood.

23

Halsey laughed helplessly, feeling as if he'd blundered into a carnival fun house where skeletons jumped out from dark corners. Bailey must have come up here with that little firefly flashlight she carried, seen the outlines of the mannequins in the distance, and thought she'd discovered the Delbrooks' crazed slaughter of two innocent people. "What am I going to do with that woman?" he asked the cat, which only narrowed its eyes in response.

But something about the mannequins puzzled him. Obviously they were intended to represent the bride and groom on the top of the wedding cake. Presumably they were stored inside the float until the parade was about to begin, when they would be mounted on top. It took Halsey a moment to realize what was odd about the figures. What he'd at first taken as the bride's gown was actually a petticoat, and the groom's formal trousers and shirt were unaccompanied by a jacket. Were the costumes to be completed at the parade assembly site?

Halsey remembered the flutter of white he'd seen atop the float before he entered. Were the rest of the costumes still up there? If the mannequins had been up top fully dressed in the first place, why would anyone have brought them down here wearing only part of the costume?

Halsey swept the light over the bottom of the layer above. There appeared to be no access to the upper layer. How did they get the figures up on top of it? From the outside with a ladder? He walked toward the front of the float, pressing experimentally against the ceiling in a few spots, but it didn't give.

The cat provided the answer. It had been watching Halsey uneasily as he moved around the area, backing farther away as he approached. When Halsey was within a dozen feet, the cat spat viciously, twisted backward, and vanished in a flash of light.

24

Halsey blinked as the sun poured through the side of the structure. With its Houdini-esque disappearance, the cat had knocked down a loosely draped sheet of canvas covering an opening to the outside of the structure. Halsey kicked the canvas aside and stepped through the opening onto the top of the first layer.

To the right of the opening he'd come through was a rose trellis laden with more hubcap flowers. A closer look revealed the trellis was actually a ladder attached to the side of the float, leading to the top of the second layer. A similar trellis gave access to the float's pinnacle. He was unable to back off far enough to see more than the edge of the top layer, but the white material he'd noticed from the ground continued to swirl out in the breeze.

Bailey's small flashlight was lying at the bottom of the trellis. Halsey set the emergency lamp down and began to climb. As his head cleared the edge of the top layer, the breeze flung the white material into his face. He batted the stuff back, realizing it was the hem of a wedding gown, heavily embroidered and extravagantly strewn with large plastic beads intended to simulate pearls. His heart began to thump heavily, in a way he could not attribute solely to the climb. He climbed another couple of steps, and froze.

The bride atop the float stared sightlessly out over the street behind him, her head resting against the back of the elaborate throne on which she was seated. Her crown of plastic orange blossoms had slipped askew, and the panel of gauzy material descending from it floated in the breeze in front of her, alternately veiling and revealing her face. Her brown hair fluttered against her lips, which were slightly parted as though interrupted in the middle of a word, a word she'd been confident would have resulted in a far different outcome. The cat Halsey had frightened was curled up in her lap, thin yellow crescents showing through its slitted lids.

Halsey heard a roaring sound in his head, and had to shut his eyes to block out the sight for a moment. When he opened them, Iris Morland was still sitting there, palms flat on the arms of her throne, wedding ring glinting in the morning sun.

With a conscious effort, Halsey turned his head to look at her groom. He was slumped forward, leaning away from Halsey. The formal jacket gaped open, and his shirt was stained a dark red. Even with the face averted, Halsey recognized the man. Iris Morland and her lover, Halsey thought. Their killer, not content with ending their lives, had put them on display for the whole town to see.

CHAPTER 4

Cecil Atkinson was afraid, a feeling not common with him, but he kept his confident expression in place as he wrapped up his presentation to the Honeymoon Falls town council. There were only five of them present: the Delbrook sisters hadn't shown up, but their presence or absence didn't make a difference either way.

"The creation of the Honeymoon Falls campus of Pacific Western College will give the town an academic institution you'll be proud of. You have before you the architect's drawings, and of course, the letter of accreditation from the government recognizing the college as a duly constituted body with authority to conduct degree-granting programs."

Atkinson took a sip of water to combat the dryness that kept invading his mouth. If they scented the truth, he was finished. He had an irrational sense of looking down at them while they besieged his stronghold, searching for the way in, the way to topple him. Atkinson drew a deep breath and gave them his most presidential smile. It was time to start offering the carrots.

"Of course, the impact on Honeymoon Falls, both as an academic and commercial center, will be significant. In addition to the hundreds of jobs created during the construction phase, we can expect up to five hundred new students from outside the community in the first year, and the number will likely double in succeeding years. This will create a sharp increase in demand for products and services from local businesses, and the college itself will be a handsome tax base for the town."

Edna Sigurdson was leaning forward eagerly—the old harpy could smell money a mile off. Art Selby looked sullen as always, but there wasn't going to be any opposition from him; his resort would make a killing as student accommodation during the tourist off-season. And both Art and Edna had good reasons for not wanting too close a scrutiny of anything to do with the mill site. Iris had fulfilled her part of the deal with those two, at least. She'd extracted a fortune from him to do it, but he wouldn't have to pay her another dime now. And after Herb Collinson's private talk with Atkinson a couple of weeks ago, his support was also certain. Wendell Baker would buy in too. Only the Mayor, Selena Coyle, remained unreadable.

"I suppose they'll need a lot of shoes," Baker said. "I'll have to lay in a supply of those Nike things they seem to wear to everything."

"We'll need to talk about an exclusive contract for floral decorations at the graduation ceremonies," Edna said. "And an on-campus flower shop."

"Of course," Atkinson assured her. "It's solely due to this council's generous gift of the old mill site that Honeymoon Falls will have an institute of higher learning. It's only natural that those with the foresight to help create such a magnificent community resource should share in the rewards."

"Five hundred students, you say?" Edna's jaws opened and closed, like a whale inhaling a massive concentration of plankton.

"And, don't forget, there'll be fifty or sixty administrative and faculty positions—all well-educated professionals with high-paying jobs. And they do buy flowers," he added, giving the old hag a final prod.

"The problem is, Dr. Atkinson, that you don't seem to have progressed much further than the architect's drawings." It was

Selena Coyle's cool voice cutting through the air. "You said six months ago you had government and private funding in place, and all you needed from us was the land, which we've agreed to. When is the building going to start? Where are all the construction jobs?"

Atkinson took another sip of water. Their eyes had all narrowed suddenly, he noticed. He kept the smile in place.

"Well, of course, we've had problems with the government grants being slow in coming." He gave a regretful shrug. "That's just how government is, I'm afraid. And big projects like this do run into unexpected delays."

Selena wasn't letting go. "When *do* you expect to get the grants? Council's approval was conditional on them being received by the end of this month."

Damn the woman. Why did she keep harping about the grants? Had Iris let slip any hint of his difficulty in persuading the sticky-fingered bureaucrats who controlled them that he couldn't increase their usual cut and still survive?

"The grants will arrive in the next couple of weeks," he said. *Stall,* he thought. It was all he could do for the time being. He projected his presidential smile at all of them. "And now, if there are no more questions, I've got an urgent meeting in Vancouver, so I'll let you get on with your usual business." He bundled his papers into his briefcase and started toward the door.

"Dr. Atkinson?" It was the Coyle woman again. "We'd appreciate your coming back at the end of the month to show us the grant approvals."

"Of course," he said instantly. He nodded to the others and left the council chambers.

Selena Coyle buttoned her jacket over her ample bosom and came to a decision: she would definitely not run for mayor again when her second two-year term ended three months from now. The venality exhibited by Edna and Selby made her sick, and none of the others seemed to have the slightest concern about what Atkinson was up to either. She'd developed a peculiar pain above her cheekbones, as if someone were squeezing the backs of her eyes with pliers.

Edna Sigurdson's voice ground on relentlessly. Not content with securing a monopoly on supplying flowers to the new college, she was plumping for a bylaw restricting the granting of business licenses for florists to those who'd been operating such businesses at the onset of The Theme.

"Ha! You mean, to *you*," Wendell Baker said, whacking pipe dottle into an ashtray.

Edna glowered. "And why not me?" The prominent vein clusters over her long jaw began to pulse, signaling readiness for combat. "Who provided flowers to every wedding and funeral for sixteen years before The Theme, at prices that barely covered my overhead—" Wendell made violin-playing motions, causing Edna's voice to rise an octave.

"You know it's true," she said. "And you'd have lost that pathetic shoe store when the mill closed if I hadn't thought of how to make this place catch on."

Stung, Wendell bit back. "No more pathetic than the roses you used to pinch from behind Mrs. Milliken's house to fill out those puny wreaths you supplied for funerals."

Edna's narrow green eyes bulged. "That's a goddamn lie!" She slammed her hand on the table. "You started that story, you lying—"

Selena knew she should intervene, but the pills that were keeping her from screaming hysterically were making her want to sleep. The babble of voices blurred, and the only words she could distinguish from time to time were references to *The Theme*. The Theme was the reason for the town's continued existence, perhaps even for Selena's.

After bankruptcy eliminated Connor Tarlech's shingle mill, the only major employer in the community of 6,000, the town's demise had been only months away. In the frantic scramble for survival, a chance remark of Edna's about the tourists she'd seen at Niagara Falls had sparked a revelation of biblical dimensions in the populace. The road to salvation was suddenly clear, and it was paved with tourists. In a blaze of enthusiasm, what was then the town of Winslow had been re-christened Honeymoon Falls. Surprisingly, however, the new name did not result in a rush of well-heeled visitors, and the town continued on the same grim path to extinction it had been travelling under its prosaic former moniker.

It was Selena who'd understood that more than a name change was required. She'd hectored the provincial government into providing money for advertising, barged into conventions to promote the town's wedding theme events, and blanketed every international travel organization and news service with stories about "The Romance Capital of the World."

The only opposition to Selena's ideas had come from the colony of performers, writers, and academics who, attracted by the distress-sale prices of the departing mill workers' houses, had flooded into town to establish summer homes. To the Colony, tourists meant recreational vehicles with vulgar bumper stickers rolling down the main street ejecting beer cans at exhausted ballerinas or sculptors recuperating from the demands of their art. Their cavils were quickly swept aside by unemployed mill workers and small business owners facing ruin, and any lingering hopes the Colony held of derailing Selena's plans were smothered by the instant and remarkable success of them.

It was still Edna who was revered as the town savior—her inspired observation had passed into legend—but Selena was regularly referred to as "our forward-thinking young mayoress"

31

in Lucy Mitchum's *Town Talk* newspaper. Not that Lucy's little paper carried a lot of clout—people read it mainly for the hilarious typos and continuity errors. Still, her support ensured recognition of Selena's efforts wasn't entirely swamped in the swell of approval for Edna.

Ironically, Selena would never have entered politics if Connor Tarlech hadn't ended their relationship a few months before his bankruptcy. She was not dismissed cruelly—his blue eyes were kind, the deep voice considerate. And it was true, as he gently pointed out, that there'd never been any discussion of anything permanent, and she'd known there'd been other women before her. Still, the nights spent in his bed with his long body moving confidently above her had seemed to imply some kind of promise, an assurance that she could not be supplanted.

The pain subsided, replaced, to Selena's surprise, by anger. The bankruptcy of the mill and the obloquy it brought on him had not assuaged the feeling. She was determined to strike back at him, and in some oblique way making a success of revitalizing the town that his failure had doomed satisfied that need.

As Selena's success grew, Connor's fortunes declined even further. While facing down the fury of the unemployed millworkers, he tried several ill-fated ventures after the bankruptcy, the last a charter fishing business. That, too, had ended disastrously when his boat burned to the water line one night while he was in Vancouver collecting a group of Spanish sport fishermen. It was arson, of course; no one was surprised. Selena had watched the fire flaring over the water with satisfaction, not even realizing until later that she might have been watching his death.

Shortly after Selena's second term as mayor began, Connor disappeared from Honeymoon Falls, supposedly for a job in some remote country where he could begin anew. Iris Morland, the woman he'd left Selena for, had obviously dealt with the end of her affair better than Selena had: she'd replaced Connor almost immediately with TV host Arnold Reifel. But then everyone knew Iris's husband, Kenneth, was too spineless to protest anything she did.

Selena refocused to find Wendell and Edna still trading barbs, and Herb Collinson regarding her curiously. He was a taxidermist; Selena had once been in his basement workshop which was full of dismembered animal parts. He lived with his widowed mother in a house that smelled of formaldehyde or whatever preservative it was he used, and it took an effort of pure will for Selena to force her mind from Hitchcockian scenarios whenever she picked him up for council meetings.

Selby was staring at his hairy knuckles, the habitual object of his regard whenever Selena's jacket was buttoned. He owned Honeymoon Heaven, a rustic log cabin resort at the north end of what locals still referred to as Winslow Lake, but which had been renamed Bridegroom Bay. In the last election, he'd been elected with the support of only slightly fewer voters than Edna, who'd topped the polls ever since she became the originator and patron saint of The Theme.

"You're damn right, Edna," Selby was saying now. "What the hell are we here for if not to get rid of crap that gets in the way of making a profit? Bottom line is, unless we make money, the town dies." He gave Selena a challenging look. "Nobody can argue with that."

"Words to live by," Selena assented, and began briskly outlining the agenda for next week's meeting, leaving Selby, as usual, wondering whether to react to the mockery in her voice.

His covert assessment of her chest so evidently dominated his thoughts that she'd begun to find it comic—he sometimes lost his train of thought in mid-sentence if she shifted position while he was speaking. Perhaps witnessing all that newlywed lust at the resort had unhinged him. Sometimes, when he was particularly aggravating, she would aim her breasts straight at him and project *make-my-day* thought waves at him. "One more word," she imagined threatening while his neurons melted, "and I let these babies loose."

Selena supposed Selby would become mayor if she didn't run again. The idea was depressing, considering his view of the council as a kind of Chamber of Commerce chapter dedicated solely to the promotion of local business, especially his own, but she supposed there could be worse choices.

Cora and Irene Delbrook, for example, who hadn't even shown up this morning. All Cora cared about was being able to call herself "Councilor" and queen it over local civic gatherings. Irene never went anywhere without a black, yellow-eyed tomcat draped over her shoulders like a stole, its long plush tail flipping unnoticed against its mistress's plump cheek. At times she looked so utterly vacant it was as if she were off on some kind of astral travel, concentrating on sounds only she could hear. Perhaps it was her son, Gary, she was thinking about—at twenty-five he was completing his second six-month sentence for car theft.

If the Delbrook sisters were not mayoral material, neither was Wendell Baker. At seventy-five, he was still amazingly vigorous, but he directed his energy so exclusively into feuding with Edna that it seemed to be his sole pleasure in life. His maliciously pointed attacks skewered her like arrows dipped in curare, bloating her with fury.

Edna, of course, could have won the mayoral race without trying, but Selena suspected that Edna knew the council wouldn't tolerate her bulldozer approach for long, and she was too canny to allow herself to become the focal point for voter dissatisfaction. It was bad for business to have angry homeowners blaming you for cracked sidewalks or unfilled potholes. Even the new mall had been controversial, in spite of the concessions Selena had negotiated: space for the council offices in which they were sitting, a library, promises of employment for local residents.

"Time to go," Selena said, scooping papers into her briefcase. "I've less than an hour to get home, change, and get to the park for the start of the Wedding Daze parade." She knew she would not be attending the parade—even the pills couldn't keep her going that long, and she could feel the crash approaching with the speed of light.

Selby and Edna were already heading for the door, closely followed by Wendell and Herb. Selena locked the council room door and caught up to the others who had paused in front of Edna's new shop while she slid the steel accordion doors open in preparation for the start of business.

"Rents are hellish, of course, right inside the main doors like this," Edna observed, leading the others in. "Still, I think it'll work—honeymoon couples are willing to pay top dollar for everything."

"And you're the one to charge it." But here Wendell needled to no avail—the thought of profits always put Edna in a good mood.

"You bet I am," Edna agreed, glancing approvingly at the pink and white letters spelling out *Edna's Bridal Bouquets*. She pulled a canvas bag containing the store's cash float from her carry-all and set it by the register.

Selena was finding the scent of the flowers cloying and was beginning to move toward the exit when a small green car glided slowly by outside. Selby noticed it too.

"Customers arriving already," he said. Like Edna, the sight of people prepared to spend money buoyed his spirits.

A moment later, a black pick-up truck entered the lot and sped toward the door. The green car had also decided to claim the spot in front of the door, and buzzed determinedly toward it. The pick-up's motor roared a challenge, but the driver of the car was equal to it—both vehicles managed to arrive in the same spot at exactly the same time, accompanied by the sound of squealing brakes and rending metal. This was followed by the usual coda of slammed doors and ranted obscenities.

Without speaking, they all moved toward the mall doors. The couples from both vehicles were obviously newlyweds. The brides had each placed restraining hands on their spouse's biceps, and were exchanging awkward smiles, while the men bellowed at each other in two different languages. Selena sighed. "Better get mall security here before they start throwing punches."

"I'll call from the shop," Edna said, starting back toward her store.

Selena nodded and hurried to her car. Thank God she'd parked away from the entrance, she thought. If she'd been delayed by the accident, she'd never have made it home.

Inside, Edna Sigurdson hurtled up and down the mall lanes shrieking with rage, completely ignoring the scattered customers who'd begun to trickle in. Blinded by fury, she took several wrong turns before locating the Security office. She burst through the door and slammed into Eddie Novak with a full-body block that knocked them both off balance.

"What the hell is going on?" she screeched, as Eddie fumbled his glasses back into place. "What the hell is going on?"

CHAPTER 5

Hermione Hopkins regarded her naked ninety-five-year-old body in the bathroom mirror with interest. Really, it was quite remarkable, she thought, how her skin, which had sagged distressingly throughout her seventies and eighties, seemed to be tightening around her long bones like shrink wrap. Her breasts, small even during pregnancy, and always liberally padded during her early film career, seemed almost to have retracted into her chest, leaving only the dark brown nipples slightly protruding.

She ran her hands over her ribs, feeling the outline of each one. Her skin was lined, of course, and worn-looking, but soft still, something like old chamois. Some faint scars—gall bladder and appendix incisions, now visible only if you looked in the right place. No, the texture of her century-old flesh was not so bad, she decided, although the speckled, yellowish tinge was unappealing, and body makeup would be required to mask the mottling that had begun a few years earlier.

If she did it. She laughed out loud as she thought of Shelagh's reaction when Pierre Blondin, the young Quebecois director, had brought up, ever so carefully, the idea of having the matriarch Hermione was playing in a scene in which Felipe, the Mexican stable hand, would undress her in the foyer of her mansion, and then carry her up a marble staircase to her bedroom.

Blondin, Shelagh, and Hermione were drinking tea at the

kitchen table in Hermione's ramshackle old house. Hermione liked the house for a number of reasons, not the least of which was that it predated her. There were so few things, she told people, that were older than she was nowadays. Stairs, Blondin had explained to the two women, were of course a Freudian symbol for intercourse, so the scene would both imply the relationship between the two characters and provide a striking visual image—the matriarch's expensive clothing in a heap below, while Felipe carried her naked body up the long sweep of marble stairs. It would also be, he said, *un hommage* to the famous staircase scene with Rhett and Scarlett in *Gone With the Wind.*

Hermione stared at Blondin with delight. The Frenchman's battiness was enthralling. An octogenarian Scarlett? Rhett as a Mexican peasant? The urge to giggle was irresistible, and she was forced to manufacture a series of gentle coughs to disguise her amusement.

Shelagh's eyes, the same bright blue Hermione's still were, had locked on Blondin's face as though it were something the dog had thrown up. Her short, silver hair seemed to tighten around her scalp, and her lips twisted scornfully.

"There is no such scene in the script. My sister would never have considered"—here Shelagh shot a censorious glance at Hermione's softly coughed accompaniment—"would never have even read, such revolting suggestions."

"*Oui, Madame* Tarlech, it's not in the script," Blondin conceded with a shrug. "Many things that will be in the film are not in the script. That is the way I work. The way many directors work."

"The Mrs. Forrester character is eighty-five—four years older than I am." Shelagh's voice had begun the arctic drop that could suck warmth from a freezer. "The Felipe character's age is not stated, but the actor playing him is in his fifties."

Blondin held up a forefinger. "Late fifties, *Madame*," he said. "And Mrs. Forrester is only eighty-two—Hermione will be a little too beautiful for a woman of such an age, but we shall work around this." He smiled charmingly at Hermione, who smiled charmingly back. Shelagh caught the exchange, and her vocal temperature dropped several more degrees.

"Many people know that Hermione is ninety-five. They will find it disgusting that someone her age should play such a scene, particularly with a man young enough to be her grandson."

Hermione was about to protest the *grand*son reference when Blondin turned to her. He was a handsome man, better looking than many actors, with a powerful physical presence. His thick dark hair framed a strong-featured face slightly hawk-like in profile. She suspected he was a bit vain about his body; his expensive clothes were close-fitting, and the tanned flesh of his muscular torso showed through the thin cream-colored silk shirt he wore.

"And what is your feeling about the age?" he inquired.

"Well, the age does concern me." Hermione paused—she was extremely good at pauses, critics had commented on it more than once—and waited until they were both leaning forward slightly. Then she reeled them in.

"I'm afraid that a man in his late fifties is apt to have a heart attack carrying me up all those stairs." Hermione treated them to her innocent look, at which she was also extremely good.

Blondin's dark eyes flashed delightedly. "You will do it!"

"You old fool," Shelagh said. She jerked an earring off (always a bad sign, Hermione knew) and began to tap it on the table. "Does Iris Morland know what you're doing to her book?" she demanded.

Blondin looked uncomfortable. "It is in the book, this scene," he replied.

Shelagh's eyes narrowed. "It is not," she said, rapping the

earring on the table with each word.

"Yes, yes," Blondin insisted.

"No, no," Shelagh mimicked. She bent below the table and fumbled in a raffia carryall. A moment later she slammed a copy of *Mrs. Forrester* down in front of Blondin with such force that his teacup leapt from its saucer like a startled hare.

"Show us," she challenged.

Blondin leafed slowly through the book for some time, then handed it back to Shelagh. She read aloud:

Felipe eased the heavy mink from Mrs. Forrester's shoulders. "I'm going to lie down," she said, and started up the stairs.

Shelagh sniffed and handed the book back to him. "You'll have to do better than that."

This time Blondin smiled, looked her straight in the eye, and bent the two halves of the book back until the spine cracked. Shelagh gasped incredulously. Still smiling, he handed the book back to her. She took it automatically, and its broken carcass hung in her hand briefly until she let it drop to the table.

"I tell the story my way," Blondin said. His smile made the ferocity with which he spoke chilling.

So should I do it? Hermione asked her reflection now. Her cheekbones were still good too, she noticed. With reasonable lighting she'd have no problem playing an eighty-two-year-old woman. She'd leave the hearing aid off, naturally. Hair a bit thin, that was the only problem—she'd started wearing turbans with gauzy veils trailing from them when that began, but it would look absurd to be naked except for a turban. A wig would be required.

Contrary to Shelagh's assertion, a staircase scene had always been in the script, although it had not included any nudity, nor indeed, any intimacy between the characters. Being carried up the stairs would eliminate the problem that had first occurred to Hermione when she read the script—she could not possibly climb them unaided; she needed a cane to navigate any distance, even on level terrain. Now her ascent was no longer an issue, if she did what Blondin was asking.

But *naked*? she said aloud to the mirror. Blondin had told her the scene would be tastefully lighted, but her body would be clearly seen. And Shelagh would hit the roof when she found out that he was not going to end the scene at the bedroom door as originally planned—it would continue with the characters in bed. Hermione loved the freedom to behave irresponsibly that extreme old age had bestowed, but perhaps this really was going too far?

She no longer cared what anyone thought of her, but there was Shelagh to consider, and Shelagh's son, Connor. If he ever came back to Honeymoon Falls, or even North America, what would he think about everyone seeing Auntie Hermione starkers? Would he think it was repulsive? She loved that boy—God, it was a sign of her own antiquity that she thought of him, at forty-four, as a boy, Shelagh's love child, the only time she'd ever known Shelagh to do anything rash. That had always been Hermione's territory—the utterly risky and improvident actions that succeeded just often enough to make the gamble exciting.

And doing the scene would be an exciting gamble. Blondin was only thirty-four, but his Quebec film company had produced two scandalously decadent films already. The last one had won an international film prize, and started the publicity mill grinding. Opinion was divided on whether his films wallowed in perversity for shock value, or merely reflected the reality of the times. That debate would pale beside the uproar sure to be generated by his concept of Mrs. Forrester and her passionate affair across age, class, and racial barriers. Oh, it was risky, risky. A celebration of human sexuality, if he pulled it off. A grotesquerie if he didn't.

"It is what the book is about—love," Blondin said. "The many kinds of love. You'll see that if you read it carefully."

Hermione had no intention of doing so. Long ago she'd learned a film performance depended on three things—the script the screenwriter provided, what the director demanded, and the actress's invention. Anything else just got in the way. She did wonder, though, why Blondin seemed so upset when Shelagh demanded to know whether he had Iris's approval for the scene. In spite of her bravado with Shelagh, Hermione knew she was going to find being naked on the set very hard. Had Iris retained some sort of script approval? If so, and Iris demanded cuts, would Hermione's nude scene wind up as a few feet of freak show film bootlegged to cult film festivals?

Hermione decided there was only one way to find out about Iris's control over the film. Iris was coming to lunch this afternoon. She'd met Iris, of course—the Colony was too small for them to have avoided each other even if they'd wished to. Hermione had heard the woman was something of a slut, but her mind was certainly razor sharp, and she did not strike Hermione as the type to give information without getting something in return. And what a writer would want, Hermione thought, was *material*. Consequently, Hermione had decided to play her gargoyle persona—the ancient theatrical hag. The role had the advantages of being both entertaining and, she hoped, opaque enough to keep Iris from discerning too much of her motives.

Hermione heard the phone ringing outside in her bedroom, and Shelagh's voice answering.

"No, she isn't here yet. Just as well, Hermione's still not ready." The last sentence was deliberately louder than necessary, and aimed at the bathroom.

Oh God, was it noon already? Hermione pulled an old chenille bathrobe on and opened the door. She seated herself at the vanity and rummaged through a drawer for a turban that would complement the green brocade caftan she planned to wear. She settled finally on a violet satin that enhanced the color of her eyes. Holding it poised above her bare old scalp like a crown, she asked, "Who was that on the phone?"

"Kenneth Morland. Iris apparently wasn't at home last night when he called, and she isn't answering now either."

"Oho, she must have a new one on the string," Hermione chortled, tucking stray wisps of hair under the turban.

"Hermione," Shelagh said.

Hermione glanced at Shelagh's reflection in the mirror, and noted Shelagh had both her earrings off and was rolling them between her palms like worry beads. One earring off was bad; both off meant trouble for someone, usually Hermione.

"What is it, Shelagh?" Hermione asked, trying to keep a note of aggravation out of her voice, and not quite succeeding.

"About the scene—"

"Oh really, Shelagh," Hermione interrupted, making no attempt to conceal her annoyance now. "This is *too* much when I'm racing to get ready!"

Hermione really didn't think she could bear to hear Shelagh start up again about the nude scene. There was in Shelagh's disapproval an implication that the scene was disgusting because it showed an old person's body, and that infuriated Hermione. Did Shelagh really think that her own body and Hermione's were so unsightly?

"You'll be ready long before she gets here," Shelagh said.

"You know, Shelagh," Hermione said, going on the attack, "Blondin makes a lot of sense when he says that if people are going to see nudity in films anyway, it's time they began to see real bodies at all ages, not just those of the young."

"That's a load of codswallop, and so is he," Shelagh said, eyeing Hermione's reflection disdainfully. "Whatever he's telling you, that scene is intended to create publicity for his trashy film."

Hermione was well aware that a significant part of Blondin's philosophy was opportunistic—he hoped to overcome her hesitancy about the scene by persuading her she was doing something artistically worthwhile, and perhaps he was even rehearsing with her the line he would take with the press. Certainly a bit of scandal would not be a handicap in promoting the film, but whether he truly believed what he said or not, Hermione did.

"There's truth in what he says, nonetheless," Hermione said, leaning forward to apply mascara.

"Perhaps," Shelagh conceded. "My God, you're not going to wear orange lipstick too, are you? Aren't purple, green, and orange pushing things just a little too far? You look like a cross between a pirate and a broken-down old whore."

"Exactly the effect I was aiming for," Hermione said grandly. She returned to the attack. "I know you think that at my age I couldn't possibly be sexual, and don't think I haven't realized that's what's bothering you about the scene."

The doorbell rang and Shelagh clamped her earrings back on her lobes.

"That'll be Iris," Shelagh said. "For God's sake, don't let her know what an ass you're letting Blondin make of you."

CHAPTER 6

BAZAAR DEATHS SHOCK TOWN

The horrifying murders of two prominent Honeymoon Falls residents cast a pall over our town's celebration of Honeymoon Daze. Dead are Iris Morland, 39, and Connor Tarlech, 44. Mrs. Morland, a well-known figure in the literary world, was the author of four novels, and another about to be published.

Lucy Mitchum frowned and reread what she had tapped into the computer keyboard. She changed the first word to *bizarre*. The story was bound to arouse national media interest, and while she was willing to play the rube to boost circulation in Honeymoon Falls, she was not particularly anxious to appear illiterate to the entire country. Anyway, she'd already provided the usual quota of snicker fodder for the Colony with the heading over the letters to the editor. *Pen is Mightier Than the Sword* it said—or had, until she'd deleted the space between the first two words.

Mr. Tarlech, former owner of the Tarlech shingle mill, was thought to have been in business overseas, but police sources have advised this reporter that he had maintained a low profile since returning to the area about two weeks ago.

Low profile indeed. That's a hot one, Lucy thought, gulping tea from the mug beside her. What he'd actually been doing, according to Will Halsey, was hiding out at the abandoned mill, knowing he'd be risking his neck if he set foot in town. The unemployed mill-workers who'd seen their jobs and pensions disappear in Tarlech's bankruptcy would definitely have wanted a word with Connor-boy as to just where all that money had gone. Chief among them, former mill foreman and current mall security officer, Eddie Novak. Lucy set the mug down and resumed punching the keyboard. She had less than two hours to get the copy to the printer if she was going to have the paper on the streets Wednesday morning.

During an interview with this reporter today, Police Chief Will Halsey advised the bodies were discovered atop a float that town councilors Irene Delbrook Rasmussen and Cora Delbrook were taking to the Honeymoon Daze parade site. Both women remain secluded at their home, unavailable for comment. Mayor Coyle did not attend the parade ceremonies due to illness, and was likewise unavailable for comment.

Halsey had not actually given Lucy an interview, nor had she spoken to Selena—her phone had rung unanswered. Lucy had, of course, been at the parade, and it was Edna Sigurdson who'd said she must be ill. Actually, Edna had implied more than that—"Selena's so high-strung, you know," Edna said, with an insinuating smile that tugged her leathery cheeks up toward her ears.

Of course, no one had known until after the parade was well under way that anything was wrong. Lucy was waiting with Edna, Wendell Baker, and Art Selby by the park bandstand for Selena to arrive. Outside in the parking lot, Myrna Brokaw, the parade marshal, was organizing the order of the floats and the various groups of costumed performers who would be marching on foot.

"Shotgun wedding group—where are you?" Myrna yelled

into the throng. Three men and a woman presented themselves, the woman exaggeratedly pregnant in a cheap floral print, clutching a nosegay of plastic violets and wearing a straw hat. One of the men wore bib overalls and carried the shotgun; another was outfitted in preacher's garb and shepherded a reluctant groom.

The group went off to the starting line, and Myrna began calling for the Brides from Many Lands to assemble. They were followed by Edna's Bridal Flowers float, the Honeymoon Falls Natural Splendor float (a representation of Bridegroom Bay against a background of six-foot evergreens, among which could be spied various examples of Herb Collinson's work), a convertible containing Miss Honeymoon Daze (Officer Bailey's daughter, Nicole), and various other floats representing local businesses.

Art Selby's float was a gigantic, red, heart-shaped hot tub, in which frolicked four female guests from his resort. The lucky girls had been personally selected by Selby on a day their new husbands had succumbed to the lure of an all-day fishing trip and left them unattended. Wendell Baker and Selby were practically licking their lips, Lucy noticed, as the girls squirmed excitedly in the foaming jets; their bikinis, all but invisible to begin with, made even more so by the water. *Your Haven, Honeymoon Heaven,* said the lettering on the side of the float.

The parade had been delayed well past the usual starting time of noon, while they waited for the wedding cake float—the parade's centerpiece—to arrive. By 12:30 the crowd was getting restless and beginning to drift away, so there was no choice but to let the parade get underway. As the high school bugle band marched off at the front of the procession, Chief Halsey had driven slowly up to where Lucy and the others were just beginning to disperse.

One look at his face told Lucy that there was serious trouble.

She stood in a small circle with Edna, Wendell Baker, and Art Selby, while he explained the utterly bizarre situation to them. Even Edna was stunned into silence.

Selby was the first to recover. "Great—right at the beginning of the season."

"I'd like to talk to Mayor Coyle," Halsey said.

"So would we," Edna said. "She was supposed to perform the ribbon-cutting and give a speech. I had to step in at the last minute, totally unprepared."

Wendell snorted. "You've only got one speech, and you've been giving it for fifteen years. The only preparation time you need is however long it takes to blow the dust off it. *'Fellow citizens of our beautiful town, it is with great pleasure that I—'* "

"Shut up, you old bastard," Edna said.

Selby was still worrying about the impact on the tourist season. "This is going to be kept quiet, I hope," he said. "No one's going to come to a place where they have to worry about being killed."

Halsey allowed the silence to stretch out before replying. "The discovery of the dead bodies of two prominent people on top of a parade float *is* likely to attract a fair amount of attention."

The contempt in his words, coupled with the formal politeness of their delivery, was like a stiletto with a point so fine that vital organs were ruptured before one was aware the skin had been pierced. Lucy relished the discomfited expressions that surfaced on the others' faces when they finally recognized the thrust.

Halsey touched Lucy discreetly on the arm and drew her away from the others. Lucy was disconcerted by how much she enjoyed the touch of his hand on her bare skin. Everything about him—his dark hair, the physical confidence he exuded, even the slight distance that rarely left his eyes (the result, she'd heard, of a painful divorce)—was triggering emotions more suited to a moony teenager than a woman of thirty-two.

"Do Kenneth and Shelagh know?" Lucy asked, thinking of the awful impact the news would have on them.

"I'm on my way to speak to Mrs. Tarlech. We haven't been able to locate Mr. Morland yet."

The last phrase struck Lucy's ear in a peculiar way. "Haven't been able to locate him? You don't mean he's a suspect?"

"We don't know where he is," Halsey said, avoiding the question. "We're still trying to find him."

Lucy felt shudders overtake her as another thought occurred to her. "My God, how could Cora and Irene have driven that thing all the way into town without realizing what was on top of it? And Officer Bailey? You know, Chief, I never really believed the stories about her, but I can't help wondering where her eyes were."

"The Delbrooks picked up the float shortly before sunrise this morning. It was dark, the float is twenty feet high, and no one had any reason to inspect the top of it. Officer Bailey had been on shift all night and was focused on the danger the float represented to other traffic on the freeway. And she did discover the bodies at the station."

In fairness to Bailey, Halsey was about to add that she was still at the station checking on Kenneth Morland's whereabouts, even though her hands were still shaking, but thought better of it. People expected cops to be capable of remaining in control no matter how grisly an event they experienced.

Lucy sighed doubtfully, but didn't pursue the issue of Bailey's competence. She spoke briskly to dispel the lingering sensation of his touch.

"Why on earth would Cora and Irene go out there at that time in the morning? Surely it couldn't take more than an hour to bring the float into town, and the parade doesn't start until noon."

"They were trying to avoid traffic," Halsey said.

Once the presence of the bodies had been discovered, the truckers had been only too happy to drop their complaints, rather than be delayed by a murder investigation. Halsey took their phone numbers, photocopied their licenses, and sent them on their way. The Delbrook sisters, shattered by the discovery of the cargo they'd unwittingly transported, were driven home by Officer Larsen, and called on by their doctor, who prescribed a sedative. A helicopter with a police photographer and two homicide detectives was dispatched from Vancouver, and airlifted the bodies to the coroner's office. By the time the chopper arrived, it had been after 10:00 A.M., and fortunately the gathering parade had diverted the attention such activity would normally have attracted.

"I need to tell Mayor Coyle what's happened as soon as possible. She doesn't answer her phone. Do you know where she is?" Halsey asked.

"Edna's probably right," Lucy said. "She must be ill, or she'd have been at the parade."

"Thanks. I'll try her again later." Halsey headed for his car.

"Wait, I'll come with you," Lucy called, suddenly realizing that she was letting the biggest story she was ever going to see walk away. Halsey kept going as though he hadn't heard.

Lucy grabbed her phone, only to discover the battery was dead. Fortunately, her change purse was full of quarters. She raced to the phone kiosk at the park entrance. In rapid succession she called Selena, Kenneth Morland, and Shelagh Tarlech, none of whom answered. She tried Arnold Reifel's number and got his wife.

"Marjorie? It's Lucy Mitchum. Could I speak to Arnold, please?" Lucy was not about to waste time explaining the reason for her call; let Arnold do that. Not that Marjorie seemed to care.

"He's not here," Marjorie murmured.

Lucy frowned. Marjorie's usually cool voice sounded slightly odd.

"Do you know where I can reach him?" Lucy asked.

"Well," Marjorie said after a long pause, "you could always try the studio in Vancouver." The first syllable of *studio* was elongated to at least twice its normal length, and *Vancouver* was uttered with a sinuous intonation suggesting an exotic foreign language.

My God, Lucy realized, the woman's crocked. "Could you give me the number?" she asked.

"Oh, I don't think so," Marjorie said, offering no reason why she couldn't.

Lucy had never heard anything about Arnold Reifel's wife being a drinker; clearly something cataclysmic had occurred. Lucy suddenly understood what it was—Marjorie had finally twigged about Arnold and Iris. Lucy didn't much care for Marjorie, but she could imagine the woman's pain.

"Look, Marjorie—I—I'm really sorry," Lucy said, wondering how to break the news about Iris's death.

"Oh, don't be," Marjorie said. "I was obviously meant to go through life being a laughingstock. Iris was just the person chosen to make sure it happened."

Lucy had begun to feel chilled. "Nobody's laughing at you, Marjorie. This is all so horrible. I'm sure Iris meant nothing to Arnold—I know he couldn't have meant anything to her—it was just a stupid, meaningless affair. But I think there's something you need to know. I hate to break it to you over the phone, but—"

"*Affair?*" Marjorie interrupted.

Lucy's stomach lurched. Surely she hadn't misread the situation? What on earth else could Marjorie have been talking about?

"Affair?" Marjorie screeched so loudly, people waiting behind Lucy to use the phone began to look interested. Marjorie was cold sober now, Lucy realized. "What the hell are you talking about?"

Oh, Lord, what had she done? Lucy scrabbled frantically to retrieve the situation. "Nothing—nothing, Marjorie. I'm confused—I meant to say Connor, not Arnold. I've just had a dreadful shock, well we all have really. Irene and Cora too." Lucy babbled on, hoping Marjorie's mind was sufficiently muddled by drink to forget her faux pas.

"You see, Irene and Cora didn't show up at the parade, and then Chief Halsey drove up and told us—that is, Edna and Wendell and Art and me, that there'd been a terrible accident; well, not really an accident." Lucy paused for breath. The silence at the other end of the line was not encouraging. She could hear glugging noises, almost as if Marjorie were swigging from a bottle.

"I guess there's no way to break this gently—Iris is dead," Lucy said, capitulating at last. The silence at the other end stretched out endlessly.

"Marjorie?" Lucy asked.

The silence was finally broken. To Lucy's horror, she realized the shock had made the other woman hysterical. Peals of laughter filled the receiver against Lucy's ear.

"Oh, quit trying to cheer me up," Marjorie said.

CHAPTER 7

It was after two, and Halsey was driving toward Hermione Hopkins's house where a neighbor had said he might find Shelagh Tarlech. He considered and dismissed the idea of grabbing a coffee at the Doughnut Hut before continuing. The damned place was turning into his second home, he thought. No wonder his belt was cutting into his gut like an anaconda tightening around a pig.

He'd always craved sweet stuff, but until a couple years ago, it had never been a problem. His lean, muscular frame burned calories like a high-efficiency furnace. Vivien was always complaining that he could empty a dessert cart and never show it, while she gained weight if she took an aspirin.

Then he noticed the dry cleaner had shrunk his pants. He complained the second time it happened, but the problem continued. *Cheap material,* he thought. He discovered the truth when he was getting his annual physical and the doctor asked him to step on the scales. The dial spun between his toes like a roulette wheel, until the needle quivered at 216 pounds—twelve pounds over what he'd weighed since he was a teenager. He'd jumped off as if he were standing barefoot on a hot stove and stared at the scale in disbelief.

And nothing—not jogging, not lifting weights, not starving himself—made the problem go away for good. The extra pounds gave ground slowly, grudgingly, only to return the minute he let his guard down. Vivien didn't seem to notice the change, although later he realized she was already so preoccupied with The Actor, she wouldn't have noticed if he'd been trundling his gut around in a wheelbarrow.

One night he dreamt he found an abandoned semi, its entire trailer filled with jelly doughnuts. He climbed inside, wading happily in the tempting, spongy sea, filling his mouth with the delicious swollen orbs, biting through the sweet dough into the luscious jelly centers. Suddenly he was back in the doctor's office, only now he filled the entire office, and she was trying to force the scale beneath his incredible bulk. He jerked awake with a gasp to find Vivien propped on one elbow, eyeing him curiously.

"Bad dream?"

He shuddered, sliding his hands down to his belly, which, thank God, was the same size it had been when he went to bed.

"You kept muttering something like 'not the sales—not the sales.' "

"Scales," Halsey mumbled.

" 'Scales?' " Vivien queried. "As in 'Scales of Justice'?"

"Exactly," Halsey said.

Marjorie Reifel knew she had made a terrible miscalculation, not in what she'd said to Lucy Mitchum—that would result in minor gossip, soon forgotten. It was what she'd done Saturday that would ruin her. One of the few times in her life she had given in to her emotions, not stopped to think, and now she was going to pay a terrible price. Perhaps it had already begun to be exacted—Arnold hadn't returned home last night. She paced frantically, Iris's duplicity burning in her like fever.

There had to be some way to recover the situation. There *had* to. The wine bottle was empty, she saw. She strode to the liquor cabinet and flung it open. She passed up the gin and scotch, which were cheap brands poured into bottles with more expensive labels, and grabbed the brandy bottle by the neck. Wrenching off its cap, she put the bottle to her lips and gulped a mouthful that slammed down her throat and left her gasping. She looked at the bottle, astonished. In her entire life, she had never done such a thing. The warmth of the liquor began to spread through her, and she took the bottle to the sofa and sat cradling it in her lap.

Marjorie supposed Arnold might have spent the night at his first wife's place, that nitwit Eleanor, who still called occasionally to tell him he should have her on his show to talk about the healing power of crystals. Hard to believe he could have had the patience to put up with her for twelve years, let alone have been genuinely fond of her. The ridiculous woman had even wanted to attend Marjorie's and Arnold's wedding—with their daughter, yet. Marjorie had had to put her foot down pretty firmly there, although she'd been unprepared for the residual resentment that surfaced every time she and Arnold quarreled.

"It wouldn't have killed you to at least let Carrie come," he said, for months after their wedding. Eight years later, she still had to be careful not to veto too many weekend visits from his precious Carrie, or he put the record on again.

"Take an interest in her—let her get to know you," he was always urging.

He seemed oblivious to the fact that Carrie, at fifteen, was precisely at the stage Marjorie found most repulsive in the human growth cycle—sullen, spotty, utterly self-absorbed, and mesmerized by the pleasure of offending as many adults as possible. Parenthood evidently blinded one to any possible defect in one's offspring, or else Arnold felt her behavior was justifiable retribution for his leaving her mother. Perhaps he even thought Marjorie deserved a share of it, having been the "other woman," a designation whose Victorian overtones always amused her. As if Arnold could afford to be self-righteous: It was bad enough when a man cheated on you with his ex-wife, but he hadn't even stopped there. And, unlike Marjorie, he hadn't bothered being discreet—only her steadfast pretense of ignorance had saved her from enduring the indignity of being commiserated with.

With Eleanor and the brat draining Arnold dry, she was lucky to have been able to acquire the historic Presbyterian manse she'd persuaded Arnold to buy. He'd finally agreed only when she showed him how much cheaper it would be for him to live in Honeymoon Falls and commute to Vancouver to tape his television show. Now the problem was to finish renovating it, especially if Arnold lost the show.

"They wanna ghost," he'd told her a week ago, after the party she'd thrown to celebrate his birthday and show off the considerable changes she'd made in the house.

His speech was slurred after he'd drunk most of a bottle of whiskey. It amazed Marjorie that when Arnold drank his formidable television articulateness degenerated into such sloppy gobbles. There was no point in asking him to repeat things when he was like this; he simply became more incoherent, and angry into the bargain. She listened intently; when he talked about "them" or "they," he was talking about the network, and it was nearly always bad news. This clearly was a bad news time.

"A woman," he spluttered.

Marjorie considered these utterances carefully.

"A ghost?" she said.

" 'Swhat I said. Go-host. Bitch Go-host."

A co-host. They wanted a woman to co-host the show. Who? Arnold didn't know, although his muddled conjectures involved blondes with large breasts. Arnold had been hosting his public affairs show, *Reifel Range,* since shortly before their marriage, and while it could never have been said to be popular with a mass audience, it had endured, supplying some unfathomable need of the government-owned network. It appeared, however, that demographic surveys showed the audience for Arnold's show was mainly aging white males, and the network was attempting to broaden the show's appeal. Hence, the co-host loomed.

Arnold had been assured that he would still get the lion's share of the spotlight, even after the co-host was in place, and that there were no plans to cut his salary or change the format of the show. He'd not had to tell Marjorie of the emptiness of such promises. At forty-eight, Arnold was not likely to have too many big-earning years left; foolish as it was, he'd been relying on the show to see him through to retirement. And had his blood-sucking family not seriously undermined his resources, Marjorie reflected bitterly, she and Arnold might not have to contemplate a future of such reduced expectations.

Selena Coyle lay in her front hall in the fetal position, weeping with a wretchedness she had never known was possible. Her throat and chest were a searing mass of pain from the violent sobbing she had done since she entered the house, and her heart felt as if it were being squeezed into an ever smaller space by an anguish that continued to expand mercilessly within her. Her eyes burned as though hot coals had been forced under their lids.

The misery had struck the moment she opened the door, and she'd barely managed to kick it shut before she fell to her knees. The blackness flooded through her—the rage first, burning like fire, and then the terrible grief.

"Connor," she whispered. She had emptied the well of her self-control at the council meeting; she couldn't possibly pretend for a single minute more. She was helpless in the grip of the agony of last night—his voice asking her to come to him, and

then the final, awful moments that meant he was gone forever from her life.

She dragged herself to the phone and tried calling the Delbrook sisters, hoping they'd be able to fill in for her at the parade, but their telephone rang unanswered. There was no answer at Art Selby's place either, nor at Herb Collinson's. She phoned Edna's flower shop and left a message, but so far there'd been no response. All at the parade, she supposed.

Quite abruptly, Selena stopped caring, and began to think about a bottle of pills the psychiatrist in Vancouver had prescribed. She'd taken only a few at the time, because they made her so groggy, but she'd never thrown them away. What had he said? Dangerous if too many were taken, wasn't that it? Especially if combined with alcohol. She knew there was a full bottle of whiskey in the sideboard in the dining room. She got up and went to get it.

Herb Collinson folded a taxidermy text open to an illustration of a moose and began to assemble the lightweight fiberglass framework over which he would stretch the moose hide. Around him on benches, he had the pieces that he would fit together to finish the job—the head with its enormous antler rack, the plastic eyes, which he would fit in the now empty eye sockets, and the four legs stacked neatly in a pile. Beside them, he had an opened bottle of Moosehead beer, his fifth, which he had taken from a small refrigerator he'd installed once his mother had become dependent on her walker and was no longer able to get down the stairs to snoop through his basement workshop. He ignored the phone ringing behind him; he wanted to be left to finish the job in peace.

While he worked, he thought of Selena, as he did most of the time now. He knew she had no idea how much he thought of her—he was well aware she did not think of him in the same way, that she considered him only a friend, perhaps not even that—more of a co-worker. She could not see him in any other light because she was still besotted with Connor Tarlech. But that would surely end soon now, and there was no reason why she would not come to an appreciation of Herb's qualities. Sitting next to her at council meetings, or in her car, Herb had to fight the urge to put his arms around her, to murmur the tender words that welled up in him whenever she looked at him. When she was the target of Art Selby's leering glances, Herb could feel the rage boiling in him, and elaborate fantasies of retribution taking shape.

He took a long pull on the beer. He was beginning to feel light-headed and disoriented. He stared at the moose, whose feet appeared to be running in the opposite direction as its massive upper body. It looked almost as if its lower half had anticipated the bullet waiting ahead and, unable to persuade the noble head to turn back, had taken matters into its own hands, or in this case, feet. Suddenly he realized what was wrong—he'd attached the legs to the moose's body with the backs of the legs facing toward the front of the animal. He laughed helplessly while the beer foamed through his nose.

Then he thought about Connor Tarlech's boat and Art Selby's resort. Who was to say that Art Selby might not decide to leave town too, he wondered. Still laughing, he rummaged in the fridge for another beer.

"She was a bitch," Peggy Atkinson's companion said, hoisting the pitcher of martinis interrogatively at her.

Peggy nodded and arranged the sheets so they displayed her breasts to better advantage. Like her, the speaker was naked, and clearly enjoying her appreciative regard of the fact. In fact, he seemed to be almost demanding it, posing provocatively in front of her. Now that she thought of it, he always took off his own clothes first, never hers. Still, he was ten years younger than she was, so perhaps it was best he wasn't demanding she display the same level of exhibitionism. She increased the tension on the sheet beneath her breasts, lifting them slightly.

"True, she is. But I thought you were once such close friends," she said teasingly.

"Why should I have refused what everyone else has had?" Blondin said. He approached the bed, holding only one glass, she saw.

"Oh, I don't know if that's fair," Peggy said, concealing her enjoyment of his remark with the air of one determined to be even-handed. Men didn't respect catty women. "She's had a few liaisons, and she's never bothered to hide them."

She put up her hand for the drink, but he pulled it back with a grin, took a swallow, and held the glass high over his head. Fascinated, Peggy watched the play of muscles in his arm and chest.

"She was a bitch," he said, still smiling at her.

It was delicious the way he'd got his tenses wrong again—*was* instead of *is*. Peggy knew better than to comment though—expressing anything other than admiration for his skill in any area made him furious. Certainly she could not have disputed his mastery of the activities in which they'd just engaged.

Peggy saw there would be no drink until she agreed with him. Not that she found it difficult—she had always disliked Iris, and the dislike had turned to loathing after she found out about Cecil's furtive fling with her. It was giving her great satisfaction to revenge herself on Cecil in his own bed, while she listened to Blondin vilify Cecil's paramour.

Peggy laughed. "She's a bitch," she agreed. "Now give me the drink."

Blondin lowered the glass and rested it against his chest.

"Come and get it." He tilted the glass until the liquor trickled in a thin stream down his chest to his navel.

Peggy came and got it.

CHAPTER 8

Shelagh Tarlech's car was parked in front of her sister's house, and Halsey pulled up behind it, wondering how he could get Shelagh alone to break the news to her. He always felt as if he had his finger on the trigger of a bomb in these situations, and had to find the proper moment to detonate it.

Shelagh looked surprised when she answered the door. "I thought it was Iris Morland," she said, startling Halsey.

"It's about Mrs. Morland," Halsey said.

"She's not coming, I suppose, and she's sent you to tell us," Shelagh said, contempt at his allowing Iris to treat him like an errand boy showing clearly in her face. She had not stepped back from the door, and obviously did not expect he would want to come in.

"She's not coming," Halsey agreed. "May I speak with you for a moment, Mrs. Tarlech?"

"I suppose," Shelagh said, not yielding her position. He remained silent until she gave a grudging nod toward the interior.

Her manner altered the moment he stepped in; the hostess now, she turned toward him with a smile. "Please come into the living room. I'm afraid it's a mess, but my sister is studying her script in the kitchen."

She led him into a room remarkable for its untidiness. Two long green velvet sofas were heaped with books, clothing, blankets, coffee mugs, and cushions, with here and there a hollowed-out space like a nest. The debris had overflowed onto the small ornately carved tables that bracketed the sofas, as well as a large flat-topped trunk in the center of the room. The glass doors in a huge mahogany breakfront revealed a jumble of tarnished plaques, trophies, and statuettes engraved with Hermione's name.

"Hermione's been reorganizing her theatrical memorabilia," Shelagh said. "The cleaning woman will have a fit when she sees this."

She seated herself in one of the vacant burrows, and indicated another opposite her to Halsey. She was remarkably incongruous among the disorder. Her well-cut gray linen suit and turquoise blouse emphasized the elegant line of her slender body and still-shapely legs. *Well-maintained,* was the thought that went through Halsey's mind. Of course, she could afford to be; it was rumored her shadowy first husband, Conner's father, had been a millionaire film producer in Hollywood, and her second, Amos Tarlech, had started and run the shingle mill in the days when it made money. Her show business career had not been as successful as her sister's, and she'd been performing comic impersonations of more famous performers in a Vancouver supper club when she caught Amos's eye. No one knew whether the first husband was still living, although Amos, of course, had been dead for years. Now the man he'd brought up as his son, and to whom he'd given his name, was dead also. And Halsey had ahead of him yet the job of telling this woman what had happened.

"Mrs. Tarlech, I'm afraid I have some very bad—"

"Darling, I'm so sorry I've kept you waiting!" The voice soared into the room ahead of its owner, great bold tones treading the air, every syllable enunciated as though the speaker were declaiming Shakespearean dialogue.

Halsey turned to the double doors that stood open between

63

the entrance hall and the living room. An apparition appeared, framed in the exact center of the doorway. The arms were borne upward on great, billowing green wings, the head crowned with a purple turban crested with an enormous yellow topaz. He thought for a moment the figure had a parrot perched on one shoulder, then perceived it was merely a gigantic blue and red earring. It was Hermione Hopkins, he saw at last, although her get-up reminded him of one of those garish mechanical gypsies in fortune-telling booths on the midway. She had always been somewhat unusual in her dress, but her present appearance was truly staggering.

"Uh—" he mumbled, getting to his feet. "Ms. Hopkins—" He regretted the *Ms.* immediately; not only was it a ridiculous locution for a woman of Hermione's generation, but it came out *miz* and made him sound like a yokel. Out of the corner of his eye, he could see Shelagh Tarlech's mind had already started to work on his incomplete sentence.

Hermione laughed throatily. "I thought you were Iris Morland," she said, unconsciously echoing her sister's comment earlier. "But how *nice* to see you anyway, Chief."

Hermione surged forward, her brightly colored outfit streaming behind her. Halsey was amazed to see how quickly she was moving; he knew she normally walked with a cane. It wasn't until she gripped both his hands in hers that he understood she'd simply flung herself forward, risking the chance she might not reach him before falling. The old girl had guts: she'd begun the performance, and she was going to put it across even if the expected audience wasn't present.

She sank only infinitesimally more quickly than was entirely graceful into the space Halsey had vacated when he stood, and glanced up at him with a look that conveyed her conviction that he was the most charming, most brilliant of men, the look she had perfected over three-quarters of a century on countless stages.

Hermione's neon get-up and great pipe-organ voice were deliberately actressy, Halsey thought. They drew attention to a technique effective enough that Hermione could allow it to be seen, even spoof it slightly, and still dazzle. Like the disorder around her, Hermione was meant to provide some kind of sensory overload. In spite of the circumstances that had brought him there, Halsey could not help smiling his appreciation.

Shelagh's voice behind him was a cool reminder. "You said you had bad news."

Halsey looked awkwardly from Hermione to Shelagh. He'd not anticipated having to tell what he'd come to say in front of Hermione; he didn't know how she would take the news, or what affect such a shock at her age might have. He looked at Shelagh and raised his eyebrows questioningly. She returned his gaze without any change in her own.

"Bad news?" Hermione echoed. The voice was concerned, but still light, firmly in control: a plot point was about to be put across with authority. "Something's happened to Iris, hasn't it— that's why she hasn't come. A car accident?"

"Something has happened to Mrs. Morland," Halsey confirmed, beginning the slow circling in toward what he had to tell them. "I'm afraid it's more serious than a car accident. She passed away this morning." He felt uncomfortable with a euphemism that had always struck him as ridiculous, but he knew the word *dead* hit people like a hammer blow, and *murdered* could not be said at all.

"Passed away? Of what?" Hermione asked. Her manner combined surprise and slight disapproval, as if Halsey had begun improvising in the middle of a scene. "She was a young woman—why would she die?"

"She was . . . shot to death," Halsey said, given permission to use franker terms by Hermione's use of the word *die.*

Hermione gasped with real shock. "But she was coming here." She looked around distractedly, as though Iris might in fact be somewhere present in the jumble of items around them. "Are you quite sure?" She seemed suddenly diminished, even the vibrancy of her clothing appearing to fade in the disordered room.

"I'm afraid so, Miss Hopkins," Halsey said. He looked back and forth between the two women. Shelagh had not reacted to the news in any visible way. When she spoke, her voice was composed.

"You didn't come here to tell us that Iris died."

Halsey glanced at Hermione, whose hands were pressed together as if in prayer. Every finger had an enormous ring on it, fake rubies, emeralds, and diamonds prisming light into her lap.

"Mrs. Tarlech," he said reluctantly, "are you sure—"

"Tell us!" Shelagh shouted. Hermione started.

"Your son, Connor, was with her. They're both dead."

Shelagh uttered a strangled, incoherent moan that sounded as though something were tearing inside her. Her hands tensed into claws, blue veins standing out prominently. Halsey watched helplessly as the woman's face twisted in pain, turning her instantly from assured matron to grieving Fury.

"*She* killed him," Shelagh said, her eyes flashing blue fire at Halsey.

"She?" Halsey inquired, uncertain of the reference.

Shelagh's jaws worked convulsively. "Iris . . . that *creature* . . . she killed him because he didn't want her."

"Mrs. Tarlech, you have to remember that Mrs. Morland was also killed the same way," Halsey said.

"Then it was him—that disgusting, crawling husband of hers! He killed them both because he couldn't control his slut of a wife! Where is Connor?" Shelagh demanded. "What have you done with him? I want to go to him." She tried to rise from the sofa, but her knees buckled and she fell back.

"Mr. Tarlech's body—"

"*Body*," Shelagh echoed despairingly. "No . . ."

"He and Mrs. Morland . . . they've been sent to the coroner's office in Vancouver for—"

Halsey stopped before he said the word *autopsy;* it was clear Shelagh understood the reason. While Halsey quickly sketched the bizarre circumstances in which the bodies had been found, tears leaked from her eyes, small clear drops sliding down without disturbing the carefully applied make-up, collecting briefly at the corners of her mouth before falling finally onto her hands. She must be in her eighties, Halsey thought, yet only now did she seem like an old woman. Considered in the light of her sister's great age, she had always seemed, if not middle-aged, at least not elderly.

"For heaven's sake, Shelagh, surely you realize this is all a mistake?" Hermione's voice startled them both. It was back to full projection, and it was brooking no nonsense.

Shelagh looked up instantly, and Halsey saw with dismay that hope was struggling to surface in her face. He turned to Hermione.

"Miss Hopkins, I'm terribly sorry, but there's no mistake."

"Not about Iris, perhaps," Hermione said. "But it wasn't Connor you found with her." She flashed a smile at him. She had taken hold of the scene and was going to steer it to its proper conclusion. "Connor is in Brazil. There is no way he would have returned here without contacting Shelagh and me. That boy adores us, you know."

Halsey sighed. "It was Mr. Tarlech, Miss Hopkins. I personally identified him—you may remember I investigated the fire on his boat a couple of years ago. I spoke with him a number of times then, and I recognized him immediately. As well, his wallet and identification were still in his pocket."

"It's a mistake," Hermione insisted. "We'll call him. We'll call him right now. Shelagh, what time would it be over there now?"

Shelagh slumped back against the sofa. "There's no point in calling," she said.

"No point in anything," she repeated, as the tears again began to slip down her cheeks.

CHAPTER 9

Beneath his shock of sandy hair, reporter Kenneth Morland's sharp-featured face was impassive. Still, Halsey got the sense of rapid, chaotic mental activity behind the prominent brown eyes. Not a physically strong man, Halsey thought, but then the murderer had not had to rely on strength to accomplish the killings.

It was late afternoon after the discovery of the bodies, and the two men were seated in Morland's living room. From the study upstairs came barely audible sounds of a constantly ringing phone and Morland's recorded voice murmuring a request for callers to leave a message after the tone. Morland folded his wiry arms across his chest and waited for Halsey's next question.

"Did your wife have any enemies you know of?" Halsey asked.

"Enemies?" Morland brooded for a moment. "She made a lot of people angry."

"How did she do that?"

"Her affairs—she played the men off against each other. And when she was finished with them, she always made sure people knew what fools she'd made of them."

"Did you express any objection to her affairs?"

"You don't think I *liked* it, do you?" Morland said, gripping the arms of his chair. Two dark splotches appeared over his cheekbones, the color so deep they resembled burns. "But at least I thought no one else knew. I didn't realize she'd made

69

everyone regard me with contempt—" His voice halted abruptly.

Halsey recognized the humiliation boiling in him. After Vivien told him about The Actor, he'd realized how many times she must have been lying when she said she was staying overnight with friends, or traveling to meet the gallery owners who sold her paintings. For a while, all he'd been able to think about was how many people must have known, each time they saw him, that he was the stock character of farce—the deceived husband.

"Do you have any idea why Mrs. Morland became involved with other men?" Halsey asked. It was a question he'd never been able to answer in his own case; he wondered if Morland could.

Morland's fingers tightened on the chair arms. "I think she saw them as experiments. She wanted to see what people would do when pushed to their limits."

"Including you?" Halsey asked.

"Not at first, I don't think."

"But later?"

"I suppose," Morland conceded. The bitterness in his expression was unsettling.

"Do you own a gun, Mr. Morland?"

"No."

"Ever owned one?"

"No."

"Where were you last night?"

"Here until around ten P.M. Then I left to catch the ferry to Victoria for an early interview this morning. Officer Bailey reached me there at my office around noon, and I flew back."

"Were you by yourself last night?"

"Yes."

"Did you see or talk to Mrs. Morland last night?"

"No."

"Did you know where she was?"

"No." Had Morland hesitated slightly before answering?

"You called Miss Hopkins this morning, and asked to speak to your wife. How did you know she'd be there?"

"Iris told me a few days ago she'd been invited."

"Do you know the names of any of the men she was . . . seeing?" Halsey asked.

"The only one I know about for sure was Arnold Reifel. There were others, but I can't be certain who they were." Morland folded his arms again and a muscle in his jaw twitched. His eyes darkened and his gaze swung to the étagère that held Iris's collection of mechanical figures.

Halsey followed his glance, noticing a brilliantly colored and intricately designed castle on one of the shelves. The structure was about two feet tall, made of polished metal and minutely detailed: every plank in the drawbridge was separately cast, and figures could be glimpsed through the arrow slits, each individuated and in perfect proportion to its position in the structure. At the very top of the castle, leaning over the parapet, were the king and queen, painted faces frozen beneath their gilt crowns. The costumes and the positioning of the figures atop the structure were eerily reminiscent of the situation in which he'd discovered the bodies.

"It's a game," Kenneth said.

"Pardon?"

"The castle. It's a game. Iris put it out to amuse the guests at the party."

Kenneth rose and brought the structure carefully to a low table between them. "It's like a three-dimensional jigsaw puzzle. It's very difficult to put together because all the pieces are connected by some type of elastic string, so you have to move one piece without disturbing the others. Working together, it took several of the guests nearly an hour to finish it Saturday night. Iris could assemble it in minutes."

"I suppose the intricacy of it appealed to her, being a novelist," Halsey said.

"That might have been part of it," Kenneth said. "But what she really liked was this."

He found a small knob near the base of the structure and pulled. The king and queen immediately tumbled backward out of sight, and the entire structure collapsed in on itself with a tinny clatter. Halsey gazed at the rubble in astonishment. There wasn't a single recognizable piece in view—even the bodies of the king and queen had disintegrated into individual fragments.

"Once people had it all put together and were standing around admiring it, she'd make it collapse."

"Didn't people start refusing to play?"

"Only those who knew about it. They stood back and enjoyed watching Iris startle the others."

Kenneth scooped the pieces of the game into a neat pile. "Iris's game," he said, his eyes darkening again. "Her very favorite."

Halsey regarded him closely, considering how to continue.

"Mr. Morland—there was another body discovered with your wife's," Halsey said finally.

He had not told Morland this at first, wanting to give him time to adjust to the idea of his wife's death before he was forced to start considering the implications of her body being discovered with its companion.

"Both of them were dressed in the wedding clothes the mannequins on the float should have been wearing." Halsey paused, noticing a change in Morland's demeanor.

Kenneth Morland's eyes had become suddenly watchful. His whole body was as motionless as those of certain lizards that camouflage themselves by blending in with their background. Seeing this, Halsey understood how Morland had been able to succeed in the cut and thrust of investigative journalism—he could become inanimate at will, attracting no more notice than a chair or filing cabinet, while observing everything around him.

"The man was shot also." Halsey paused again. Morland's attention seemed to be focusing on Halsey like a camera lens. "A friend of your wife's, I believe."

"Connor Tarlech," Morland blurted. Halsey's eyebrows rose. "How did you know?"

"Lucky guess," Morland said. "A man has to have luck sometimes, don't you think, Chief?"

After Halsey left, Morland sat in his office staring at his computer screen. As if of its own volition, his hand replaced the disc in the answering machine with the one lying on his blotter. He flicked the *play* switch.

"Kenneth dear, it's me," Iris said. *"It's Sunday evening and I'm in Vancouver—"*

No, you're not, Kenneth thought.

"—and I just wanted to let you know I have an interview Monday morning—"

Liar.

"—so I won't be home until around noon on Monday."

You won't be home then either.

"Remember, I'm viewing the ancient ruins in the afternoon—"

Hermione Hopkins.

"—hope to see you either before or after then."

Liar.

She went on speaking with the utmost assurance, until he slammed his hand down on the *eject* button and the disc catapulted from the machine. He flung it savagely against the wall.

Clever Iris.

Clever, clever Iris had been completely unaware that the message immediately preceding hers made it clear that every

73

word she uttered was a lie. All the time she was telling him she was in Vancouver, she was with Tarlech at the mill.

It was unfortunate he'd blurted out Tarlech's name to Halsey, but ever since he'd first heard the message, it had pounded in his head like a drum beat. Halsey hadn't pressed the issue, but Kenneth knew he wouldn't forget about it. Halsey had asked if he could look through Iris's study, and with Kenneth's permission had taken her computer and the guest list from the party Iris had given Saturday evening to mark publication of her new novel. Some of the guests might have information that would assist in the investigation, Halsey said. Kenneth supposed that meant they'd all be questioned.

The whole time they stood in Iris's study, Kenneth was all too aware of the disc lying on his blotter across the hall. What would he do if Halsey asked to search his office? He'd already denied knowing where Iris had been last night. He'd been a fool to leave the old disc in plain sight. Not that it was the only way he could be caught in a lie; the person who'd left the first message on it might implicate him also.

But Halsey hadn't asked for anything more. He stood at the door for a moment, as though he knew there was more that Kenneth hadn't told, finally leaving with a polite repetition of his condolences, and a request to stay in touch. As soon as he left, Kenneth erased the incriminating earlier message, but he been unable to resist playing Iris's lies over and over. Even now he could not bring himself to obliterate her voice. He put the new disc back in the machine and tossed the old one in the wastebasket.

Tarlech. He'd thought that was over with long ago. He knew Iris had moved on to others after Tarlech disappeared. Reifel, for example.

He'd discovered her affair with him by arriving home unexpectedly. As he passed through the living room, he knocked one of Iris's mechanical figures off the étagère.

The figure his elbow had sent to the floor was a small tin mouse, painted dark green, with bits of red glass for eyes. Kenneth knelt behind the sofa, retrieved it, and wound the tiny key in its belly to ensure it still functioned.

He stood as he heard Iris's voice, and found to his astonishment that she was naked. She was standing with her back to him, facing the door into the hall. From the kitchen came Arnold's voice inquiring about drink glasses.

Flummoxed, Kenneth dropped behind the sofa, peering out past the end. A moment later, Iris was on the floor beneath Arnold, eyes closed, her face exhibiting the uncontrolled hunger of some devouring insect. Her high-pitched shriek as she climaxed startled Kenneth into relaxing his grip on the mouse, and with a determined *whirrr* it sped from his hand and skimmed across the carpet straight for the couple, red eyes flashing reflected light, clockwork motor buzzing excitedly.

Iris's head swung toward the source of the noise. Kenneth could see her face turning to him in the space between the sofa and the floor, but was powerless to move. She opened her eyes and looked directly into Kenneth's. And laughed.

But she wouldn't laugh anymore.

CHAPTER 10

Millicent Mountjoy stood in the immense carved doorway of her Spanish-style house in Vancouver, directing a cool glance at Halsey. She was somewhere in her fifties, he guessed, although her striking appearance made her age seem irrelevant. She wore an elegant black jacket and slacks, the severity of the outfit relieved only by a line of engraved silver buttons on the jacket. She was easily six feet tall, and the narrow high-heeled pumps she wore let her stand eye-to-eye with Halsey.

"She knows," she said. "Kenneth called yesterday. And the Delbrook sisters."

"May I speak to her anyway?" Halsey asked. "She may be able to help with the investigation."

Millicent's glance hardened. "She's in no state to be talking to anyone."

"I'll leave whenever she wishes," Halsey promised.

"Yes, you will," Millicent said. She hesitated a moment, then moved aside and let him in, her heels knocking with military precision on the terracotta tiles in the foyer. She pointed to an archway on the left. "Wait in there," she ordered. "I'll see if she wants to talk to you."

The living room was startling after the austerity of the foyer: the walls were a radiant turquoise, hung with an amazing collection of vivid orange and red papier-mâché carnival masks. The furniture was upholstered in a butter-colored leather that felt soft as skin when Halsey sank into one of the armchairs. A long, low table in the center of the room supported a sculpture of two nude women reaching up for some unseen object above them.

The room didn't seem to fit with Millicent Mountjoy's personal style, and Halsey wondered if it reflected Enid Regular's influence. It wasn't until Millicent led Enid in that Halsey understood the point of the room. The opulent brilliance of the colors and the unbridled sensuality of the furnishings made Millicent's stark figure dominant over all of it; no matter where she moved in the room, one's eyes automatically focused on her.

Beside Millicent's commanding figure, Enid looked raddled. She was Iris's younger sister, but right now she looked older than Millicent. She wore a shapeless green sweater pulled on over a wrinkled gray skirt, and she'd stuffed her bare feet into frayed huaraches. Mascara had run down her face and been wiped away clumsily, leaving smears across her cheeks that looked like ashes. Her red-rimmed eyes regarded Halsey dully.

"I'll be just across the hall," Millicent said to Halsey, giving him a cold stare. "Remember, you don't have to talk to him," she said to Enid. "Call me if you need me." The sudden shift in vocal temperature was striking. She kissed Enid's smudged cheek and left.

Halsey had stood when the women entered; now Enid gestured him back to his chair. She sank onto the sofa, drawing her legs and arms inward, appearing as drab as a wood beetle against the vibrant yellow of the sofa.

"I'm sorry to be troubling you right now," Halsey began. "I'm just hoping there might be something you can remember about your sister's party or anything else about her that could be helpful in our investigation."

"About who killed her, you mean," Enid said. Her voice was harsh, seeming to scrape her throat as it emerged.

Halsey nodded.

"I'm an alcoholic. Did you know that?"

"No," Halsey said, startled by the non-sequitur. He realized the manner he'd assumed was caused by sedatives was due to something else.

Enid sagged back, her fingers twisting restlessly in her lap. She picked up a scarlet cushion and cradled it against her chest.

"We hated each other, Iris and I. From the time we were girls, she could get anything she wanted. She was the *normal* one; even the fact she slept with any man she felt like wasn't held against her. When our parents found out I worshipped my female professors, they stopped talking to me. Guess who told them.

"She could make me do anything—write to the Honeymoon Falls council to support her denunciation of the wedding-theme stuff she loathed, or personally deliver her manuscripts to her publisher, as if I were some kind of servant. I was utterly spineless when Iris was around."

Self-contempt choked her into silence. She pressed the cushion against her face, then dropped it on the floor, stroking her gray cheeks absently for a moment. "I say we hated each other, but I suppose that wasn't always true. She paid for my detox treatments; I lied to Kenneth for her. So sometimes we got along. But never for long: there was always a sting buried somewhere in whatever Iris did for you, even if it was just a feeling she was enjoying orchestrating your life."

She lapsed into silence again, then lifted her arms as if imitating one of the sculpted figures before her. "Help me up, will you? I want to show you something."

Halsey supported her into the hall. Millicent appeared in front of them.

"I think it's time for you to go," she said to Halsey.

"No, no, it's okay, Millie," Enid said. "We're going to my

room. I want to show him the letter."

For the first time, Millicent's composure slipped. "Enid, you don't know what you're doing right now. Please, let me get rid of him," she said, grabbing Enid's arm. "You don't *have* to do this."

"Yes, I do," Enid said, shaking her off. Millicent stood aside but remained in the hall, watching their halting progress.

"Now *she* loves me," Enid said. "Even the drunken wreck that I am right now." She swung around and called out "Don't you, Millie?" before turning to face Halsey with a woozy smile. "But I'll be better soon—this has happened before, you know. The psychiatrist told me this is just an *episode*!" she said.

"I'm sure it is," Halsey agreed, supporting her unobtrusively as she wove down the hall, and wondering what Enid had that seemed to evoke alarm in the imperturbable Millicent.

Enid shoved her door open, and once more Halsey was surprised by the decor. This time, however, the view was not impressive: even with the curtains closed, Halsey could see the room was a pigpen. Clothing was trampled underfoot, dirty glasses and plates of half-eaten food were abandoned on the bed, and lurid paperbacks were scattered through the mess in tattered clumps. The room reeked of stale liquor. The *episode* had been going on for a while.

"I know who killed Iris," Enid said, flinging her arms open dramatically. "And it's all my fault!"

Oh hell, Halsey thought. He might have known it wasn't going to be anything useful. Millicent's concern probably just meant she didn't want Halsey to see the squalor Enid was living in.

"Why do you say that?" he asked, keeping his tone polite.

Enid stumbled to one dim corner and fumbled on a light. She pawed at a pile of clothing atop a desk, finally uncovering a computer monitor and printer.

"I've been staring at it all day," she said, sounding almost sober. She punched a button on the keyboard and a second later the printer started to hum. "Here," she said. "I told him. And he killed her."

The paper contained only two lines:

She's making a fool of you. If you don't believe me, ask her what she's doing with Connor Tarlech at the mill.

Halsey stared at the words. "How did you know Tarlech was back?"

"Fluke," Enid said, slumping into the chair before the computer. "I was going to Los Angeles, and I happened to pass the two of them leaving the Vancouver airport in Iris's car. They didn't see me."

"When was this?"

"About a month ago. Iris had just shown me a draft of her new book, and one of the characters was a caricature of Millie. She said she'd take it out, but you could never trust her to do what she said. So when I saw a chance to cause trouble for her, I jumped at it. But now she's dead." Stifled whimpers began to slip from Enid's lips. "Oh, God, I swear I never meant for him to kill her."

"Of course not," Halsey agreed. "Who did you send this note to?"

Enid stared at the words on the monitor as if hypnotized and made no response. Then she leaned forward and began rubbing the screen, as if she could erase the words with her hand. She appeared to have tuned out everything around her. Halsey waited for a moment, then when he saw she didn't intend to say more, took a risk.

"*Enid!* Who did you send this to? Tell me right now!"

The door flew open behind him, and Millicent sprang at him with pantherish fury.

"Get out!" She yanked his arm. She was remarkably strong, and she forced Halsey off-balance with surprising ease. *"Get out now!"*

Halsey struggled to regain his footing on the lumpy mess beneath his feet, but didn't resist her when she thrust him toward the door. He'd been there only with their permission and had no legal right to insist on questioning Enid further. Just before he exited, he got Enid's answer.

"Arnold Reifel," she whispered.

CHAPTER 11

"Where were the bodies discovered?"

"On a parade float."

"What kind of float?"

Halsey ignored this.

"What was the cause of death?"

"Both victims died from gunshot wounds to the chest, inflicted with a .32-caliber pistol."

"Who discovered the bodies?"

"Officer Lydia Bailey, of the Honeymoon Falls Police Department."

"Is it true Iris Morland was killed because of information contained in her new book?"

"I have not seen the manuscript yet, but we have no reason to suppose it has any connection with her death."

"Are you pursuing any leads at this time?"

"The investigation is proceeding as expected."

"Have any suspects been identified?"

"Not at the present time."

Halsey watched himself speak into the sea of microphones bobbing below the television cameras. It was 6:00 P.M. Tuesday evening, and the report playing now on the small portable set at the station resulted from the questions he'd answered while he'd run the gauntlet to his car after the press conference in Vancouver. Halsey and Bailey were drinking coffee while Larsen finished off the remains of the Chinese take-out they'd ordered.

Bailey pried open another carton and offered it to Halsey.

"Doughnut?"

"Good idea, Lydia," Halsey said, helping himself to a lemon-filled beauty.

A few seconds later, he realized Larsen and Bailey were both looking at him in surprise. He was shocked to find the doughnut had disappeared.

"Guess I was still hungry," he said, mortified.

Bailey held the box out again, a little cautiously this time, as if afraid her hand might disappear with the contents.

Halsey shook his head and averted his eyes from temptation. The one he'd just bolted down was probably worth two hundred extra sit-ups tonight. And one more performance like that and his doughnut obsession would be out in the open.

On-screen, the grilling continued. A blonde head cut through the shoal of reporters like a dorsal fin until its owner, Delia Bendel, a Channel Five reporter, was so close to Halsey that only her microphone separated them. Her long, thin face turned up to him, eyes glinting.

"Isn't it true," Delia demanded, "that the total Honeymoon Falls Police Department consists of only three people?"

"Uh-oh," Larsen muttered, as Halsey tersely agreed with the woman.

"And isn't it also true," Delia continued, "that none of them except you have any professional training?"

Bailey, who'd been looking pleased since Halsey's reference to her finding the bodies, muttered an obscene suggestion at Delia so startling and out of character that Halsey was forced to bite his lip to keep from laughing. Larsen choked on a mouthful of sweet-and-sour pork and dabbed a napkin at the ends of his mustache, which were tinged pink with sauce.

"That's *not* true," the on-screen Halsey said.

"Are you denying that your staff consists of a former

83

hairdresser and a truck driver, and that neither has a university degree?"

"Everybody, including television reporters, was a former something," Halsey said, fixing the woman with a level stare. "Some of the best detectives I've known haven't had a university degree."

Delia Bendel was not to be deflected. "You have a double murder on your hands that is commanding national attention. Do you really expect to solve it with an amateur police force?"

"They're not amateurs, any more than you are," Halsey said.

"Wouldn't it be better to forget your ego," Bendel said, "and call in the RCMP?"

"Wouldn't it be better for you to check your facts before you ask questions like that?" Halsey replied. The steel in his voice caused the smallest furrow of uncertainty to appear between Delia Bendel's eyes, but she forged onward.

"Meaning what?" she challenged.

"Meaning that this morning I was sworn in by the RCMP as a special investigator in charge of this case, with the full resources of the force at my disposal." Halsey fired his broadside straight at her, and she was swept away as the mob of reporters surged forward to demand details.

Larsen whooped with satisfaction. "Blew her right out of the water," he said. "What an idiot. She's been on Channel Five all day going on about the 'sleepy little town awakened by a shocking crime.' Made us all sound like rubes."

"On the national news, we were a romantic little town paralyzed by fear," Bailey said.

"It'll get worse," Halsey warned. He held up the two daily papers he'd picked up in Vancouver. One, a tabloid, was headlined *DEATH OF A BRIDE AND GROOM*. The other, more sedate, contented itself with *FAMOUS WRITER MUR-DERED*. Both were liberally sprinkled with quotes from the press conference he'd given Monday evening after the bodies had been discovered. Under a subhead of *Police Baffled,* the tabloid quoted Halsey saying that the investigation was proceeding but no suspects had been identified. Halsey had always hated that *police baffled* phrase. It surfaced inevitably when there were no immediate arrests, and conjured up in his mind the image of a large, dumb dog trying to recall where it had buried a bone.

"We haven't heard the last of Delia Bendel either," Bailey said. "She's been out here all afternoon, asking honeymooners how they feel about the murders."

Sure enough, scenes began to appear on the television of hand-holding couples emerging from the hiking trails in the vicinity of the mill. Delia sprang forward with a dramatic account of the discovery of the bodies.

"Is this still the 'Romance Capital of the World' for you?" she inquired, shoving the mike in their faces. "Can you think of love when death has swooped so close?"

"Ah, jeez," Bailey muttered. "If only death would swoop on her."

"The phone's been ringing all day," Larsen said. "Selby called to complain because he's getting calls from honeymooners wanting to cancel their reservations. Mayor Coyle wants to talk to you as soon as possible. And there's a whole stack of messages on your spike from reporters all the way to New York and back. Apparently the Delbrook sisters were on a remote hook-up to a tabloid TV show in California today, describing how they discovered the bodies and promising to devote themselves full time to solving the crime. Said it was their civic duty as town councilors."

"*They* discovered the bodies! That's a hot one," Bailey said. "They'd have driven right through town with them on the float if I hadn't pulled them over."

"Oh, and Lucy Mitchum called," Larsen said. "Wants an interview too, for some TV show."

"Lucy's on retainer from the All News Network to provide exclusive coverage on the murders," Bailey said. "Let's hope she gets things straighter for them than she usually does."

"They'll all have to wait until the resources the RCMP promised get here," Halsey said. "I've asked for two officers for the course of the investigation. They'll be here tomorrow morning."

Larsen frowned and became interested in scraping the last of the pork from the bottom of the carton. Bailey thumped her coffee mug down on the desk and glared at Halsey.

"So in spite of the fact that I discovered the bodies, I don't get any chance to work on the case," she said. "Some outsider will come in here and just take over—is that it?"

Larsen snickered into the sweet-and-sour carton.

"You might swoon," he said, tasting the fringe of his mustache. To both his and Halsey's surprise, Bailey only smiled.

"Did I mention that your mother was in today?" she asked. "She brought her little boy's laundry in."

Larsen's fair skin flushed from the roots of his hair to the base of his throat. "What did you do with it?"

"Nothing," Bailey said. "Told her to put it in your locker."

Now Larsen's face blanched. "She couldn't—it was locked!"

Bailey smirked. "Worried mommy might see your dirty magazines?"

Larsen rose abruptly and strode from the room. They could hear him fiddling with the combination lock in the alcove off the hall where the lockers were located.

Halsey looked at Bailey. "That wasn't nice, Lydia. Mrs. Larsen's a religious woman—"

Bailey nudged a brown paper package tied with string from under the desk. "The boy wonder's undies," she said. She booted the package over to the end of the desk at which Larsen had been sitting. Halsey sighed.

Larsen stomped back in. "It was locked. What the hell are you up to?" he demanded, glaring at Bailey.

She smiled pleasantly and sipped her coffee, ignoring him. Halsey pointed to the package on the floor. Larsen flushed again, scooped the package from the floor, and took it back out to his locker. A moment later, he slumped into his chair, grabbed the take-out carton, then flung it down when he realized it was empty. He directed what was intended as a malevolent glare at Bailey, but succeeded only in looking sulky. He opened his mouth to speak, but Halsey'd had enough.

"You started it," Halsey reminded him.

"As I was saying before I was so rudely interrupted," Bailey said, "you're bringing in someone else to work on this, and shutting me out?"

Before Halsey could respond to this, Larsen spoke up.

"Look, Will. How do you think we feel about being passed over for a chance to work on something besides parking tickets or directing traffic on parade day? It's not as if we're ever likely to have another opportunity to get this kind of experience. I know we might not seem like real police officers to someone with your background, and sometimes we—I—act like an asshole, but we are serious about being good cops. I know we're kind of a joke sometimes, but that doesn't mean we want to be."

Halsey listened to Larsen with surprise verging on amazement. It was the first time he'd heard him speak without the immaturity that made him hard to take seriously. Even more surprising was the fact that Bailey was nodding agreement. There was silence for a moment while Halsey considered.

"If," he said at last, "*if* I let you work on the investigation, it would be on the condition that the first time you embarrass me, you're back to your regular duties." He looked straight into Bailey's eyes, then Larsen's. Both met his gaze evenly.

"Agreed," Bailey said. Larsen nodded solemnly.

"And *everything* you learn on this investigation is confidential," Halsey added.

Bailey bridled. "Why wouldn't it be?"

"Of course," Larsen agreed.

God help us, Halsey thought. He began filling them in on the interviews he'd conducted.

"Did Mrs. Tarlech or Miss Hopkins say what Tarlech was doing here?" Larsen asked. "Wasn't he supposed to be over in—" He waved an arm, denoting some vague foreign location.

"Hermione didn't know he was here. I think Shelagh did, but she wasn't saying anything, and at the time, I didn't want to press her. I'll be talking to her again."

"Was he staying with Shelagh, do you think?" Bailey asked.

"No, we found enough evidence at the mill to make it clear he was hiding out there."

"*We?*" Bailey asked. She was clearly suspicious of any potential newcomer to the scene.

"Detective Carol Wilson from the homicide squad who flew out from Vancouver, and me," Halsey said, annoyed. "*We*"—he swooped on the word with the same paranoid emphasis she'd used, and was just tired enough to take satisfaction in the faint flush of embarrassment it produced— "*we* found suitcases with his clothes, letters from various financial institutions, canned food. He'd been there for a few weeks."

"Doing what?" Larsen asked.

"One of the things we have to find out, obviously."

"What about Kenneth Morland?" Bailey asked. "Do we know where he was when his wife was killed?"

"Says he was on the midnight ferry to Victoria. Didn't see anyone he knew, and spent the night alone in an apartment he keeps there."

"Convenient," Larsen commented.

"Possibly true also. The murders occurred in the middle of the night. Most people would be home in bed."

"He could just as easily have taken an early ferry Sunday morning. And he knew it was Connor Tarlech who'd been killed with his wife, not Arnold Reifel." Bailey shook her head. "*Lucky guess,* my rear end."

"He's a reporter, Lydia. He could have learned all or part of the story from half a dozen different people."

"If he already knew, why let you go through the whole routine of telling him?" Bailey asked, unconvinced.

"Shock, maybe," Halsey said. "Or he didn't know all of the details. Or perhaps he wanted to find out what I knew."

"What *do* we know? About what happened to the victims, I mean?" Larsen asked.

"The coroner's report shows both Morland and Tarlech were killed by shots to the chest fired from the same .32-caliber pistol. Tarlech was shot twice: apparently the first bullet was deflected by his left arm, probably as he raised it in a defensive gesture. Morland was shot at very close range—three or four feet; Tarlech from about ten feet. About six to ten hours elapsed between the time they were killed and the time they arrived here."

"Did the homicide guys find anything useful at the mill?" Bailey asked. "Fingerprints? Blood? Anything that didn't belong to the deceased?"

"Blood, of course, but only the types belonging to the victims. Judging from the locations of the blood stains, they were shot in what used to be the old paymaster's office on the second floor. Tarlech appears to have been camping out there, probably because it has no windows, so he could have light without it be-ing seen from outside. After they were killed, the bodies were loaded onto a hand truck and hauled outside onto the receiving dock. The top of the parade float was just slightly below the level of the dock."

"What the hell was the float doing out there on MFR property in the first place?" Larsen asked.

MFR was the company whose takeover of the timber license had put Tarlech out of business, and given the damage that action had inflicted on the town, the company was not popular. The acronym stood for Matcor Forest Resources, although some locals freely expressed the idea that it was an abbreviation for an obscenity suggesting an improper relationship with one's parent.

"Ever since MFR took over the timber license from Tarlech, they've worked overtime to polish their reputation in town. They lent the truck, an old beater that's been sitting out there for years. And they let the kids who built the float have any lumber they could scrounge from the site to put it together."

"Do they still have power out there?" Larsen asked. "I thought they mothballed the whole place when they got the timber rights."

"There's still a generator in one of the sheds, but Tarlech hadn't been using it—too noisy probably. He had a gas lantern in the office."

"Prints?" Bailey prompted.

"The only recent ones were from Iris Morland and Tarlech. There were others from mill staff from several years ago."

"What about footprints? Whoever killed them couldn't have walked around in there without leaving some trace," Larsen said.

"Not much help there either. It rained earlier that night, and the ground outside was watery muck. Lots of smeared mud splotches, none of them clear enough to take a decent impression. Same with the road outside. We found the victims' cars in one of the outbuildings, but no sign of them driving up."

"I presume the float and the clothes on the bodies were also examined," Bailey said. "Nothing there either?"

"Nope. A couple of hairs were retrieved from the sleeve of the bridal gown, but they appear to be from Tarlech. At some point, his head must have rested against Iris Morland's body after the costume was put on her."

Halsey was glad the float had been disassembled and taken to Vancouver. He'd hate to have it sitting in back of the station, attracting gawkers like flies to a carcass, and reminding them all of what they'd found on it. He glanced at Bailey. Her breathing had quickened slightly when she mentioned the float, and she was pale, obviously recollecting the moments leading up to the discovery of the bodies. However, her expression was set in lines that made it clear her own body was not about to be allowed to slip its moorings again.

"So the killer came in, shot them, and left without leaving any sign of his presence," she said.

"Or hers," Larsen said.

"Hers?" Bailey demanded. "Hers who?"

"Doesn't have to be a man, you know," Larsen pointed out.

Bailey flipped a hand dismissively. "I'll bet a month's pay against your stack of dirty magazines it was."

"I don't have—" Larsen began, but Halsey cut him off.

"John's right, Lydia," Halsey said. "Don't forget that Iris Morland had plenty of female enemies. And Tarlech had broken off affairs with more than one woman."

"Including Her Worship, our esteemed lady mayor," Bailey said. "Does that make her a suspect too?"

"No, but it doesn't rule her out, either," Halsey said.

Larsen's eyes had bugged at the mention of the mayor. "Mayor Coyle and Connor Tarlech?" But . . . she's the *mayor.*"

"It was before she was mayor, if that's any comfort to your

faith in local officialdom," Bailey said. "And just so it doesn't come as a shock to you later, it isn't *really* the Easter Bunny that leaves the basket of candies behind the sofa."

Larsen shot her an angry glare and clamped his jaws together while she continued.

"Although I suppose she might have hoped it would resume. I wonder if she knew he'd returned." She looked at Halsey with a malicious glint in her eye. "Have you asked her where she was Sunday night?"

"I'll be talking to her again soon. She was ill yesterday when I stopped by her house to tell her what happened."

"What happens next?" Larsen asked Halsey. "I mean, what do we do?"

Halsey massaged his forehead wearily. He'd slept less than four hours since Monday morning, and he could feel an annihilating wall of fatigue approaching.

"We start investigating the people who might logically be presumed to have a motive for killing Iris Morland or Connor Tarlech."

"Her husband, I guess," Larsen mused. "He might have been mad enough to kill both of them."

"Or any of her other lovers," Bailey put in.

"Other lovers?" Larsen said, eyebrows raised. "What do you mean? She didn't ever seem like a . . . a . . . that kind of a woman."

"You mean she didn't wear fishnet stockings and stand under a lamp post?" Bailey inquired. "There isn't anybody in town, except maybe her husband, who couldn't name at least three men who were involved with her at one time or another," she said, and proceeded to name names.

Halsey sighed. "Remember, everything that's discussed here is confidential."

"Including the stuff about the Easter Bunny," Bailey said.

Larsen turned to Halsey. "I want you to know that I appreciate your confidence in us, and no matter how unprofessional she is, I'm still going to work with her, and we're going to do a good job."

It was Bailey's turn to clench her teeth. Nonetheless, when she finally spoke, it was to echo Larsen's promise.

Halsey nodded. "I expect no less," he said.

He didn't tell them he'd known from the beginning he'd have no option but to involve them in the investigation. As he'd explained to RCMP Commissioner Jim Harrelson, it would take an outsider forever just to learn what was common gossip in Honeymoon Falls.

What he could not deny, however, was the truth of Delia Bendel's public slurs on Larsen's and Bailey's lack of experience in a major criminal investigation. Privately, he had to concede even more of a problem with them: their judgment was often unseated by their inability to control their personal rancor.

"But if they can't get information from the locals, nobody else will either," he'd told Harrelson. "They know those people."

Harrelson had mulled over the situation and suggested appointing Halsey special investigator. In addition, he'd agreed to provide two extra officers to police Honeymoon Falls while Halsey and his staff worked on the case, as well as putting the RCMP's research and investigative facilities at his disposal.

"You realize that if you don't produce results quickly, I'll have to replace you," Harrelson had warned. "The media's going to chew my ass big time while this is going on."

Halsey didn't need to be told it was going to be no cakewalk. Somehow, he was going to have to juggle assignments between Larsen, Bailey, and two new staff, keep as much of the regular police work done as possible, and solve a double murder.

While avoiding negative publicity.

Before profits from the season were seriously affected.

With sufficient involvement of Larsen and Bailey to help both of them grow into real police officers.

Without offending local VIPs who happened to be suspects. Shouldn't be too hard.

CHAPTER 12

Lord, what is the matter with me, Lucy Mitchum wondered. Halsey'd taken her by surprise when he called to ask if it would be convenient for her to talk to him about Iris Morland's party, and she'd asked him over right away. She must have seemed so transparently eager—she could only hope he'd put it down to journalistic curiosity.

She hung up the phone knowing she should clean the entire house, get her hair done and buy a dress that would dazzle him. She settled for frantically brushing her hair and discarding everything in her closet as too dressy, too casual, or too tight, with the result that she was still tugging on a pair of black slacks when she heard his car pull up outside. She couldn't find the belt for the slacks and it was too late for shoes; she ran barefoot from the bedroom, yanking the door shut on the mess behind her. She paused for a second at the front door, took a deep breath, and opened it.

"I was wondering when you'd get to me," she heard herself say. She felt the warmth rising in her face and cursed the fair skin that made it impossible to hide. "I mean . . . please come in."

Halsey stepped inside and smiled down at her. She had a charmingly abstracted look, which suggested he'd interrupted her in the middle of something important, but she didn't seem to mind. He recalled her cool professional image at the parade site, and thought how much more attractive she was when she hadn't made any effort. The soft glow of her complexion set off her wide blue eyes, and her bare feet and casual shirt and slacks projected an appealing insouciance.

"I appreciate you seeing me on such short notice," he said. "I'll make it quick."

Lucy stopped herself just in time from assuring him her whole afternoon was at his disposal. She led him into the living room, deciding that while it might be dusty it should at least be tidy, considering how little time she spent in it.

"Coffee?" she inquired. Oh God, she didn't have any. "Tea?"

Pick tea, she implored silently. He did. She fled to the kitchen, leaving him to contemplate the photo gallery her parents had assembled to record her progress from grade school through university.

She plugged the kettle in, rinsed mugs under the tap, and dropped the tea bags into them directly. She'd had a brief vision of using her mother's good china, but quickly realized the idea was excessive for what was supposed to be spur-of-the-moment hospitality.

"Can I help?" he called.

"No thanks," she said, forcing calmness into her voice.

During her brief marriage, she'd lived in a large house with her stockbroker husband and maintained it like a showplace—it was the one thing he hadn't complained about.

Now one bedroom, and another room she'd converted into an office, seemed more than enough. She visited the kitchen occasionally to make tea, but went out for meals, or ate take-out in front of her computer. Neglect, along with a thin layer of dust, had settled on most of the other rooms. Sometimes the remnants of her former housekeeping standards surfaced like sad-faced ghosts and prompted frenzied cleaning jags, but the results were always ineffectual, as if somehow the house knew she did not have the firm hand of her mother, who'd kept everything gleaming.

"Your parents must be very proud of you," Halsey said when she returned.

"They're in Arizona," Lucy said absently, setting mugs of tea down on the low table between them. Were those toast crumbs in the sugar? She pried open the carton of milk. "I'm afraid I'm out of lemon." In fact, she couldn't remember the last time she'd had it in the house.

"Are they enjoying it there?" Halsey asked, sugaring his tea.

"Where?" Lucy asked. Those *were* toast crumbs. Fortunately, Halsey didn't seem to have scooped any of them up. His uniform shirt tightened around his broad shoulders as he leaned forward to set the spoon down. "Oh—yes, they love the retirement community there."

"So you've taken over the paper permanently, I imagine," Halsey said.

"Yes—yes, I have. It's out three times a week now, and finally beginning to turn a small profit. I'm still paying the bills by designing and testing computer software."

"Wish I'd known there was an expert so close to home," Halsey said. "We put up with a glitch in one of our programs for months until we could get someone in from Vancouver."

"I'd be glad to look at your system any time," Lucy said.

Oh God, why did everything come out sounding like she was talking about something else? She felt the color rising in her face again. Act like a grown-up, she admonished herself.

Halsey set his mug down. "I understand you were at Iris Morland's party a couple of weeks ago. Did you notice anything unusual that evening?"

"Not really," Lucy replied, relieved to find some capacity for normal speech returning. "I'd just returned that evening from visiting my parents, so I didn't get to Iris's until around ten thirty, and by that time the fun was pretty much over."

"The fun?" Halsey inquired.

"Oh, Iris always had the knife out for someone, and apparently that night it was Marjorie Reifel. The strange thing is, I don't think Marjorie had even been there, but none of the few people who were still around would explain what had been going on. And I got the distinct feeling Iris was about to start in on me—she had that air of barely suppressed glee she exhibits when she's about to do her great white shark routine."

"Any idea why she'd attack you?"

"Nope, but I'll find out," Lucy said. "I was in Vancouver troubleshooting a computer network for most of last week, and of course the big news this week is the discovery of the murders, so I haven't had time to tap my usual sources." She grinned as she uttered the last phrase. "Us crack crime reporters talk like that, you know."

Halsey laughed. "Yeah, us cops do too."

Lucy was suddenly thoughtful. "You asked me if anything unusual happened at Iris's party, and I just thought of something—when Iris announced her book was dedicated to him, Kenneth called Iris a bitch. Right in front of everyone."

"Presumably this wasn't his usual behavior?"

"God, no. Kenneth is famous for being Iris's doormat."

"What did Iris do?"

"Laughed as though she'd just drunk a quart of warm blood."

"Have you seen or talked to Morland since the party?"

"Nope. I called him right after I left the parade site, but all I got was the answering machine, and the tape was full so I couldn't even leave a message. I suppose everyone in town had been calling. Not that I imagine he'd be willing to talk to me anyway. Right now I imagine he's pretty gun-shy—" She broke off, horrified. "Oh, God. I mean, he'd naturally want to avoid anyone from the press."

"Do you think Marjorie knew about her husband's affair with Iris?"

"It's hard to imagine she wouldn't have known. Maybe she felt she was in no position to criticize."

"What do you mean?" Halsey leaned forward, intent.

Lucy caught the faint hint of his aftershave and for a moment was distracted by a vagrant impulse to run her fingers along his jaw, trailing the scent down his throat to the knot in his tie.

"I was up on the hill behind Honeymoon Haven taking pictures of Bridegroom Bay for *Town Talk*. I saw Art Selby drive up with Marjorie."

"You think they were having an affair?"

Lucy turned her palms up. "All I know is Marjorie ducked out of sight until they drove into Selby's garage. I was still there when they left, and Marjorie pulled the same duck-and-cover maneuver." She frowned. "Does it mean anything to your investigation, even if they were?"

"Can't tell at the moment," Halsey said. "Right now I'm just gathering information. I won't know until later if any of the pieces fit together."

Lucy leaned toward him. "Will you keep me in mind for anything you can share? *ANN* is a real pit bull and there doesn't seem to be much meat to feed them right now."

Halsey smiled. "What's a nice girl like you . . . ?"

Lucy laughed. "I sometimes wonder myself. I guess it's a kind of challenge. I don't know if I want to be a television reporter, but I'd like to prove I could be if I wanted to." She paused for a moment. "Maybe we could meet from time to time. To discuss the progress of the case?"

"I take it you haven't adopted Delia Bendel's view that there hasn't been any," Halsey said.

"Can't stand the woman. Every time I see her roll into town with her million-dollar satellite linkup and her own hairdresser,

I'd sell my grandmother to scoop her."

It was Halsey's turn to laugh. "I'm not that crazy about her myself. But she's not the only one who's not impressed. Town council isn't thrilled with what's happening either."

Lucy snorted. "Edna Sigurdson and Art Selby don't give a damn about finding the murderer. Their idea of progress is what's recorded on their cash register tapes at the end of the day. And the rest of them, with the exception of Selena, wouldn't know what to do with the murderer if he turned up at a council meeting and confessed."

Halsey smiled. "Now that would make a good headline for *Town Talk*."

"Instead of the ones like 'Edna Sigurdson Appointed Head of Sneering Committee,' you mean." Lucy laughed. "That was an accident, but it got so much attention sales rose nearly twenty-five percent. Now I throw in a few goofs on purpose, just to give people a laugh."

"My favorite was the caption on the picture of Reverend Slater fixing the church floor with salvaged planks," Halsey said.

" 'Old Broads Take on New Life in Reverend Slater's Hands,' " Lucy supplied.

"Did he get mad?"

"Nope. He was still laughing when he called to ask permission to reprint the article in the church bulletin."

Lucy admired the smoothness with which he'd diverted her request for updates on the investigation, but she was not about to give up yet. She decided to try an avenue that might have a more direct appeal for him.

"So, will you help me fry Delia Bendel's phony hide?" she asked.

Halsey's amused glance made it clear he recognized both her refusal to be distracted and the astuteness she'd shown in selecting her lure.

"I'll pass on anything I can, but the pickings are likely to be slim for the moment," Halsey said. He stood up. "I've taken up enough of your afternoon."

"Not at all, Chief," Lucy said. *Not at all, William,* she thought. She led him to the door, and they stood facing each other for a moment. She felt her nervousness returning. They were so close, and she could smell his aftershave again. He opened the door and held it ajar for a moment. His expression seemed tentative, as if he were thinking about asking her something further. She smiled encouragingly.

"Well," he said slowly. "Thank you for the tea."

CHAPTER 13

Shirley Novak shoved the vacuum cleaner over the worn broadloom in Kenneth Morland's office and wondered how his wife's death would affect her employment. It could go either way, she supposed. Morland might sell the house and leave Honeymoon Falls, or he might stay and require her services more than once a week.

It would not be the first job she'd lost, if she did lose it. Shirley was not a good cleaning woman; she hated housework and had always done as little of it as possible in her own home. Eddie never seemed to care, same as she hadn't minded how much he drank, as long as he paid the bills.

Their daughter, Pearl, used to complain she was ashamed to bring friends home because the house was a pigsty, and Eddie was always slumped in his underwear in front of the TV belching, and sometimes worse. She even came home one day and told them that her high school guidance counselor said she came from a dysfunctional family.

"My functions are all a-okay," Eddie said, accompanying his assurance with a demonstration that sent Pearl to her room roaring with fury.

Eddie, at fifty-four, had been only a year away from early retirement when the mill went under four years ago. The pension fund they'd both relied on turned out to have disappeared into the magician's bag of tricks employed by Connor Tarlech's creditors. Shirley still did not understand how this could have happened—something to do with a bad investment in South American currencies, apparently, and a shell company that had gained control of the company that held the pension contributions. A lengthy police investigation found enough evidence to prove Tarlech's involvement in the shell company, but not enough to prove criminal intent. The only thing certain was that the money was irretrievably gone.

It took almost a year before she and Eddie realized what was going to happen to them. Until then, they'd both assumed Eddie would have to keep working for years to come—a bitter enough pill to swallow when retirement had seemed within their grasp. Slowly they came to realize that even that wasn't the worst that was going to happen.

The fact was that nobody was going to hire Eddie. He'd run a planer machine at the mill for thirty-two years, and he was too old for any of the trade schools. No one wanted him anymore—tough Eddie, the shop steward, head of the grievance committee at the mill, the bellowing bull that no one crossed. Gradually, the prospects of a life made up of leisurely summer boat trips down the coast, wintering in Arizona, occasional flights to Reno or Vegas, receded until they disappeared from view.

It was on the last trip in the Winnebago that Shirley realized how serious their situation was. They didn't go to the R.V. park as usual; it was too expensive. Instead, they found a spruce grove off the Washington interstate and pulled in for the night. She'd been awakened by a noise sometime in the night and instinctively reached out to Eddie, only to find he wasn't beside her. Heart hammering, she listened to a series of low gasping noises, as if there were something outside struggling to pull air into its body.

"Eddie," she whispered into the darkness. "What is it?"

There was no answer. She got up and padded silently to the

103

front of the vehicle and looked out. He was sitting outside on the bumper, back to her, and from his fixed attitude he seemed to be watching whatever was causing the disturbance. She looked past him, trying to pierce the darkness and focus on what he was seeing. It wasn't until she realized his shoulders were heaving that she understood the sound was coming from him.

Heart attack was the first thing that flashed into her mind. Or he'd drunk too much and was being sick. When she realized he was crying, she swayed dizzily, feeling sick herself. She had never, ever seen him do that. While she twisted her hands together, frightened, pitying, uncertain whether to go to him or let him alone, he turned and saw her standing inside. They stood with the glass between them, looking into each other's faces. It was only then she realized that their old, unexciting, satisfactory lives had ended, and all that was left now was the struggle for survival.

When they came back, they sold the Winnebago. A few months later, the boat went, then her car. Eddie started doing handyman jobs, and Shirley worked at Honeymoon Heaven for a while, until Art Selby fired her for falling asleep in one of the rooms she was supposed to be cleaning. Since then she'd done housework during the summer months for the only people in Honeymoon Falls who hired others to do their own work—the Colony people. Thank God Eddie'd got the job at the new mall; it paid just enough that Shirley might not have to keep working.

Shirley kicked the vacuum into the hallway and started pushing it to the utility closet. It rolled forward in unwieldy loops, crashing into the wastebasket she'd set outside the office door to empty later, spilling the contents in her path. One wheel caught on something in the mess, and when she yanked it free, she saw it was a CD. In spite of the rough treatment, it looked okay. Maybe Pearl could use it to record that crap her friends called music.

She dropped the disc in her pocket, crammed the vacuum into the closet, and scrabbled the mess on the floor into a garbage bag. She flung the wastebasket back under Morland's desk. As she straightened up, she glanced out the window over the desk.

Lucy Mitchum was still out there, standing in front of a camera crew and gesturing toward the house. Shirley would have to slip out the back way, she supposed. They'd pestered the life out of her when she arrived, but when she found Lucy was the only one getting any money out of it, she brushed by with what everybody said on TV: *no comment*. She'd have to be stupid to antagonize Kenneth Morland for nothing. Not that the pittance she was getting from him was so important, but having access to his house might be. Who knew what one of those big TV shows might be willing to pay for whatever she cared to offer. A tour of the house, say. Now that might be rewarding enough to be worth getting fired for.

On her way out, she tossed the garbage bag into the trash can behind the back fence and walked up the lane, humming cheerfully. She'd been in the house for less than ninety minutes, but Morland would never know, and there was no reason she couldn't charge him for the usual three hours.

Chapter 14

"Yes, I knew he was back."

Selena Coyle pushed the Wednesday morning edition of *Town Talk* away from her until it slid over the edge of her kitchen table to the floor. She spoke carefully, as though each word might shatter the fragile composure she'd managed to muster. Her eyes were fixed on her small hands, which lay palms down on the tablecloth, like birds that had fallen to earth. She was dressed casually, her pallor accentuated by a shapeless black shirt. Halsey wondered if the color had been chosen deliberately, or if she'd simply pulled on whatever was available when she got up.

"You'd seen him?" Halsey prompted.

She sighed wearily and closed her eyes for a moment.

"He called." Her eyes opened, and her gaze slid over him, coming to rest again on her hands.

Halsey waited.

"When I heard his voice . . ." The sentence trailed off. "I thought he was going to tell me he still cared about me. Wanted me back." She gave a brief, self-mocking laugh that ended in a gasp, quickly stifled.

"What did he want?"

"Council documents from the time when MFR took over the timber license. Asked if I'd bring them to him at the mill. I took copies to him on Sunday night." Selena looked at him directly for the first time. "I know that makes me a suspect."

Halsey refrained from comment. "Do you recall the time you got to the mill?"

"A little after ten thirty. He asked me to come when it was dark, so no one would wonder what I was doing there. He said he had to keep out of sight until he could . . . 'prove himself,' I think he said."

"What did he mean by that, do you know?"

Selena shook her head. "I really didn't think about anything, except that I'd be seeing him again." She lifted her ravaged face to Halsey. "I couldn't seem to get the knack of living without him. Even after he was gone, I thought of him all the time—there was never room for anyone else."

Halsey knew what she meant. Your past losses hung on you like old rags, warning off anyone who might come too close. After a while, no one did.

"Was the stuff you copied any use to him?" he asked.

"No. That was before the town had a mayor, and there was just Edna Sigurdson and Hannah Spofford looking after things. There were no proper files kept. All I could find was some cartons of old receipts, tax rolls, and letters from various provincial ministries."

"Nothing on the timber license?"

"No." Selena turned her palms up. "Does it matter now?"

"It could explain what drew Mr. Tarlech back here. And that might point to who killed him. I'll have to get someone to check through all the records you've got, just in case."

"The boxes are locked in cupboards in the new council chambers," Selena said. "I'll give you the key."

"Who actually owns the mill site now?" Halsey asked. "MFR?"

"Yes. But they had no interest in operating it once they got the timber license. They turned the site over to the town on a fifty-year lease for a dollar a year rather than pay taxes on it.

That's how we were able to accommodate Cecil Atkinson's request to use it for his college." Selena frowned as she mentioned Atkinson, but offered nothing further.

Halsey hesitated before asking his next question, suspecting he was approaching the part that had devastated her. He watched her face for a moment, and she looked up suddenly.

"Go ahead," she said.

"What happened when you got to the mill?" Halsey asked.

"He was waiting for me inside the door at the front of the main building. He led me up some stairs into a little room he was living in." Selena paused. "God—it was so wonderful to see him again," she said. The longing in her voice was almost palpable. Her eyes filled, and for a moment she was silent. Finally, she took a deep breath and continued.

"He said he'd received information that Edna Sigurdson had been involved in having his timber license withdrawn and awarded to MFR. He was hoping the council records would show some irregularity that would force the Forests Ministry to open an enquiry and restore the license to him."

Halsey's eyebrows rose. "He thought Edna Sigurdson engineered the closure of the mill?" he asked. "Did that seem likely to you?"

Selena sighed. "Not really. Edna'd skin her own mother for a buck, but her only source of income was that flower shop. She was certainly smart enough to know that a mill closure would turn Winslow into a ghost town and put her out of business. When the mill did close she almost went bankrupt. Until The Theme took off, she was planning to move down to Vancouver and open a store there."

"Did Mr. Tarlech tell you how he got the idea Edna was responsible for the loss of the timber license?"

"No. But I know where it came from." A hectic flush appeared along her cheekbones, standing out in startling contrast to her pallor.

"I threw myself into his arms and just started babbling— telling him how much I loved him and that I'd do anything for him, if only he wouldn't leave me again." She stared into Halsey's eyes. "I begged."

Halsey averted his glance, unable to watch the naked emotion that burned in her.

"And then," she said, forcing the words out, "Iris walked in."

Halsey felt the hair on the back of his neck prickle. Something told him that Iris Morland would have relished such a scene, and Selena's next words confirmed his feelings.

"She'd been there the whole time, gorging on my humiliation. The moment I saw her, I knew she'd brought Connor back with the story about the timber license. It was clear they'd resumed their relationship."

"I ran out of the building. Connor followed me out and jumped in the car as I was driving off. He was begging me to help, but I was so enraged by how he'd let me debase myself in front of Iris, I wouldn't listen. We must have travelled a couple of miles before I stopped and ordered him out. The last I saw of him, he was walking back toward the mill."

Selena slumped back in her chair and stared fixedly over Halsey's shoulder, as though she were watching the scene play out behind him. She fumbled a couple of capsules from a pocket in her blouse, swallowing them quickly before Halsey could offer to get her some water. His recollection of the whiskey on her breath the last time he'd seen her must have shown in his expression, for she laughed suddenly.

"I finished the booze on Monday, Chief."

"Would you like me to call someone?" Halsey asked. "You shouldn't be alone at the moment."

"I'm fine," she said. "I'll be seeing my doctor later today."

"We can finish this another time," Halsey said.

"No," she said. "It's got to be now. I can't do this again. Please," she said, seeing he was still reluctant. "Just keep going."

"Just a few more questions then," Halsey said. "Can you recall the time you left the mill?"

"It was eleven thirty when I got home, so it must have been about quarter past when I left."

"What did you do when you got home?"

Selena sighed. "I suppose he told you I called."

He? Halsey wondered. "Why don't you tell me about it," Halsey said.

Selena's mouth twisted. "I left a message on his machine." She looked down at her hands. "I'm not proud of this. I told him who Iris was with."

Halsey took a chance. "Did you also tell Mr. Morland where they were?"

"Yes."

Halsey kept his expression neutral. Morland had specifically said he hadn't known where Iris was on Sunday night. So much for his "lucky guess" about her companion being Connor Tarlech.

"What did you think he would do?"

"Oh, probably nothing. Kenneth couldn't do anything with Iris. But at that moment, I hated Connor and Iris so much, I had to do something to strike at them, or I'd have gone crazy. Maybe I just wanted to make someone else feel as bad as I did. Oh God," she muttered. She was silent for a moment, close to exhaustion. "There's something else," she said finally.

"I also called Eddie Novak at home and told him where Connor was."

CHAPTER 15

"Yeah, the crazy broad called. So what? You think I got up in the middle of the night and went out there on a wild goose chase when I had to be at work the next day?"

Eddie Novak was seated with his back to a row of television monitors, chin thrust forward aggressively, thick lips twisted into a sneer. His large-knuckled hands rested on his legs, fingers drumming a slow, truculent rhythm against his knees. Behind Novak, people disappeared briefly from one screen, only to appear suddenly on another, tracked by cameras tucked discreetly into lighting fixtures and decorative friezes high on the walls of the lanes leading through the mall.

"You must surely have been interested to hear Tarlech was back in town," Halsey observed. He was leaning against the door to the office, there being no place to sit other than the chair Novak occupied.

"Oh, I'da been *interested*, all right. And so would a lot of the other guys he screwed." Novak's eyes swelled in their sockets, and his hands tightened into fists. "Yeah, I'da been interested—if I hadn't figured she was ready for another spell in the loony bin."

"You didn't believe Miss Coyle?"

Novak snorted. "I ain't among the ones who think her brain's on the same scale as her knockers. Everybody knows she went off her rocker when Tarlech dumped her for mattress Morland."

"You must have known she'd been telling the truth when the

111

bodies were discovered," Halsey said, masking his distaste for the man. Novak's contempt for Selena Coyle appeared unabated by the fact that he owed his current job to her success in attracting the mall's investors.

A malicious grin spread across Novak's face. "Yeah. Turned out she was right after all. Well, even a stopped cuckoo clock is right twice a day."

"What time did she call you?" Halsey asked abruptly, hoping to puncture Novak's satisfaction.

"I dunno—close to midnight."

"Anybody else hear the phone?"

"Shirl heard it first—the phone's downstairs and I'm a heavy sleeper. She figured the night guy here was calling, so she woke me up."

"What exactly did Miss Coyle say when you answered?"

"Said Connor Tarlech was at the mill."

"Those were her exact words?"

"I don't remember her exact words—I just climbed outta bed, remember? I think she said my name first, like she wanted to make sure she was talking to the right person. Then she said about Tarlech being at the mill. Then she hung up."

"Did she identify herself?"

"No. She didn't have to, I knew her voice."

"You're sure it was her?"

"Listen, I heard her talk lots of times. It was her."

"What about the telephone connection itself? Was the transmission clear? Did you hear anything in the background while she was talking?"

"Sounded same as always. And I didn't hear anything except her."

"What did you do after the call?"

Novak grinned again. "I went back to bed."

"Did you tell your wife about the call?"

"Nothing to tell. Anyway, she was sawing logs the second I headed downstairs."

Halsey pondered this for a moment. Selena Coyle's call pinned down Novak's whereabouts at midnight, since both of them agreed Selena had called him at home, and Novak's wife would no doubt confirm the time of the call. On the other hand, Selena could have been anywhere at the time, even the mill. Maybe she was telling the truth about being there, but not about what she'd done there. Telling part of the truth would account for anything that might be found at the mill linking her to the crime.

"I'll have to confirm what you're saying with your wife," Halsey said.

"Go right ahead," Novak said and swiveled his chair around to face the monitors. Halsey watched over his shoulder for a moment, then turned and left.

Had Novak really just gone back to bed, as he said? Was it likely that, after hearing the man who'd destroyed his future had returned, he'd be able to go calmly back to sleep?

And even if both he and Selena Coyle had been at home at midnight, the mill was no more than thirty minutes away from either of them. Or from Kenneth Morland, who'd lied about not knowing where Iris was.

The *ANN* van was sitting directly outside the main door of the mall, and he could see Lucy Mitchum buttonholing people as they left. He was about to change direction when she spotted him and beckoned frantically for him to come over. He could have ignored her, but sooner or later he was going to have to talk to some of the media, and at least with Lucy he could rely on there being no personal attacks on his staff.

Lucy was looking particularly attractive, Halsey noticed. Her dark red hair was set off by an elegantly cut green suit that afforded a discreet glimpse of cleavage in which a pearl pendant nestled. In spite of her glossy appearance, however, Lucy was nervous.

"Thank you so much," she said, gripping his elbow as if she were drowning.

Halsey wondered if her new employers were getting fed up with reports featuring nothing but the outside of Morland's house and shopping mall gossip. Over her shoulder, he spotted Delia Bendel and a Channel Five crew approaching.

"Make it fast, Lucy," he warned.

"You got it," she said. She'd spotted Delia too. She began speaking rapidly into the microphone.

"I'm talking with Chief William Halsey, who has been appointed Special Investigator into the murders of Iris Morland and Connor Tarlech. Chief Halsey, can you tell us the status of the investigation so far?"

"We have several promising leads we are pursuing at this point," Halsey said, beginning the say-nothing formula these occasions demanded.

"Do you expect to be making an arrest soon?" Lucy maneuvered herself between Halsey and the Channel Five camera as she spoke.

"It's too soon to say, but we are hopeful," Halsey returned, beginning to edge toward the parking lot.

Delia Bendel was actually shoving people out of her way as she streaked toward him.

"When can we expect your next press conference, Chief?" Lucy asked.

"As soon as we have something specific to announce."

Halsey stepped into the crowd, ignoring Delia Bendel's shrieks of protest, which were counterpointed by Lucy's relieved voice wrapping up their encounter.

As he drove away from the mall, a fleeting smile crossed his face. At least the interview with Novak hadn't been a total loss.

CHAPTER 16

As promised, Harrelson's additional resources had arrived in the persons of Helen Stewart and Tom Silas, a Kwakiutl Indian. Both were newly minted officers from the RCMP training college, clearly anxious to impress their new colleagues.

"My God, they're just kids," Larsen said to Halsey and Bailey.

Halsey had to suppress a chuckle at this comment, and Bailey's guffaw indicated she was barely resisting the urge to point out that they were only a couple of years younger than Larsen.

Halsey had smothered a sigh as they followed Bailey out to see the town they'd be patrolling. God only knew what would happen with two fledgling officers on the streets of Honeymoon Falls. He'd had enough trouble with Larsen and Bailey, and they at least had some experience.

However, there'd been no problems in the first week, and Halsey was hoping his luck would hold. What the new recruits lacked in experience they made up for in sheer effort. Working the usual twelve-hour shifts, with the station phone patched through to the patrol car, they'd kept law and order intact in Honeymoon Falls while Halsey and the other two worked on the murders.

Both Stewart and Silas were taken aback at the number of reporters cruising the streets. Coming at the height of the season, the media influx had resulted in an acute shortage of accommodation. Foul-tempered reporters were forced to double up with their most-hated competitors in the Bridal Suite Hotel's heart-shaped vibrating beds. Adding insult to injury, they found themselves contemplating this repulsive intimacy in the mirrored ceilings of their rooms every time they awoke. Punch-ups over blanket-hogging were becoming common, and one grizzled journalist had dislocated his thumb in a struggle with his roommate for supremacy over the TV remote. They were showing even less restraint on the streets of Honeymoon Falls.

"Some awful little creep with a ponytail offered me ten thousand dollars for pictures of the bodies," Helen Stewart said. "Then he kept telling me to moisten my lips and unbutton the top of my shirt while he ran ahead of me taking pictures."

"I'd've moistened *his* lips," Bailey said, clenching a fist.

"That Bendel woman seems to have it in for you, Chief," Silas said. "She was asking why you'd leave the RCMP to work in Honeymoon Falls. Keeps implying you got fired for incompetence or drinking on the job."

Still smarting over Halsey's snub at the mall, Delia Bendel had ambushed Larsen and Bailey on the street and demanded their opinion of how the murders had affected Honeymoon Falls' romantic atmosphere. Bailey snapped that it was a stupid question, while Larsen earnestly explained that he didn't think the romantic atmosphere had altered. When the resulting exchange aired, it was salted with references to Larsen as "Honeymoon Falls' Handsome Heartthrob" and to Lydia "No-Time-For-Romance" Bailey.

Halsey had gathered them all together and warned that every move they made and everything they said was going to be the focus of intense media scrutiny from now on.

The Handsome Heartthrob scowled. "It doesn't matter what we say, they turn it around so we look stupid," he warned Stewart and Silas.

"That's why you don't say anything," Halsey replied. "Refer

all questions to me."

"Got it," Stewart said. Silas nodded agreement.

Halsey was still struggling with the embarrassing matchmaking impulse he'd had when he first saw Helen Stewart, a pretty, fresh-faced blonde, and Larsen together—they seemed so right for each other. Neither of them appeared to notice it, however.

The only person who betrayed any partiality for Larsen was the last one Halsey wanted to see it coming from—Bailey's daughter, Nicole. Ostensibly, Nicole came to the station to get a ride home with her mother after spending time doing homework with friends living nearby. Halsey had noticed, however, that Nicole only seemed to do homework with those particular friends when Larsen was at the station. She and Larsen would chat while Bailey got ready to leave.

"It was wonderful the way you introduced me in the parade," Halsey heard her tell Larsen.

"Um, I believe all I said was 'Ladies and Gentlemen—Miss Honeymoon Daze,' " he said, rearranging a clump of notes on his blotter.

"Oh, but the way you *said* it," Nicole breathed.

The girl was not yet eighteen, and Halsey shuddered at the thought of the explosion that would occur if her mother even suspected her daughter was interested in Larsen. Larsen appeared to be exhibiting only polite friendliness, but there wasn't that much difference between the girl's age and his own, and Halsey understood the impact of large doses of admiration on an immature male ego. He'd dropped a hint to Larsen about the danger.

"Apple of her mother's eye," Halsey said, nodding at the girl as she and her mother left the station one evening. "Lydia's got her heart set on Nicole becoming a teacher."

"Nicole wants to be a model," Larsen replied. "She flipped out when Lydia wouldn't let her wear a bikini in Art Selby's parade float."

Larsen grinned briefly, whether at the thought of Bailey's battle with her recalcitrant daughter or something else. Halsey hoped it wasn't because he was picturing the girl in the garment in which her mother had forbidden her to display herself—an image Nicole had obviously taken pains to plant in Larsen's mind. Halsey had let the subject drop, uneasily aware that it wasn't resolved.

He forced his attention back to Selena's and Iris's phone records. He'd obtained a warrant for the information the day after Iris's death. Selena Coyle's records showed a one-minute call to Kenneth at 11:33 P.M. on June 6, the night of the murders.

Iris's records showed she'd made two calls to Morland's number. One had lasted from 11:38 P.M. to 12:09 A.M., and the other from 12:31 A.M. until 2:04 A.M. Long calls for that time of night, Halsey reflected. No wonder the battery was dead when the phone was found at the mill.

Selena Coyle had seen Iris alive around 11:15. Shortly after Selena's call to Kenneth Morland, Iris made two calls to Morland's number. Since she wouldn't have left messages of such length, it seemed logical she'd had a conversation with someone. If she had, that meant she was still alive at 2:04 A.M.

But why would Morland deny receiving the calls?

Halsey pondered a possible sequence of events. Morland listened to Selena Coyle's message and then received Iris's first call. She tried to lie about her whereabouts, but since he already knew where she was, Iris was caught. They argued, Morland demanded she come home, she refused and terminated the call. Later she called again. To apologize and ask forgiveness? Not likely, given Iris's character. To turn the screws even tighter? Perhaps. Judging from the length of the call, the discussion must have been intense. Then what? Morland, pushed beyond endurance, drove to the mill and finally ended his tormentor's life?

Of course, the phone records in themselves didn't establish that Morland had received the calls. In the absence of any proof Morland was in his house that night, his lawyer would no doubt argue Iris could have been speaking to someone else at Morland's number. After all, she was known to be a woman who conducted simultaneous romantic intrigues—it was entirely possible she'd find it exciting to give one lover the run of her house while her husband was away, as well as call him there while she dallied with Tarlech. Even Halsey couldn't deny such a situation was possible. *Reasonable doubt,* it was called.

But Halsey was sure of one thing—Morland was lying about the calls.

Halsey sat up suddenly, thinking of his interview with Lucy. What had she said about phoning Morland? He grabbed his notebook and rifled through the pages. When she'd called Morland right after the parade at noon, the machine was full and she couldn't leave a message. But when Halsey'd been at his house later in the day, his answering machine was responding to repeated calls. Somewhere between Lucy's call and the time Halsey'd spoken to him around 4:00 P.M., Morland had replaced the disc.

And if the disc was full when Lucy called, that must mean it contained Selena's and Iris's calls from the night of the murders. Odd as it seemed, Iris must have left messages long enough to cause the disc to fill to capacity. But why? And more important, what had Morland done with it?

Halsey dialed Morland's number at the newspaper and attacked as soon as he answered.

"Selena Coyle says she told you where Iris was on the night of the murders. I have telephone records showing her call and calls from your wife. It's to your advantage to tell the truth and all of it."

As Halsey hoped, his blunt approach caught Morland off guard.

"Okay, okay," Morland conceded. "I listened to Selena's message. It was on the disc just before Iris's. So what—it doesn't prove anything."

"Proves you lied when I asked if you knew where your wife was that night," Halsey fired back, hoping to keep Morland off balance.

But Morland had regained his equilibrium. "It proves nothing of the kind. I listened to those messages for the first time just before you arrived on Monday afternoon."

"I want that disc," Halsey said.

"I erased it and threw it in the garbage."

How convenient, Halsey thought. Selena could vouch for the fact that the answering machine had been on when she left her message, but there was nothing but Morland's word Iris hadn't spoken to him.

"Why?" Halsey demanded.

"Because I couldn't stand listening to Iris's lies, that's why!" Morland said.

"What did she say?

"That she was in Vancouver."

"What else?"

"She wouldn't be home until late Monday, after visiting Hermione Hopkins."

"And?" Halsey pressed.

"That was all," Morland said.

"It took her"—Halsey calculated the length of Iris's first call—"thirty-one minutes to say that?"

"Of course not. The call lasted only a couple of minutes."

"What about the second call?"

"That was the second call. Selena's was the first."

"Mr. Morland, your wife's phone records show she made two calls to your number—one from eleven thirty-eight to twelve oh nine and another from twelve thirty-one to two oh four."

"Then the records are wrong," Morland said. "I have to go. I've got a deadline to meet."

The line clicked in Halsey's ear as Morland hung up. Halsey frowned. Morland was no fool; he knew the records didn't prove he'd spoken to Iris. And perhaps he hadn't. But that didn't mean he wasn't at home listening to the calls as they recorded, and making murderous plans.

Why would Iris have left such ridiculously long messages? Did she know Morland was there listening to them? Halsey pondered a sequence of events. Iris called Morland and when he refused to answer began taunting him about her affair with Tarlech. Later, she called again to deliver more of the same, goading Morland until she finally pushed him over the edge and he went to the mill and killed them both. He put them on the parade float to send a final public notice that he wasn't the complaisant fool everyone thought, drove to Vancouver, and caught the early morning ferry to Victoria.

Why would he lie about the length and number of Iris's calls? Like the disc, that piece of the puzzle was missing. But Halsey was instinctively sure of one thing: the disc led to the murderer. Halsey made a note to check the garbage pickup times for Morland's neighborhood. If it hadn't been bulldozed under already, there might be a chance of recovering the disc, and even blank, there was a chance the high-tech wizards at the Vancouver crime lab might be able to recover something from it.

Halsey rubbed his eyes wearily, jumping as the phone rang at his elbow. The button over the unlisted line was lit. Expecting Larsen or Bailey, he cursed inwardly as Edna Sigurdson's voice poured into his ear like a load of gravel, drowning out the lilting violin music in the background.

"You better get down here, Chief," Edna said. "One of the brides has spotted a flasher."

"Officer Silas—"

"Said to call you," Edna interrupted. "He's out at Honeymoon Heaven breaking up a fight between some guy's girlfriend and his wife. The flasher'll be gone before he can get over here."

He'd be gone before anyone could get there, Halsey knew— that was the nature of the beast. Still, there was no point in arguing with Edna. She was the hostess of the nightly True Romance Dance in the park, an event where, not coincidentally, the men were pressured to present the women with long-stemmed roses from Edna's barrowful of pricey blooms. He was surprised the flasher issue had even registered with Edna while she was raking in cash; it was like a shark being distracted from a blood-soaked carcass by a strand of seaweed.

"Be right over," Halsey said. He stuffed a handful of doughnut holes in his shirt pocket and climbed into his car.

"She's gone home," Edna said when he arrived. "But she said the creep was in the bushes over there." She pointed to the darkened end of the park, where enormous clumps of rhododendrons and buddleia afforded shelter. "Fortunately, she didn't seem too upset, so I don't think anyone else noticed. And I gave her a discount coupon for the shop to make her feel better."

"I'll go have a look," Halsey said. "But he probably took off as soon as he got a reaction."

"I'd like to see the pervert try something like that with me," Edna said.

Me too, Halsey thought. Edna's glower would laser a flasher's manhood off.

Halsey prowled through the shrubbery around the park perimeter, moving silently along the narrow paths, but, as he'd expected, found no one. He made another pass, finishing up just inside the greenery, and stood watching the couples through the branches. The dance ended at midnight, which was now only a few minutes away. The thought made him realize he hadn't had any supper. He dug a couple of the doughnut holes out of his pocket and popped them into his mouth. *Too many doughnuts,* a mean little voice in his head warned. *They're gonna have to bury you in a boxcar if you keep this up.* He pulled his gut in hard as he chewed.

The couples nestled close together, eyes closed, moving to a slow waltz under the colored lanterns strung across the makeshift dance floor. A mirror ball turned above them, shimmering their dream-like movements with flecks of colored light. The pale moon sailed overhead, silvering the leaves of the trees, the light seeming to retreat wherever it encountered darkness.

"Do you dance, Chief?" Lucy asked, emerging from the shadows near Halsey.

Halsey started, gulped the last doughnut hole hastily, and wondered if she'd seen him scarf the other two. He didn't dance; he still remembered Vivien saying he made her think of a moose on a pogo stick when he took to the floor. On the other hand, it was a slow number, it was dark, and he wasn't in uniform so people would be less likely to stare. Lucy was wearing a pale pink sundress, and her red hair glistened as if it were decked with rubies every time the light from the mirror ball floated over her. There was nothing else he wanted right now, Halsey realized, except to feel her body against his.

He smiled and held out his arms. She stepped into them, and they joined the slowly turning couples. The sundress was backless, and with the hand holding her he could feel the delicate bones of her spine shifting beneath her satiny skin as they swayed against each other. Her hair brushed his jaw as she glanced up and smiled. He should say something, he thought, but he couldn't think of anything, except the perfumed scent rising from her hair.

"Your hair . . ." he murmured, amazed at the feeling it aroused in him. She moved its silky mass against his chin in response.

Their slow perambulation had brought them to the darkest corner of the dance floor. He drew her slightly closer, stepped onto the grass, and leaned down and kissed her. They drifted gradually away from the others, until all Halsey was aware of was a kind of slow-motion carousel of dancers and colored lights in the distance. He led her behind an enormous clump of fragrant buddleia and kissed her again.

The final bars of the music drained out of the loudspeakers, succeeded by a brief silence in which a faint rustling in the buddleia branches grew more purposeful. They jerked apart just before Cora Delbrook's hatchet face thrust itself through the greenery, incongruously framed in delicate pink blossoms.

"Oh, there you are, Chief Halsey. Edna said you were checking out the perimeter. Can't be too careful with a murderer on the loose, of course. That you, Lucy?"

"Yes," Lucy said, subtly retreating farther into the darkness.

Halsey remained where he was, struggling to regain his composure.

"So," Cora said to Lucy. "I suppose you're trying to beat Delia Bendel to an interview with the Chief. Well, has he given you what you were after?"

"Not yet," Lucy said demurely.

CHAPTER 17

"Well, as Iris's parties go—or rather, went—it was pretty typical. There was the Adoration of the Author, celebrated by her publisher Pieter Rempel, the Veneration of Her Latest Holy Word in pre-publication blurbs from other Rempel clients, and finally the ritual humiliation of an unsuspecting victim."

Peggy Atkinson shot Halsey an ironic glance. "And, of course, one got to observe her former lovers eyeing each other and calculating where they fit in the line of succession. Great theater." Her throaty voice floated the words into the air in the patio where they were seated.

The Atkinsons' names had followed Lucy Mitchum's on Iris Morland's guest list. Halsey hadn't been sure how much he would learn from any of the guests, nor how willing they would be to talk. Fortunately, this one at least was willing to divulge details that some might be tempted to withhold to avoid maligning the living or the dead.

"And were people able to make accurate assessments, in your opinion?" Halsey asked.

"Oh, I think there was a pretty general consensus among the onlookers that Rempel belonged to an earlier period, and that in the current group, Connor Tarlech, Arnold Reifel, and Pierre Blondin came after my husband. Whether all of the men involved were aware of the exact sequence, I can't say."

"Your husband was involved with Mrs. Morland?" Halsey was astonished at the casualness with which she had tossed out the reference to Cecil Atkinson.

"Mmm," Peggy said.

"This didn't bother you?"

"Somewhat," Peggy said. "I'd always warned him that Iris was dangerously good at manipulating people, and to find that he had connected her with me through him was infuriating. I knew she'd find some way of using that connection sooner or later."

An interesting reaction, Halsey thought. Most women would have been upset to find their husband preferred another; this one was angry because she felt herself jeopardized.

"And did she? Use the connection?"

"No," Peggy said. "But only because somebody killed her first." The corners of her lips twitched very slightly.

"Was there anyone who didn't hate the woman?" Halsey demanded.

Peggy laughed. "An excellent question, Chief Halsey." She thought for a moment, then said as though trying to consider every reasonable possibility, "Her husband, I suppose. Although people were beginning to speculate the poor sap had finally woken up—apparently he'd taken to phoning around town asking people if they knew where she was—so who knows?"

"Is Kenneth Morland a sap?" Halsey asked.

"Not in the way people think," Peggy said. "He wasn't an idiotically blind cuckold, at least not toward the end. He knew she was having affairs, but somehow he seemed able to accept it."

"You say he wasn't a sap in the way people think," Halsey said. "In what way was he a sap, then?"

"He loved her."

The answer was as direct as all her others, but lacked their bite, and underlying it Halsey heard for the first time a wistfulness, the kind of tone people use when a loved one cannot be persuaded against doing some utterly foolish and self-destructive thing.

Peggy slid her fingers through her thick dark hair and laced them behind her head. She studied Halsey for a moment, and then smiled.

"You're wondering if I had an affair with Kenneth Morland," she said.

Halsey laughed. She really was amazing—she'd guessed where his mind was heading before the thought had quite formed in his head.

"You could do one hell of a mind-reading act."

"Far too dangerous an occupation," she said lightly. "The answer is *no*. Oh, it occurred to me after I found out about Iris and Cecil, but it never came to anything. Kenneth probably hasn't had an affair with anyone, if you ask me." She stood up. "Would you like some coffee?"

He nodded and watched her walk away. She was wearing pink shorts and a pink and white striped top, both of which fit a trifle more snugly than she would have preferred, Halsey suspected, although she was not overweight. She wore no makeup—the faintly etched traces of her habitual expressions had been visible as she sat opposite him in the morning sun. A few lighter strands in her hair might either have been gray or due to sun bleaching. She was perhaps five or six years older than Halsey, and she was, he thought when she returned, gorgeous. A wave of longing passed over him, the likes of which he hadn't experienced since the first months after his divorce.

"Doughnuts," she announced. "I want them, I need them, and I intend to have them. Don't try to stop me. I have hot coffee and I'm willing to use it." She set a black-lacquered tray on the glass-topped table. In addition to a half dozen old-fashioned sugar-coated doughnuts, it held cups, cream, sugar, napkins, and the pot of coffee she was using to back up her warning.

127

"I'll overlook your threatening an officer of the law as long as you share the doughnuts," Halsey said in his toughest voice.

"Certainly, Officer," she replied. "I intended to let you have one anyway."

He had two, while she continued to fill him in on Iris's party.

"Cec and I got there about nine-thirty—neither of us wanted to go, but he felt he had to. Couldn't stand the idea of facing Iris among her stud farm by himself, I guess." She laughed as Halsey choked on a mouthful of hot coffee.

"You seem awfully matter-of-fact about their involvement," he said. "Most wives would have made his life hell on earth."

"What makes you think I haven't?" She grinned at him. "And is that experience talking?"

He smiled back, but refused to be drawn.

"You have to understand that academic couples sink or swim together. Cec and I have been married for twenty-five years, and I've done the whole faculty wife routine in all its boring clichés: edited his thesis—though back then we both admitted only that I typed it—sucked up to the professors' wives when he was starting out, got pregnant the minute he got tenure, raised the children, gave the innumerable boring dinner parties for his colleagues and the endless boring cocktail parties for his students."

Halsey knew he was asking the next question to satisfy himself, not for the investigation.

"Why?" The word seemed to spiral up in the air between them.

Peggy gave him a look that let him know she too recognized the question was personal rather than professional. Her eyes, a lovely deep brown flecked with green, clouded over as if she were contemplating the long history of her marriage. She thrust her empty hand out, palm upward, in a gesture that indicated she had no answer.

"I don't know," she said at last. "I loved him? His success was mine too? I drifted? All of the above?" Her hand dropped back onto the table, where the long, tanned fingers drummed for a moment, then stilled.

"And you?" she asked, not to be denied now that he had opened the door.

"Divorced. She found someone else."

She echoed his earlier question. "Why?"

"She was a painter. He was an actor. I was a cop. All of the above. Hey, this is easy."

"I think we've got a theme show for Oprah," she said. *"People with no idea why their lives worked out the way they did."*

A jay rocketed between them as though underlining her words in the air. They laughed, following its flight into the cherry trees that bordered the garden beyond the patio. The garden was beautiful, the shrubs and flowers set against a background of boulders and logs that both contained and displayed them. In winter, Halsey realized, when the plants were dormant, the stones and logs would form a sculpture that gave character to the otherwise featureless terrain.

"Did you do this?" Halsey asked, gesturing at the garden.

Peggy nodded. "Once Robert and Anna went to university, I needed a project. I love sitting out here looking at it. In the winter, when the flowers die—"

"It looks like a sculpture," Halsey finished.

"You wouldn't make a bad mind-reading act yourself," she said. He could see she was pleased he'd recognized the essential character of the garden, and he felt absurdly proud, as though he'd impressed a favorite teacher. *Careful*, he warned himself. The woman was possibly involved in murder—things were moving far too fast. And she was married. The Actor hadn't given a damn about that, nor had Vivien appeared to give it much thought, and nearly three years later he still remembered how that felt.

"You were talking about Iris's party," he said, reluctantly returning to his investigatory role.

"Oh, we're back in real life," she said. "What a shame. I was enjoying myself." She scooped the last doughnut from the plate and regarded him thoughtfully while she munched. *God, she even eats great,* Halsey thought with dismay. *What's going on here?*

"Well," Peggy said, licking sugar from her lips, "once we got there, we did the obligatory rounds. Iris was surrounded by her usual coterie, except for Marjorie Reifel, which I thought was a little odd—the two of them were thick as thieves the week before at Marjorie's party for Arnold's birthday."

"Can you tell me who else was there?"

"Not everyone. But I remember seeing Pieter Rempel, Lucy Mitchum, Edna Sigurdson, Kenneth of course, Shelagh Tarlech—which I also thought odd, because I'm pretty sure Shelagh intensely disapproved of Iris's involvement with Connor. I suppose Connor must have persuaded her to take a message to Iris. Pierre Blondin, the director. That dancer, Zuza something, who did the nude Swan Lake. And some famous poet whose name I never did get, but who created quite a stir when he seized Kenneth in his arms and gave him a great smacking kiss on the lips for being Iris's inspiration. Apparently the new book is dedicated to Kenneth. Shouldn't you be writing this down?"

Halsey tapped his temple. "Photographic memory." He'd make notes later—nothing made people clam up like someone writing down their every word. "Was Arnold Reifel there?"

"No, but then there was no need for him to be when he could see her any time he wanted." Peggy sipped her coffee. "It crossed my mind the reason Marjorie wasn't there was that she'd found out about the two of them. The odd thing is, I was surprised she took it so hard. I never imagined she'd like it, but I thought she'd have borne almost anything to keep on Iris's good side."

"Was that so important to her?"

"It was everything to her—she wants to be accepted. She can't seem to understand that needing anything from anyone is the mark of the leper as far as the people whose acceptance she craves are concerned."

"Do you know what Iris's new book was about?"

The look of ironic detachment was back in Peggy's eyes. "No. But I believe it was called *The Rest of Esther.* Apparently it's some kind of reference to the Apocrypha—the books of the Bible that aren't generally accepted."

"Sounds like the title of a murder mystery," Halsey said. "But that's not the kind of stuff she wrote, is it?"

"God, no. I actually read two of her earlier novels. They were about women who scorned petty conventions—one abandoned her children at a rest stop on an interstate highway and took off to find herself, and the other was about a woman who underwent a sex change to spite her parents."

Halsey gave her a skeptical look. Peggy flicked a concessionary wave at him.

"All right, so maybe I simplified the plots a little. I do that when stories irritate me. It's a way of cutting them down to size. Capsule reviews: man kills boss to get to the top—*Macbeth.*"

"But they were primarily books for women?" Halsey asked, his brain idling.

"*Books for women?* What *do* you mean?" The brown eyes were glinting dangerously.

Halsey started to say he'd only meant that in his experience books about women's emotional lives were usually bought by other women, but thought better of that. "Books about women," he amended lamely.

"Books about women normally involve men too," Peggy said. Her attitude had definitely cooled. "Iris's last book, *Mrs. Forrester,* has a female protagonist, but it explores the nature of sexual and spiritual love between both men and women."

"How do you know that?" Halsey queried. "It's not one of the earlier ones."

She was startled for a moment, he saw. Then she laughed. "You've caught me—I haven't read it. You made me mad when you talked about books for women, as if women were the only ones who ever thought about their emotional lives. Next thing I knew, I was defending a writer whose work I don't like."

"I do the same thing when people talk about police brutality," Halsey confessed. "I say stuff like 'if they hadn't been some place they weren't supposed to be, they wouldn't have gotten their skulls fractured,' while a voice in the back of my head asks, *is that me talking?*"

Her expression showed him he was restored to her favor, and again he felt an absurd satisfaction. It wasn't so great, however, that he didn't notice she hadn't answered his question on the source of her information about Iris's book.

"So how do you know about the book?"

He watched the realization dawning in her eyes that, friendly or not, their conversation was part of his job. Was he wrong, or with the realization was there the faintest hint of disappointment at that fact? He hoped so. He also hoped he hadn't taken leave of his senses.

"Pierre Blondin told me about *Mrs. Forrester.* He does make it sound worth reading. On the other hand, he may be talking about his film interpretation of it."

There had been the slightest pause between the first two words, Halsey noted, as if she'd been about to use the Christian name only, but thought better of it. An expression crossed her face so fleetingly that it was gone before Halsey could assess it.

132

Peggy refilled their cups, and they busied themselves for a moment doctoring the contents. She was seated to his right, and when she reached for a napkin his fingers brushed her bare arm as he returned the sugar bowl to its place. The sugar spilled as his hand jerked involuntarily at the contact with her warm flesh. She glanced at him quickly, smiling.

"May I ask you a very personal question?" she asked.

"Yes." Halsey was astonished at how instantly he'd given permission. Personal questions had been almost impossible to answer since the divorce, but now he was going to tell this woman he'd just met anything she wanted to know about him and Vivien and The Actor. He hadn't realized until right now how much he wanted to tell someone. But that was not what she asked.

"Did you ever kill anyone?" Peggy's fingers lay lightly against her lips, as if to chastise them for the question they'd posed. "I know that's a terribly unfair question to ask anyone who might have had to do it because of their job, like asking a Vietnam vet what he did to survive." She paused for a moment. "Tell me to mind my own business," she advised.

Halsey smiled, hoping his expectation hadn't been obvious. Sooner or later everyone wanted to know your body count. Some were pleased when they found out, others disappointed. He wondered which she would be.

"I've only had to shoot two people," he said. "Two men abducted a teenage girl when I was stationed in Vancouver. I stopped them at a roadblock and they started shooting. I shot both of them. We were lucky—the girl was unhurt."

"What happened to the men?"

"Three months in the hospital, two years in prison. They were killed during an attempted bank hold-up in Seattle six months after their release."

"I'm glad."

133

"Glad they were killed?"

"No. Glad you don't have to carry the weight of being responsible for their deaths."

She spoke as if she knew something about that kind of responsibility. Her eyes rested on Halsey intently, and he watched his reflection growing larger in them as she leaned toward him. A moment later, her lips were pressed against his. The shock of her mouth on his drew him out of his chair. His senses cataloged an overwhelming array of impressions: the scent of her hair, the sweetness of the fine grains of sugar on her lips, the flutter of her long, black lashes as they brushed his eyelids, his own excitement, the thud of their hearts. They stepped away from the table, and he felt the soft skin of her arms sliding up around his neck, and the warmth of her breasts through his shirt.

He muttered a caution against her lips, but made no attempt to move away from her. Some part of his brain continued to shout warnings at him, but a long-dormant need had taken control. She pulled him inside to a stairway in the living room, which evidently led to bedrooms above.

Exerting every ounce of willpower he possessed, Halsey pulled away. "Peggy—"

"I want you," she said, absolving him. "You're not seducing me."

She grasped the pink and white top, yanked it over her head, and flung it behind her. One hand flashed behind her back with the practiced speed and assurance of a stage magician's gesture. A second later her brassiere slid from her shoulders and her full breasts swung free in front of him. The sight of her body dissolved the last remnants of Halsey's control. She put her hands up to his face, and he touched the dark tendrils of hair curling against her neck and drew her to him, sliding his hands down her beautiful bare back, feeling the wonderful heat of her flesh against his own.

"Peggy—" This time the voice was Cecil Atkinson's, and it was coming from upstairs. "Peggy, are you down there?"

The two of them froze as if turned to stone. Peggy recovered first.

"Yes, dear," she called back. Her voice was too tremulous to carry far, and Atkinson obviously didn't hear it.

"Peggy, is that you?" Atkinson's voice was closer; he was apparently coming to the landing to look down into the living room.

"Yes, dear," she called again, a little too loudly this time. Her face was flushed, and her breasts rose and fell rapidly as she attempted to regulate her breathing. She quickly refastened her brassiere, scooped her top from the floor, and jabbed a shaking finger toward the patio.

Halsey, senses reeling, strode back out to the table they'd left a few minutes ago and gulped in lungfuls of air. Behind him, he heard Peggy's voice again, wavering only slightly now.

"You'd better come down, Cecil. The police are here."

Chapter 18

Cecil Atkinson strode through the doors to the patio and thrust a hand at Halsey.

"Good morning, Chief," he said. He had a masculine, resonant voice, with the undertone of one used to being listened to. He was slightly shorter than Halsey, barrel-chested, moving forward with such assurance that he seemed to lay claim to every foot of ground on which he trod.

He brandished a sheaf of files at Halsey. "Forgot these," he announced. The smile was quick: on, off, gone.

Still shaken, Halsey managed to return his greeting with outward composure. Atkinson's gaze dropped to the patio table and the remains of the coffee and doughnuts, which seemed to Halsey as incriminating as passion-rumpled sheets. Halsey wished Peggy would get the hell back out here—he had no idea what she might have said to Atkinson before he came out.

"Didn't see your car when I drove up," Atkinson said with a questioning glance.

"One of my staff is picking me up later." Halsey gave mental thanks that he'd had Larsen drop him off at the Atkinsons'. He tried to picture Atkinson as the young untenured professor, scribbling a thesis for his wife to edit, but the image refused to take shape. Atkinson gave off none of the signs of academe; he appeared every inch the successful, hard-driving businessman.

Halsey forced himself back into his professional groove. "I'm glad you're here, actually—it's saved me another trip. I was asking your wife about Iris Morland's party, and it would be helpful if I could talk to the two of you together."

Atkinson frowned. "I'm afraid my time is pretty well booked Monday mornings," he said.

"It's about the murder of two people you knew," Halsey reminded him.

The shoulders of the expensive suit lifted casually. "I hardly knew Tarlech at all, and Iris was really just an acquaintance."

Halsey met Atkinson's eyes. "I was under the impression that Mrs. Morland was more than just an acquaintance."

"I see Peggy has served up more than doughnuts," Atkinson said. The voice had lost none of its assurance, though its temperature had dropped considerably, and there was an ambiguity in its meaning. Halsey wondered how much Atkinson had surmised. He waited, keeping his expression neutral.

"Oh, all right. I'll have to make some calls to reschedule things." Atkinson dropped the briefcase on one of the chairs and went back into the house, passing Peggy on her way out. *Darby and Joan,* Halsey thought.

Peggy smiled. "Turning out a lovely day, isn't it, Chief?" she said in a bright, public voice. A moment later, she murmured, "He's gone up to his study to make his calls."

"I won't need much longer," Halsey said, trying not to think about what was under the striped top.

She laughed. "I wouldn't have either."

Feeling flustered again, Halsey retreated to his seat at the table, then, remembering the chain of events that had begun there and Atkinson's surveillance of their repast, stood up and went over to the edge of the flagstones. Peggy came to stand beside him, and he was about to move away when she said, "He'll be more suspicious if we avoid each other."

Halsey was still flabbergasted by Atkinson's sudden appearance. "How did he get upstairs without seeing us?"

"It's like a French farce." She flicked one of his shirt buttons open, laughing as he immediately rebuttoned it and moved away. "He must have come in while we were out here, and gone straight upstairs to look for his files without realizing we were here. No sooner had he cleared the living room than we were inside. Seconds later, he's on his way downstairs while we're stripping on our way up."

"Not too funny for any of us if the timing had gone wrong," Halsey said, moving away.

"Do you think I'd have cared if he saw us? Remember when you said most wives would have made his life hell on earth for having an affair, and I asked you what made you think I hadn't? I've made him pay."

"Maybe he's paid enough," Halsey said.

She rounded on him. "Like *hell* he has. He chose her over me, the nobody, the boring housewife. The not-famous, not-talented, not-exciting *wife!*" Her eyes filled with tears. "God damn him."

She seized his arm just as Atkinson stepped through the door, but managed to convert the action into a gesture directing his attention to the garden. She was enjoying the covertness of it all, Halsey realized, with a chill that slid down his spine like ice water.

"Still, I think it's been worth it all. I sit out here for hours in the summer, just looking at the flowers." The pleasant social voice was back, the expression calm.

Atkinson dropped into the chair in which Peggy had been sitting and shoved the clutter on the table aside with a look of faint distaste. "I can give you half an hour," he announced.

Halsey returned to the table, resisting the urge to sit anywhere except in front of his own dishes. Peggy ambled about the patio, pinching leaves off the quince and azalea plants that were set in large pots.

"You and Mrs. Atkinson were at a party given by Iris Morland last Saturday," Halsey began. "Can you tell me who you saw there?"

Atkinson named most of the same people Peggy had, and included two she hadn't: Enid Regular and Millicent Mountjoy.

"Which ones were they?" Peggy asked, still snapping off dead leaves and flipping them onto the grass beyond the flagstones. Halsey recognized a dangerous undercurrent in her question, a siren tone meant to lure the unsuspecting onto reefs.

"Enid was the small, thin blonde who put away the vat of liquor. She's Iris's sister. Millicent was the older woman with the silver jewelry you admired. An optometrist, I believe." Atkinson's voice was even, but he was clearly aware of the dangers ahead.

"What sort of name is Regular?" Peggy asked. "Are you sure you've got it right?"

Peggy had returned to the table and was now sitting opposite Atkinson. She rested her chin on her interlaced fingers, regarding her husband with a watchfulness that reminded Halsey of a hawk waiting for its prey to emerge from a burrow.

"It's Iris's maiden name," Atkinson said. "As you know."

"Why, so it is," Peggy replied. "I'd forgotten that."

"Like hell you had," Atkinson said. Halsey could see his hands balling into fists below the glass-topped table. Atkinson directed a stony glare at him. "Iris and I had an affair. A very brief one."

Peggy sighed indulgently. "All her affairs were very brief, my dear." She shook her head regretfully, turning to Halsey. "I'm afraid none of her lovers had any . . . *staying power* . . . with Iris. But of course, that's all over and forgotten now," she added, with a mocking smile in her husband's direction.

Halsey was finding it difficult to watch the two of them, but Atkinson endured the acid bath stoically.

"Why did you go to the party?" Halsey asked. "Surely it

couldn't have been a comfortable situation for either of you."

Both of the Atkinsons laughed simultaneously.

"Because Iris is on the board of governors of Pacific Western College, and Cecil is a weak-willed coward who thought swallowing the constant humiliation she dished out would save his college," Peggy said, with what appeared to be genuine amusement, almost fondness.

"Because Peggy found Iris a convenient scapegoat for her failure to achieve anything meaningful in life, and she never gave up hope of seeing Iris defeated in some way," Atkinson riposted amiably.

Halsey felt the hair on the back of his neck prickle. Their exchange had the familiarity of long practice, combined with the grudging respect of one formidable adversary for another. Both seemed to relish the battle, even while recognizing the price of victory would be ruinous.

"My only failure was in allying myself with you twenty-five years ago," Peggy parried, lifting her face from her fingers. For the first time, Halsey noticed she wore no rings. A statement, he supposed.

Atkinson scoffed. "You'd have been a failure no matter whom you'd married."

"Perhaps," Peggy allowed. "But so would you if you hadn't had my help—you know what I mean, don't you dear?"

Atkinson did not change expression at this, but made no response, and Halsey got the sense Peggy had played some sort of trump card that had brought him to a halt, even if it had not precipitated a retreat.

Halsey struggled to organize his thoughts. "You mentioned the humiliation of someone at the party," he said to Peggy.

The Atkinsons looked at each other, diverted for a moment from the fray. It was Atkinson who answered.

"I suppose you mean Marjorie Reifel."

Peggy nodded. "God, it was awful. Iris really pulled out all the stops."

"You said Mrs. Reifel wasn't there," Halsey reminded her.

"She wasn't."

Halsey looked at her for a moment, feeling that the headline *Police Baffled* was slowly appearing on his forehead. Peggy laughed.

"Iris played a telephone message that Marjorie had left her," Atkinson said. "It repeated every ten or fifteen minutes over the stereo speakers interspersed with the mariachi music she was using for the party—you could even hear it outside in the garden."

The 10:00 A.M. sun was starting to make itself felt, and Atkinson was evidently warm in his suit. He picked up one of the napkins Peggy had used earlier and patted it over his cheeks, already darkening with the beard growing beneath. A few grains of doughnut sugar sparkled and dissolved over one cheekbone. Halsey glanced involuntarily at Peggy's lips, then looked back at Atkinson, but it was Peggy who took up the thread.

"It was very unpleasant," she said, shuddering slightly. "Marjorie was—I suppose you could only call it raving—calling Iris filthy names, threatening to kill her."

"I don't know if she was threatening to kill her, but she was definitely threatening her," Atkinson amended. "She screeched abuse for several minutes."

"What did Mrs. Morland do while the message was being played?" Halsey asked.

"Criticized her grammar," Peggy said wryly. "Said the college she attended must have been located in a shopping mall."

"Mrs. Morland found the message funny?" Halsey asked.

"Not exactly. She found the cruelties of life funny." Atkinson replied. "It was part of the philosophy she espoused as a writer— the exposure of real feelings. Unfortunately, Iris seemed to

141

think the only time that people exhibited real feelings was when they were forced to express what she called 'elemental emotions'—anger, hatred, betrayal."

"And she certainly inspired all of those feelings in you, didn't she?" Peggy said. "You left a few of those accusatory messages on her answering machine yourself at one time, didn't you, dear? I wonder if she played them for Connor Tarlech?"

Atkinson took the jab stoically. "Probably," he said evenly. "She played them for you, didn't she?"

Halsey stared at Peggy. "Mrs. Morland played her telephone messages from Mr. Atkinson back to you?"

"Indeed. She invited me over specially to hear them. Accidentally, of course. Turned the machine on and left me in her study to listen while she made coffee in the kitchen. Came back and pretended shock when she found me in tears."

"What did you do?" Halsey asked, stunned.

"Flung the coffee at her books and left," Peggy said. "My pathetic attempt to retaliate for what she did to me."

"Peggy, don't do this to yourself," Atkinson said. It was startling to see the change in his demeanor—the carapace in which he was sheathed seemed to have softened for a moment. Peggy ignored his attempt at consolation.

Halsey pressed on. "Did she say anything after you threw the coffee?"

"Oh, she called out sympathetic bromides after me as I ran out of her house, with her face fixed in that insufferable smirk. Dr. Mengele had nothing on that bitch."

"You said earlier the only reason Mrs. Morland hadn't been able to use the . . . connection . . . with you was that someone had killed her first. This didn't seem to you like she had used it?"

"Of course it did." Peggy grimaced and stared off into the garden. "I didn't plan to tell you this."

"It sounds like an answering machine was a deadly weapon in Mrs. Morland's hands. Were you concerned that she might try to humiliate you again?" Halsey kept his voice neutral.

Peggy's eyes met his, letting him know she understood the significance of the question, then turned to Atkinson. Her voice when she replied was also neutral.

"How could she? What else could she possibly have done after that?"

Halsey turned to Atkinson. "When did your relationship with Mrs. Morland end?"

"Several years ago, when I discovered she was involved with Connor Tarlech."

"Oh, not exactly then," Peggy interjected, animated now, her eyes sparkling maliciously. "You spent some time playing second fiddle to Tarlech, trying to win her back."

Atkinson said nothing in response. Perhaps the scene his wife had described enduring at the hands of his former mistress made him willing to allow her to expose his own humiliation unopposed. The air seemed heavier around them, charged with expectation and apprehension, as though they were both readying themselves simultaneously for attack and defense. Atkinson no longer exuded the assurance with which he'd begun the interview, and lines of weariness had etched themselves in his face.

"Mrs. Atkinson mentioned that Iris was a member of the Board of Directors of your college," Halsey said. "After your personal relationship ended, did you consider removing her from the Board?"

"Cecil remove Iris?" Peggy looked at Atkinson and laughed. "That was never a possibility, was it, dear? She was too important to the success of the college, and far cleverer than you at political in-fighting." She turned to Halsey. "Iris collected a fat fee every year from Cecil, just to let him use her name on the college letterhead as a director. People used to wonder who ran the college—Iris or Cecil. To see the two of them together, you'd never guess Cecil owned it."

Atkinson flushed with anger. "You choose to ignore the fact that it was the respect Iris had in literary circles that attracted a significant portion of PWC students and the finest faculty of any college in the country."

"For which she was very well paid," Peggy said. "Both in cash and the rich pleasure you afforded her by allowing her to humiliate you at regular intervals. My God, what a *taste* you have for bootlicking."

A muscle twitched in Atkinson's cheek, and his fists jerked up from under the table, bringing a coldly triumphant smile to Peggy's lips.

Halsey jumped in before Atkinson could respond.

"You own PWC?" he asked. "I thought it was publicly funded."

"I created it twenty years ago and I own it," Atkinson said through clenched teeth. "It's the only privately owned fine arts college in the country." He breathed out slowly and forced his hands flat on the table. "I do receive some government grants for special projects, such as the new campus I'm building."

"Grants you may never get," Peggy said.

"The government's always slow with the grants," Atkinson said. "They'll come."

"Even if the people in charge of the grants find out about the red ink in the college's books, dear? Maybe there wouldn't have been so much of it if you hadn't paid Iris all that money," Peggy said.

"Since Iris will no longer be associated with the college, there'll be no more payments. Anyway, the deal is worth millions," Atkinson said. "All Iris got was her usual director's fee of fifty thousand dollars."

144

"Which is twice what any other director would get, *and* she got it all up front, *and* once she got it she immediately slithered off and left you to do all the work."

"She'd already done what she was supposed to—persuaded council to let me have the mill site."

"And do you think she was really going to let you have it, Cecil?" Peggy needled. "Don't forget who Iris had with her at the mill."

"She couldn't have done anything to stop it," Atkinson said. "Council had already signed the letter of agreement. It's a legal document binding on everyone involved." He sagged back in his chair, running his hand slowly over his eyes.

Peggy's ferocious attack showed no sign of abating.

"Unless those grants don't come through—then the deal's off, isn't it, dear? How much longer will you be able to buffalo council into waiting? If they pull the mill site on you, all that's left is the tender mercy of the bankruptcy courts. Not even Iris to run to for help."

"You'd better shut up," Atkinson said. "You seem to forget your livelihood's at stake too. Do you need anything more?" he asked Halsey, who was beginning to feel as if he had been buffeted in hurricane-force winds.

"Just your whereabouts on June sixth, between six P.M. and six A.M. the following morning."

"Is that when—?" Peggy asked.

"Somewhere in there," Halsey replied.

"I was in my office in Vancouver. I worked until after one finishing a major funding proposal. It would have been around two-thirty A.M. when I got home."

Halsey looked at Peggy. "Did you hear Mr. Atkinson come in?"

"No. I'm a sound sleeper, and we sleep in separate rooms now."

Peggy's gaze rested thoughtfully on her husband, who had winced slightly at the emphasis with which she spoke the final word.

"Can you recall your movements earlier, before you went to sleep?"

The expression dawning on Peggy's face reminded Halsey of a wolf closing in for the kill.

"Indeed, I can recall my movements very clearly," she said, with a knife-sharp smile. She toyed with one of the cups, letting the silence grow until it crackled with tension. Halsey recollected her earlier mention of Macbeth; this was a woman with the same steely resolve as his consort. Atkinson sat motionless, waiting. When she finally spoke, it was to him, not Halsey.

"I was here, in your bed, with Pierre Blondin."

CHAPTER 19

Hi—my name is April. I've got blonde hair and blue eyes. I'm 38-22-36, and I've got long, looong legs and skin like satin. I'm just aching to feel your virile manliness—

Pearl Novak giggled helplessly into the microphone. She'd already tried twice to say the last part without breaking up, and the breathy voice she was using had started to remind her of her grandmother during an asthma attack.

"Hi, Gary," she said in her normal voice. "Thought I'd give the guards something to get excited about. Did you know it was me?"

She punched *play*, listened to her take-off of the phone-sex line, and started giggling again. Right after her final word, Iris Morland's assured voice began speaking. Pearl shut it off quickly—the dead woman's voice gave her the creeps. She'd listened to it once before, just out of curiosity, but the message lasted only a couple of minutes, telling her husband where she was. After that there was silence. Pearl's own message had already obliterated the beginning of Iris's, and soon the original would be gone altogether.

She was using a miniature recorder her father had once used to make surreptitious recordings of management comments at the mill. It was small enough to be mailed to Gary so he could play her message. She pressed the *record* button and started talking again.

"It's great about the parole hearing being moved up to

147

September—you'll be out just when I'm starting my fashion design course in Vancouver. I've already looked at a couple of apartments. Once we're settled, you'll be able to start your apprenticeship."

Gary's love of cars was well known, and although Pearl was uneasily aware that he tended to express it by stealing them, she planned to redirect it into a more socially acceptable form. On one of her clandestine visits to the prison, she'd shown him a brochure on a mechanics' apprenticeship program designed especially for ex-convicts (or "former offenders," as the brochure optimistically referred to them). If Gary had not displayed any special enthusiasm for the idea, he hadn't rejected it either, particularly when Pearl pointed out that enrollment would likely be looked on favorably at his parole hearing.

Sometimes Pearl thought of him as a wild stallion sniffing suspiciously at the bridle. She would have to lead him slowly into what he needed: stability, with someone who could sort out his life and put it in order. Not that she wanted to break his spirit or anything like that—when he flipped his long black hair off his forehead and gave her that bad-boy grin, she couldn't breathe properly—but there was no reason his energy couldn't be channeled into something productive. It was just a matter of closing off all the avenues that led to problems.

"You probably heard some of this stuff already on TV, but I'll tell you anyway. Connor Tarlech's funeral is tomorrow, June twelfth, which is weird because on *ANN* Lucy Mitchum said that would have been his birthday. Your mother and your aunt Cora are going—I guess they feel involved because of how the bodies were found. I don't think there'll be too many others going. Of course, Dad is saying they should give whoever killed Mr. Tarlech a medal. The police have questioned Dad—he's a suspect, I guess." Pearl was pleased to be able to mention a circumstance in which Gary might at last find common ground with her father.

"There wasn't any funeral for Mrs. Morland—apparently she said in her will she didn't want one. Her husband donated her body to a medical school. Gawd, imagine that—being dissected by a bunch of nerdy med students? Ugh. Mom also said Marjorie Reifel was telling people that since Mrs. Morland spent her life cutting people up, being carved up herself was poetic justice."

It occurred to Pearl that, after the autopsy, Iris Morland would not offer the medical students the same challenge she would normally have provided. Gawd, probably everything was already wrapped and labeled like moose meat in freezer bags.

"Anyway, when you get this, use it to send me a message, okay? I want to hear your voice. Love, love, *love* you!"

Pearl switched the machine off, frowning. Should she be saying anything about murder in a message going to a prison? They'd surely be monitoring everything he received. She was not concerned about any possible impact on her father, but what if they got the idea Gary was somehow involved?

She switched the machine on, and began recording details about her forthcoming graduation ceremony, jabbering on until she was sure she'd erased all the murder stuff. When she pressed *play,* Iris Morland's message and her own comments about the murder were gone.

Satisfied, Pearl slid the recorder into a stamped, padded envelope, printed Gary's name and address on the outside, and ran down to the mailbox on the corner. The envelope plopped onto the others inside, and the metal flap over the slot clanked shut. The pick-up time listed on the front of the box was 2:00 P.M. In less than an hour, her package would be on its way to Gary.

CHAPTER 20

Marjorie Reifel's voice roller-coastered through long frenzied lines of invective, soaring into eldritch screeches and plummeting to rasping obscenities.

"Whore! Bitch! Lying, plagiarizing, *filthy* tramp. I swear to God I'll make you pay for this. You'll be sorry, you cheap, sluttish—"

Halsey leaned forward and switched off the tape recorder as mariachi music began to flood from the speaker. He'd obtained the party tape from Kenneth Morland after hearing the Atkinsons' description of it. Presumably, Iris had erased the original message after copying it, since it was not among the few routine messages on her answering machine. The recorded rant was unsettling, not only for the ferocity with which it was delivered, but also because its complete lack of restraint seemed to spring from a creature whose entire center had shattered.

Marjorie Reifel sat opposite him on a sofa upholstered in ivory linen, one forefinger slowly tracing the contours of the chignon confining her blonde hair. Halsey judged her to be somewhere in her early forties, a woman still confident of her ability to attract, although the face beneath the carefully applied makeup had a pinched look. Her slender body was sheathed in a simply cut cocoa-brown silk dress that both floated and clung, spilling over her breasts and down her torso, outlining one long thigh folded over her lower leg, and ending in a flare of material that stirred softly when she swung her crossed leg.

150

Sitting bolt upright beside him was Officer Bailey, whose white shirt sleeves and navy uniform slacks contained creases sharp enough to slice bread. Halsey had brought her along with the idea that this was a good opportunity to honor his agreement to involve her in the investigation, an idea he'd seen immediately was wrong. Both women's eyes had narrowed to slits at the sight of the other, and Bailey's expression as the message played had done nothing to warm the atmosphere.

"Can you tell us when you made this call?" Halsey asked.

"Saturday morning at the mall." Marjorie's voice now was perfectly controlled.

"What did you mean by it?" Bailey demanded. "Were you threatening her?"

Oh hell, Lydia, Halsey thought, *what does it sound like she was doing, giving her compliments?*

Marjorie raised her eyebrows. "I would have thought it was perfectly obvious that I was."

"You realize the woman you threatened was killed the next night?"

Bailey leaned forward and rested her hands on the coffee table that separated them. Marjorie's face twisted into a mocking smile as she leaned forward also, mimicking Bailey's none-too-subtle attempt at physical intimidation.

"Is *that* what the whole town's talking about?" she said, her eyebrows climbing in mock amazement.

Halsey decided things had gone far enough. "Mrs. Reifel, we've got a double murder on our hands. I suggest you can the crap, and explain why you made this call."

Marjorie Reifel looked startled at the roughness of his tone. Bailey looked pleased, a fact that did not escape Marjorie's attention. "Shouldn't she be terrorizing the tourist buses at this time of day?" Marjorie said, turning to Halsey.

Bailey sucked in an outraged breath, but before she could

turn it into speech, Halsey intervened.

"You can either tell us now, or call your lawyer," he warned.

"And what if I do call my lawyer?" Marjorie inquired, leaning into the sofa cushions and stretching her silk-clad arms out across the top of the sofa back. The dark material flowed between her breasts, outlining them briefly before lifting away again.

"We'll play the message for him," Halsey said. "Then we'll play it for the Crown prosecutor."

Marjorie flipped a hand at him and the dress recontoured her body again. "Half the town's heard it already—you obviously know that Iris played it as the entertainment at her party. Do you think it matters to me if a few more people hear it?"

"Up to you," Halsey said. "I suppose it'll be played on the evening news too."

"You louse," Marjorie said. She was clearly shaken at the thought of the tape being played on television. "You know what they do with those things—they play them in an endless series of sound bites for days."

Halsey waited. Marjorie's narrow shoulders dropped slightly, although her long, slender body remained poised. She regarded them for a moment from beneath lowered lids, then seemed to come to a decision.

"Oh, what the hell," she said. "It's not as if it matters anymore. You see this"—she gestured around her—"Lots of natural woods, simple, elegant design." She ran her hand over the sofa material. "Pale colors. And to set them off, one or two classic French pieces—the lamps, the *escritoire.*"

Bailey was writing this down using a stubby little pencil that a cartoon cop might have used, and was obviously at a loss as to how *escritoire* might be spelled. Halsey took comfort from the fact that at least she wasn't licking the end of the pencil before she wrote. He saw Marjorie's mocking glance playing over her and shot her a look that warned the woman off.

"Iris . . . was a great help," Marjorie said, the mockery turned inward now. "She knew everyone who could give you a good price, and her taste was impeccable. She chose this table, for example. It's made of Norwegian pine—the carvings around the border are illustrations of Norse legends. She found it in a shop in Vancouver and had it shipped up on approval. Stores would do that sort of thing for her—all she had to do was tell them who she was: Iris Morland, the famous writer."

"What was the name of the store?" Bailey asked.

"Why? Are you planning to buy one?" Marjorie said.

"It might be important," Bailey said.

"*Sears,*" Marjorie said, with sarcasm that was obviously wasted on Bailey, who promptly wrote it down.

"You were saying," Halsey prompted.

"Yes, well, Iris could be a nasty piece of work at times. She loved to lead people on, and then pull the rug out from under them. She loved showing people up."

"How much was the table, do you remember?" Bailey now actually did lick the pencil lead, thrusting her head forward like an alert hound.

Halsey stared at her and suddenly got the picture. If playing the dumb flatfoot was going to irritate the other woman, Bailey was going to play the role to the hilt.

"Lydia," Halsey said, but it was too late.

"Get this idiotic meter maid out of here," Marjorie said.

"*Meter maid?*" Bailey swelled with fury. "*Meter maid?* I'll have you know I'm a fully trained criminal investigator, and any woman who achieves that certification has to be twice as good as any man with the same qualifications."

"My God, if that's true, the rest of you must be a dim lot," Marjorie said to Halsey.

"Could I have a word with you, Officer?" Halsey said. He

stood up and towed Bailey to the door and thrust her through it. "Game's over," he said. "Wait in the car."

Halsey returned to Marjorie Reifel's living room. Outside, he heard the squad car door slam with a sonic boom in the quiet street.

"Sorry," he said briskly to Marjorie. "Continue."

She gave him a sour look. "I've forgotten what I was saying."

"I haven't. You were talking about Iris Morland setting people up for a fall. How did she get you?"

"Surely you've heard by now," Marjorie said. "Why should I go over it all again?"

Halsey scooped the recorder from the table and stood up. "See you on television, Mrs. Reifel."

"All right, all right," Marjorie raised her hands, red-lacquered nails flashing surrender. "Sit down. Please," she added.

Halsey sat, but kept the recorder in his hand, as though he were about to leave any minute. "I'll need to talk to Mr. Reifel too."

"Then you'll have to go to Vancouver," Marjorie said. "He couldn't take Delia Bendel ambushing him every time he poked his head out the door. He stays at his ex-wife's apartment so he can get to the studio easily for the tapings. So he says."

She laughed cynically. "You probably know what people say about me—that I was some little typist bimbo who latched onto Arnold and devoted myself to pathetic attempts at social climbing."

Halsey immediately demurred, although he had, of course, heard exactly such stories.

"Oh, hell, it's true enough," Marjorie said, waving away his politeness. "Except for the bimbo part. I'm not stupid, ordinarily. But I have always wanted to be accepted into a certain kind of life, and I've found that people who live that way don't invite you into their circle; you have to fight to get in. And part of the fight involves getting people to sponsor you—vouch for you, if you like. And I knew Iris could do that for me in the Colony."

"Couldn't Mr. Reifel do that? Surely your position as his wife—"

Marjorie laughed. "Exactly the problem—I'm sick of being *the wife of*," she said, etching the phrase in acid. "When you're *the wife of,* you're tolerated, not accepted—you don't exist when your husband isn't at your side."

"How did you get to know Mrs. Morland?" Halsey asked.

"Arnold had her on his show a couple of times. She even filled in for him once as host when he was ill."

"So you became friends."

Marjorie dismissed this with a derisive laugh.

"But you expected her to—what did you call it—sponsor you in the Colony?"

"She could have. She even seemed to want to. What I didn't realize was the depths of her contempt for me, how far she was willing to go to humiliate me." Marjorie shut her eyes for a moment.

"The names you called her in that message—what made you use those particular terms?"

Marjorie took a deep breath. "I wanted to insult her, I guess. Pay her back for what she'd done to me. Perhaps I was putting my faith in the old saying that the truth hurts. I suppose I even hoped her husband might hear it and finally get the guts to throw her out."

"You believed she was being unfaithful to her husband?"

"Unfaithful to her husband!" Marjorie laughed with genuine amusement. "Really, Chief. Iris was unfaithful to the men she was being unfaithful with. She was still sleeping with Cecil Atkinson when she took up with Connor Tarlech. And she wasn't finished with him when she started with that psychotic

Frenchman—now there's your murderer if you ask me, not that he'd be the only one who ever contemplated killing Iris."

"You're referring to Pierre Blondin?" Did Marjorie know about Iris and Arnold Reifel also, Halsey wondered. Her own husband was the only one of Iris's paramours Marjorie hadn't mentioned.

"Yes, of course, Blondin," Marjorie confirmed. "Busy man, our fine film director. For once, Iris got a taste of her own medicine."

"What do you mean?" Halsey knew what she meant, but he wanted her to confirm it.

"He was sharing his attentions with Iris and Peggy Atkinson at the same time," Marjorie said.

Halsey had been surprised at his own chagrin when Peggy had skewered Cecil Atkinson with the news—he'd had nearly as much difficulty as Atkinson to maintain his composure. Peggy had been connected with Iris through more than one man, Halsey thought. And reflected that it was only luck that had kept him from becoming one of them.

"What about 'plagiarizing'?"

"What?"

"You called her a '*plagiarizing* filthy tramp.' "

Marjorie snickered. "I knew that would get her goat."

"You thought she was copying other writers' work?" Halsey said.

"Oh, not really. But when *Mrs. Forrester* was published, I noticed one small passage that was an uncanny reflection of something I happened to read a couple of years earlier in another book. In both books there's a scene where the hostess of a dinner party serves an unusual dessert—a kind of caramel trifle made to resemble a marigold in a terracotta pot. I suppose I remembered the scene from the first book because I'd thought of trying something similar, and when it turned up in Iris's book years later, I was startled."

"Did you mention the similarity to Mrs. Morland?"

"Yes, like a fool, I did. I thought she'd be amused at the co-incidence. But she was furious—said I was accusing her of plagiarizing trashy novels, and that just because that kind of stuff reflected my literary tastes, I shouldn't assume she'd be reading such trash, let alone seeking inspiration from it."

"Do you remember the name of the other book?"

"No. Just the writer's name—Amber St. Clare. I threw the book out after Iris pitched her fit."

"So why did you make the call—what did Mrs. Morland do to you?" Halsey waited intently for her response. If Marjorie had known about Iris and Arnold, this should be the point where she admitted it. But when the answer came, it was not what he expected.

"It's the fireplace," she said. She pointed to her left without looking, as though she couldn't bear the sight. "There's another just like it in the master bedroom."

The fireplace appeared normal enough to Halsey. It was sheathed in an attractive grayish-white marble that extended to the ceiling and took up most of the wall. A brass fire screen covered the opening.

Halsey raised an eyebrow. "Doesn't it work?"

"Oh, it worked beautifully—for Iris. It was the centerpiece of all my decorating plans. You see, it picks up the white in the sofas, and some of the subtler gray tones in the rug—oh, hell, as if you cared about any of that."

Halsey watched a slow tide of humiliation rise in the woman's face. He set the recorder down and went over to the fireplace. It appeared oddly familiar. He ran his hand over the surface of the facing material. It felt peculiar, not exactly warm, but not as cool as he'd expected.

"What kind of stone is this?" he asked, turning back to

Marjorie. Her face was now flushed a red that matched the nails she was digging into the arms of the sofa.

"It's not marble, of course. It's a fake—some sort of high-quality acrylic, good enough to fool anyone who isn't an expert. In fact, it fooled everyone who came to the birthday party I gave for Arnold a couple of weeks ago. Only Iris knew it wasn't real—it was another of her finds. Some friend of hers was able to let me have it at an irresistible price."

"And she told someone it was fake?" Halsey hazarded.

"Oh, no, that wouldn't have been nearly devious enough for Iris. It was her suggestion that we put people on a little, see how easy it would be to make them look foolish. She was readying the trap, but I was too stupid to see it." Marjorie's hands clenched and unclenched, the scarlet claws leaving deep indentations in her palms.

"So you and Mrs. Morland pretended what?" Halsey asked.

"Iris didn't pretend anything, although she talked as though it were something we'd both do. But when people started arriving, she just watched me pretend. Egged me on."

"To do what?"

"To tell some ridiculous story about the . . . marble . . . being the last of its kind, specially quarried in Italy and custom fitted for me."

"Did your guests believe it?"

"Of course, why shouldn't they? Why wouldn't the wife of a famous television personality be able to afford imported marble?" Marjorie clasped her arms under her breasts and stared coldly in front of her. "How should they know the famous television star can barely keep up his house payments because he's being bled dry by his ex-wife and her brat, or that he could lose his job any minute?

"Lucy Mitchum was at the party," Marjorie continued. "She asked if she could do an article for *Town Talk* on how I'd been renovating the house. I got a little scared then, but what could I say? Iris said no one would be able to tell and she was right. Lucy came back, took some pictures, and the story ran a few days later. Restoration of historic manse, and all that. With prominently placed quotes from me about the Italian quarry, etcetera, etcetera."

Halsey eyed the fireplace. There was something familiar about it that niggled at his attention, yet remained just outside his grasp.

Marjorie unclasped her arms and spoke past the bright tips of her steepled fingers. "So now the whole town knew about the fireplace. The people who weren't here had the pictures in the paper to admire. The trap had snapped shut, and I didn't even know it."

Halsey raised his hands in an I-give-up gesture. "So your party was a big success, everybody believed you had an expensive marble fireplace, you even got newspaper coverage for your decorating taste. Where's the problem?"

Marjorie's thin lips twisted into a sour grimace. "The problem was that Iris's accommodating fake marble supplier was John Dunleavy of Dunleavy Construction."

Halsey felt a light beginning to dawn. "The contractor for the new mall."

"The same," Marjorie said bitterly, "although at the time I didn't know it."

"You found out when the mall opened that Saturday," Halsey said, finally grasping the reason for his sense of familiarity.

Marjorie's face had set in an expression of remarkable hardness, her eyes like agates.

"And what you saw at the mall caused you to make that call to Mrs. Morland." Halsey said, gesturing at the recorder.

"Yes." The set expression on Marjorie's face was cracking like ice breaking up on the surface of a frozen river. "The entire

159

front of the mall—four hundred feet long and thirty feet high—
was finished with the same imitation marble. The same fake
plastic that the whole town knew I'd been claiming was price-
less special marble, custom quarried to be the *pièce de résistance*
of my decorating scheme, the acme of my taste."

CHAPTER 21

Halsey was relieved to see the squad car was still sitting outside. The entire time he was interviewing Marjorie Reifel, he'd expected to hear tires peeling away from the curb, or even the horn blaring while Bailey pounded furiously on the wheel.

She was sitting in the passenger seat, leafing through a sheaf of traffic reports, etching terse notes in the margins with a ballpoint. At least she'd discarded the pencil stub, Halsey thought, sliding behind the wheel.

Bailey put the papers down in her lap and stared through the windshield.

"I'm sorry," she said, still looking straight ahead.

Halsey didn't trust himself to reply. What was he going to do with her? Reassign her to regular duties and ask for a detective from the homicide squad in Vancouver? His justification for not bringing in experienced detectives—that local people could scope out the terrain better than outsiders—had just been blown out of the water. Bailey not only hadn't helped, she'd actually hindered.

Shrieks of excitement rose toward them as he headed back to the station along the lakefront road. The daily pedal-boat races had begun, with the brides pedaling madly and screaming directions at their blindfolded grooms, who were doing the steering. Wendell Baker's amplified voice could be heard offering advice to the competitors and commenting humorously on the action to the crowd cheering on its favorites. As usual, a few boats were headed entirely in the wrong direction, others turned slowly in circles, some slammed into each other, rebounding in erratic dips and spins, or locking together and drifting help-lessly. While the brides churned the water frantically and screeched themselves hoarse, the grooms scowled and cursed behind their blindfolds, yanking the tiller back and forth in response to instructions they could only half hear or understand. In spite of the laughter and applause coming from the audi-ence, Halsey was glad when the frenzied shrieks were finally behind them; the event had always struck him as being uncomfortably symbolic of the married state.

They pulled up at the station and walked in silently. Larsen was at the desk. Helen Stewart was out on patrol.

"Put this in the evidence locker," Halsey said, handing Larsen the disc from Iris's party.

When Larsen returned, Halsey sketched in the interview with Marjorie Reifel, omitting any mention of the contretemps between her and Bailey.

Larsen was stunned. "God, that Morland woman was a piece of work. No wonder people wanted to kill her." He looked at Bailey and grinned good-naturedly. "So how did it feel to be a real cop, doing a real investigation? The closest I've got so far is chauffeuring Will to the Atkinsons." He glanced at Halsey. "Uhh—I didn't mean to sound—"

"I didn't behave like a real cop," Bailey said. "I made a fool of myself again." She dropped the papers she'd been carrying on the front counter and sat down at her desk.

To Halsey's surprise, there was no triumph in Larsen's expression at hearing this. He looked from Bailey to Halsey, who remained grim-faced and silent.

"Well . . . I'm sure you did your best," Larsen said.

Bailey glanced at him quickly, suspecting mockery. Seeing none, her gaze softened into something almost resembling gratitude. She busied herself at her desk.

Halsey watched this exchange with amazement bordering on disbelief. Bailey admitting to making mistakes? Larsen not crowing about it? Had he entered some parallel universe, where reality had twisted out of shape? Apparently so, since Larsen's next question made it clear he intended to pass the matter off without further comment.

"We don't seem a whole lot closer to solving this, do we?" Larsen said.

"Well, it's only been four days since the bodies were found," Halsey said. "It's not like on television where they figure it out overnight." His tone was sharp, and Larsen reddened. *Easy, Will,* Halsey cautioned himself. Swallowing his anger at Bailey had just resulted in Larsen getting it in the neck.

And Larsen was right, Halsey reflected. They were no closer to solving the case. He tossed his notebook into the drawer. Bailey was working quietly at her desk, head down. Larsen was giving directions to Tom Silas, who was just heading out. Halsey waited until Silas left before speaking.

"I'm going to Vancouver on Wednesday to talk to Arnold Reifel," Halsey said. "I need the two of you to stay here and do some research."

Halsey could see disappointment surfacing on Larsen's face; he'd hoped to be asked along to help, but Halsey knew Larsen would be out of his league there. Bailey's expression hadn't changed; she'd known she wasn't going. Halsey thought for a moment, then made a decision.

"Lydia, check out a writer called Amber St. Clare. Find out who publishes her books, and see if you can talk to her. Ask her if she's read *Mrs. Forrester* by Iris Morland, and if she's aware of any similarities."

Halsey wasn't sure what the St. Clare angle had to do with the murders, but he figured anything that roused Iris's fury the way Marjorie Reifel had described was worth checking out. Besides, it gave him something to assign to Bailey, which, even if she screwed up again, wasn't likely to be fatal to the investigation.

Bailey's eyes met his, and this time there was no question there was gratitude showing in them. He let his own gaze telegraph a clear message to her: *last chance.* They both knew he didn't mean on the investigation only. She acknowledged the warning with a faint nod.

"John, I want you to interview Eddie Novak."

"Is Edna on the warpath again?" Larsen asked.

Larsen obviously thought Halsey was referring to Eddie Novak's complaint to the station on Saturday. Edna Sigurdson had been robbed, Eddie reported. She'd returned to her shop to find the bag containing her $300 cash float had disappeared while she and the other councilors were distracted by a car accident. Edna was convinced of two things: the display in the parking lot had been planned deliberately to distract them, and Eddie was an incompetent moron who'd be out of a job unless her money was recovered.

"Not because of the robbery. You can say you're still investigating the theft of Edna Sigurdson's money, but see if you can get him talking about Tarlech, or anything about the mill that might have a bearing on the murders."

Larsen looked confused. "If you couldn't get anything out of him, what's he going to say to me?"

"Maybe nothing. But if he tells the story again to someone else, he might just make a slip. Something inconsistent with what he told me, even one additional detail, might help."

Larsen's face lit up; he was going to do some investigating after all.

"And when you get done with him," Halsey said, "go ask Wendell Baker what he did with Edna's cash bag."

CHAPTER 22

Hermione shuffled unsteadily across the Persian rug and pushed a snifter of brandy into Shelagh's hand. Both women were dressed from head to foot in black, having just returned to Shelagh's house from Connor's funeral. Shelagh's veil still hid her face; as she absently raised the glass it pressed the black silk against her lips. She paused for a moment, and her left hand rose slowly and folded the veil back above her hat.

"Drink it, dear," Hermione said. She lowered herself into the twin of the wing-back chair in which Shelagh was sitting, careful to keep the contents of her own glass from spilling.

In the days since Connor's body was discovered, Shelagh had refused to see a doctor, refused any sedation, refused any help. She seemed utterly controlled, in both senses of the word: no sign of emotion escaped her, yet at the same time she appeared to be functioning at the behest of some other entity. That moment just now, when she'd moved her veil out of the way: it had looked so odd, as though the instruction for the movement had been transmitted across light years.

Shelagh swallowed some of her brandy. "How long do you imagine I have to live, Mother?" she asked.

"Why do you ask, dear?" Hermione tightened her grip on the brandy glass.

It must have been decades since Shelagh had referred to their real relationship, even when they were alone. Sometimes Hermione forgot they weren't sisters. My God, I was fourteen years old when she was born, Hermione thought. I used to leave her in the dressing room with the chorus girls when I was onstage with that bastard, her father. Called himself *Sir* Robert Walmsley—what a fool I was thinking I was going to be Lady Walmsley; even if he'd married me I'd have been Mrs. Harry Leach—how's Mrs. Leach and all the little leaches, the old music hall joke, imagine!

To keep him out of jail, she'd had to disappear while she was pregnant, returning with her "sister" after Shelagh was born. Nowadays he'd be called a child molester, Hermione supposed.

"I was thinking about how much time I'd spend in prison," Shelagh said.

"Prison?" Astonishment fluted Hermione's voice upward so she sounded as if she were doing Lady Bracknell's famous *handbag*? line. She brought it back down to a more appropriate pitch. "Why on earth would you be thinking about prison? If anyone goes to prison it'll be whoever killed Connor and—"

"Don't say her name with his." Shelagh's eyes lit with fury, the first emotion Hermione had seen in them since Connor's death.

"Shelagh dear, I miss Connor too, and you know I loved him dearly. But *she* didn't kill him. And she wasn't the only woman in his life."

"No. But she was the one who brought death to him." Shelagh drank again.

The unnatural stillness seemed to be ebbing from her, Hermione saw, but what was taking its place was not reassuring. Even as a child, Shelagh had been implacable once she'd determined a course of action, and something told Hermione that she'd embarked on one now.

"Brought death to him?" Hermione had a momentary vision of Iris leading a black-robed figure toward Connor. "What do you mean?"

"Kenneth Morland is what I mean," Shelagh said.

Hermione thought for a moment. "You think Kenneth Morland—"

"Found out what his slut of a wife was up to and vented his rage on both of them." Shelagh put her empty glass down on the table beside her and began unpinning her hat. Her movements now were brisk, purposeful.

"Oh, I can't see Kenneth Morland in that role," Hermione said. "He doesn't have the backbone to do something like that."

"Even the worm turns eventually, Hermione," Shelagh said, dropping the long, black-bead-tipped pins onto the table beside her.

So they were sisters again, Hermione thought. Just as well: she had no talent for maternity and Shelagh none for filial devotion; they were both more comfortable as sisters.

"But he called my place, looking for her—don't you remember?" Hermione objected. "You talked to him."

"Oh, for God's sake, Hermione. That proves nothing at all. It just helps make his story look better for the police. He called several other people too. If he hadn't called, the police might have wondered why he wasn't concerned at her not being at home." Shelagh's hat and veil sank into a dark crouch beside the pins. She got up and fetched the brandy. "More?"

Hermione shook her head. Shelagh sloshed a good measure into her glass and sat down again. The liquor at least seemed to be bringing Shelagh back to life again; let her pay for it later if necessary.

"Shelagh," Hermione said, "did you know Connor was back in town?"

"Yes, I did," Shelagh said.

Hermione was surprised how much this hurt. Connor, whom she had loved, had not wished to see her, or at least had not considered her important enough to know what was happening to him.

"Don't look like that," Shelagh said. "He was hiding from all the yahoos who threatened him when the mill went under."

"And he didn't trust an old woman not to babble his whereabouts to all and sundry," Hermione said.

"Oh, for heaven's sake, it wasn't like that at all," Shelagh said. "He was ashamed, can't you understand that? He'd been run out of town, humiliated in every way. He was hoping to get financing for the mill again. He wanted you to see him when he was triumphant, not defeated. It was only going to be for another few days."

"What makes you so sure it wasn't one of those yahoos who killed him?"

"Why would they kill her? And look at the way they were found—dressed up like a bride and groom on a parade float. It was meant to send a message that their involvement was known. Kenneth Morland wanted everyone to know he wasn't the spineless fool others might have thought him. It was only chance that stopped those batty Delbrook women from displaying that horrible tableau to the entire town."

"Shelagh—you mentioned Connor was looking for financing."

"No," Shelagh said, responding to the unspoken question. "Not from me." She began removing her black gloves, one finger at a time.

"You don't have any money, do you dear?" Hermione asked. "You lost it all when Connor went bankrupt."

Shelagh shrugged. "I'm eighty-one. This house is paid for, and I can qualify for the old age pension."

"Eighty-one—my God, I still remember when you left London. You were twenty years old. When was that? Sixty-one years ago—God, you're old, Shelagh." Hermione's ironic inflection made it clear whose age was really on her mind. "You were going to America to become a singing star in pictures. I was standing in the crowd on the dock as the ship pulled out, all its horns blaring. You threw a streamer down to me; we held on to it while it stretched and finally broke as the ship pulled away. I reeled in my piece and kept it in my cases, until it eventually got lost—everything does, sooner or later."

"Yes, I know," Shelagh said. "Everything does." She smiled suddenly. "Maybe I'll resume my singing career. Do you remember how I used to have Connor in hysterics when I did the Madonna imitation?"

"You were quite a good singer," Hermione said. "I always told you that if you'd only taken your talent seriously instead of doing all those comic songs and imitations of other singers—"

"I'd have had no career at all—not that it was much of one, anyway. But it did pay the bills for Connor and me when his father, Mr. Robert-Big-Shot-Film-Producer-Rankin, dumped us, God rot him."

Hermione sighed. "Men are often such pigs, aren't they? But you know, Shelagh, I never understood what on earth possessed you—you were always so infuriatingly practical. Even as a child, you used to give me that *look* whenever I was over the moon about some new male. Good grief, when I married Ackland Richardson, I remember your little face scowling at me when I walked down the aisle—you couldn't have been more than six or seven. And just as I was promising to love, honor, and obey, you stood up in your pew and announced to the whole church, 'We'll see.' " Hermione giggled. "Poor Ackland—he said you froze his blood."

Shelagh sipped her brandy. "Well, we did see, didn't we?"

"Oh, Acky was all right," Hermione said tolerantly. "He just couldn't walk by a casino without entering, and the man had the worst luck I've ever seen. We were stony broke the whole two years we were married. We both had to borrow to pay the lawyers for the divorce. But then, I always knew I had no judgment about men. You always seemed to see right through them."

"Well, I didn't see through Robert Rankin. I was thirty-four when we met, not exactly a dewy young maid anymore, and he was incredibly handsome and attentive, and he thought I could be a great comedienne. Barbara Streisand, Lucille Ball, and Carole Lombard all rolled into one, as I recall. Well, of course, it didn't happen. For three years, I played every two-bit fleabag across the United States, and one fine day when Connor was four months old, he just disappeared. I hadn't been able to work much while I was pregnant, and I suppose he realized that a thirty-seven-year-old woman who hadn't made it yet was never going to make it."

"My God, why didn't you let me know? I could have helped you. I was working steadily then in all that continental claptrap."

"Hermione, you were already helping me," Shelagh said. "You sent a check every month, and don't think I don't know how hard it was for you to manage that at times. I would have died before I asked you for another cent."

"I've been a rotten mother," Hermione said. "I should have checked to see you were all right. Even a sister would've done that."

"Nonsense," Shelagh said. "I was, after all, well past the age when I needed supervision. When I had my baby, I was almost three times the age you were when you had me, and you had no one to help you."

"Think of it—twenty years passed before we saw each other again," Hermione marveled. "You were married to Amos and living here by then."

Shelagh smiled. "Amos saw me perform at a supper club in Vancouver. *He* believed I was a star. He also took to Connor right away. I had to tell him I was a widow, of course. In those days, no man was going to marry a woman with an illegitimate child."

"He loved that boy, didn't he? I remember seeing Amos for the first time when I got off the plane. A big, bald man with a bushy mustache. He was holding Connor, who must have been three by then, and he said, 'This is my son.' I almost blurted out, 'And my grandson.' And you were beside him, so beautiful and self-assured. Did you ever tell him—"

"About not being a widow? No, but I think he knew. He never asked a single question about my first husband." Shelagh frowned and said, "Do you know, I cried when I found out that louse was dead—all I could think of was how wonderful he made me feel the whole time we were together. Amos was worth ten of him, a wonderful father to Connor, and I loved him, but—"

But you never get over the first one, Hermione thought. She'd cried too, when Harry Leach died, even though she'd been over fifty and hadn't seen him for decades when it happened—like all bastards, he'd lived to a ripe old age.

Hermione's mind veered to something that had been puzzling her.

"Shelagh—what made you change your mind about the nude scene, dear? You were so dead set against it, but the day Kenneth Morland called, you seemed almost resigned to it."

Shelagh sighed. "I knew you were going to do it after Blondin talked to you, no matter what I said. That's why I went to that vile woman's party—to tell her what Blondin was planning. I hoped when she heard about it she'd be distracted enough to loosen her grip on Connor."

"And what was her reaction?"

"Oh, she already knew about it, of course. That's why she had Blondin there. And she understood instantly what I was trying to do. She took me upstairs to Kenneth's study and showed me some papers he had in his safe. She said they were evidence that could help Connor get the mill back. Then she

171

locked them in the safe and just stood there, smiling at me. The message was clear—without her, Connor could never return."

"And now he never will," Hermione said, her throat constricting. "What are we going to do, Shelagh?"

"We're going to go on as best we can. You'll finish your picture." Shelagh took another generous mouthful from her glass. Her face had started to go slack, the lines of pain submerging.

"And you—what will you do, dear?"

"I'll work on Connor's memorial," Shelagh murmured.

"His memorial? But we've arranged for a very nice stone to be put on the grave already."

"I don't mean that kind of memorial. I mean something in a larger sense. To make sure no one forgets how he died."

"What did you have in mind, dear?"

Bringing death to Kenneth Morland, Shelagh thought. The idea was more intoxicating than the brandy. Aloud she said only, "I'm not sure yet. I'll have to think about it."

CHAPTER 23

"We *can't* fire him," Selena said. "And even if we could, it's a ridiculous idea."

It had been at Art Selby's demand that tonight's council meeting had been convened to consider Halsey's handling of the case. Selena had known from the start that any meddling on council's part would only garner worse publicity than the town was already getting, but Selby had forced her hand by threatening an off-the-record chat with Delia Bendel.

"What's so ridiculous about it?" Selby demanded. "We hired him, we can fire him—simple as that."

"Oh shut up, you fool," Edna said. "We hired him as chief of the town police force, and that's the only authority we have over him. The RCMP put him in charge of the murder investigation, and I doubt they're going to take him off it at our request."

"And how would it look if council starts trying to get rid of the RCMP's chief investigator?" Wendell Baker said. "Some of us around this table . . ." He let the sentence trail off.

"Are potential suspects," Cora Delbrook finished, over the agitated demurrals of her sister.

Other than Irene Delbrook's, all eyes swung toward Selena. She stared back at them, her flat, cold glance quickly driving theirs to other objects.

It was remarkable how quickly after the murders the hostilities among them had surfaced. It was not only the long-established feuds like the one between Wendell and Edna that had blazed up with renewed fierceness—that was to be expected when the pressure was on. More notable was the abandonment of diplomatic relations among those who'd previously managed a workable state of truce. Edna's détente with Selby was clearly over: he was referring to her every remark as stupid, and she in turn regularly told him to shut up. Only the Delbrooks' behavior was relatively unchanged since the murders, in spite of their involvement in the discovery of them.

Even Herb Collinson had gone off his rocker in Selena's car tonight. She'd been stopped for a light when he sprang on her and attempted to kiss her. Worse yet, his idea of stimulating her erogenous zones was either rooted in some Neanderthal magazine fantasy, or his seat belt had precluded an accurate aim. He'd driven his tongue into her ear with such pile-driver force, she'd expected it to emerge from the other side of her head and smack against the driver's-side window. Through it all he hadn't spoken a word, and Selena was still fighting the urge to shake her head like a dog expelling ditchwater from its ear. Collinson now sat sullenly glaring at Selby whenever the latter spoke to her.

The acrimony presently filling the chamber had developed in quantum leaps since Selena's announcement that she'd asked Chief Halsey to attend to give them a progress report on the investigation. Selby had been first to react.

"Investigation?" His face twisted in a sneer. "That's not what I'd call it. Incompetent bumbling would be a better description. Every newspaper in the country is publishing stories about the possibility of a ritual killer stalking the streets of Honeymoon Falls. My bookings at the Lodge are off fifty percent, and with every week that passes, more people are going to cancel."

"Oh God, as if you're the only one," Edna retorted. "Business is down for us all, and it's going to stay that way until this is cleared up."

"Well . . . after all . . . it's only been ten days," Irene said. "I don't think you can actually set a time limit on . . . I mean, it probably takes a while to gather clues . . . and Chief Halsey was very nice to us when that horrible Bailey woman. . . ."

Everyone ignored her, except Cora, who patted her hand comfortingly. "I've told him he should fire her," she said.

"He's not going to tell us anything anyway," Collinson said.

Irene murmured assent. "Whatever information he's gathered would have to be kept confidential at this point," she said, avoiding Collinson's gaze.

"What information?" Selby said. "I don't believe he knows any more about the murders than we do. Maybe less than some of us," he said, with an insinuating look at Selena, whose expression remained stony.

"Like you, for instance," Collinson said. "Maybe that's the reason you're so quick to point the finger at others."

Selby's dark-skinned cheeks swelled with wrath. "Listen, you freak show—"

"Oh, shut up," Edna said reflexively.

"Lucy Mitchum says there's tons of suspects," Irene said. "I guess the husband is always a suspect, so Mr. Morland . . . then there were people who didn't like her because—" She broke off, suddenly conscious that she was straying into awkward territory.

"Oh hell," Edna said. "Everybody knows the woman had more enemies than Hitler. Not liking Iris Morland was hardly a distinguishing characteristic among anyone who knew her."

"Quite right," Halsey said, entering the room.

His sudden appearance made all except Selena start. She gestured to a vacant seat beside her.

"Chief Halsey, as you know, the murders have been on all our minds to a considerable degree." Her glance was cool, her voice rock-steady. "We would appreciate hearing whatever you can tell us about the progress of the case."

Halsey marveled at the change since his interview with her shortly after Tarlech's death. Then, the bleakness of her despair seemed to have sapped her last reserves of strength. Now she seemed restored, armored against all assault, assured, even powerful. Something besides pills had put that steel into her spine, he thought. Was it the determination not to allow Tarlech's second rejection to destroy all she'd created as the result of his first? Or was it the satisfaction of having avenged herself finally and unanswerably?

Halsey brought them up to date quickly, riding firmly over Selby's attempts to interrupt.

"Like I said," Collinson muttered when Halsey finished, "nothing we don't already know."

"As I'm sure you realize, the success of a murder investigation depends to a considerable degree on confidentiality," Halsey said.

Selby opened his mouth, but was quickly overridden by Edna.

"Chief Halsey, it's come to my attention that you've alienated some extremely influential media outlets. I'm sure I don't need to tell you the impact this has on the portrayal of the situation here."

"Yeah, imagine stiffing Delia Bendel for that nitwit Lucy Mitchum," Selby said. "Channel Five's nightly newscast has a viewership of nearly a million people—did you know that, Halsey? That piddling All News Network Lucy's fronting doesn't get a tenth of that."

"Lucy treats my staff and me with respect," Halsey said.

"You don't have a clue what a ratings point means, do you, Halsey?" Selby said.

"No, but it's pretty clear Delia Bendel has explained it thoroughly to you and Edna," Halsey said, no longer giving a damn if they were offended or not.

"Shut up, Art," Edna said, cutting off Selby's outraged reply. "We all saw you slobbering over her on the six o'clock news. Imagine offering her free accommodation at Honeymoon Heaven—God, what a jackass you looked."

Selby inhaled furiously, but Wendell Baker got the next words in before he could speak.

"You should talk, Edna. Your interview with her about the funeral flowers was hardly the epitome of taste—all that stuff about wreaths made out of 'love-lies-bleeding' and 'lilies of passion.' If that didn't make all one million of Channel Five's viewers puke in unison, nothing would."

"Look, Chief," Selena Coyle said, ignoring Edna's ranted response, "every time Channel Five takes a swipe at Honeymoon Falls, more people stay away. The story's starting to appear in the foreign media, and if it keeps up, the perception that Honeymoon Falls is a dangerous place to visit is going to take hold. Once that happens—" She spread her palms. "Your job's on the line as well as mine."

"All right," Halsey conceded. "Next time Delia Bendel shows up, I'll talk to her. But if she starts that crap about my staff again, you may wish I hadn't."

"She's *from the press*," Selby said. "You just don't get it, do you?"

Halsey leaned forward and stared straight into Selby's eyes.

"And I'm *from the police*. You don't seem to be getting that."

For a moment Selby met his stare, then his glance dropped and he began examining his knuckles closely. There was a moment of silence, broken by Irene Delbrook.

"Well," she said, "I'm so glad we got that straightened out. Now, about the bridal fashion show in the mall. . . ."

CHAPTER 24

Reifel led Halsey through the hall of his ex-wife's Vancouver apartment. As Halsey followed, he caught glimpses of a study lined with books and reproductions of medieval navigation charts; an all-white kitchen with black granite countertops; and a solarium full of exotic flowering plants he knew could not be grown in other than climate-controlled conditions.

They passed through a graceful archway, which opened into an expansive room with a rug depicting intricate bird and flower designs and walls hung with paintings in a style that Halsey remembered Vivien referring to as French Impressionism.

"Chief Halsey!" the famous voice intoned. He shook hands with Halsey, gestured him to an armchair upholstered in jade-green silk brocade, and took its twin opposite.

"I need your assistance with my investigation into Mrs. Morland's death," Halsey said.

"Of course," Reifel said. "My ex-wife and daughter are out, so we can speak freely."

Had Iris been readying Reifel for immersion in one of the acid baths she had been so partial to administering? Certainly Reifel seemed to offer no real challenge to her skill—he appeared almost too easy a target, Halsey thought. The silvery hair, the confident, handsome face, even the voice, seemed excessive, as if they were a stage disguise that, seen close up, were revealed as obviously false. And yet . . . perhaps the brilliance of the disguise was that it appeared so easy to penetrate?

"What would you like to know?" Reifel asked. One hand lay lightly on the chair arm, the other on the gray sock covering the ankle resting on one knee. The faint, rhythmic flex of the raised foot in its expensive loafer was the only sign of any discomfort Halsey could detect.

"What was your relationship with Mrs. Morland?"

"As I'm sure you know, we were having an affair."

"Were you aware of any others with whom she had been involved?"

"Yes, of course. Iris was promiscuous. Perhaps that's unfair— she simply didn't regard sexual adventures as important moral issues."

"That's all your relationship was—a sexual adventure?"

"You sound like an elderly spinster, Chief." The tone was still pleasant, but something cold flickered in Reifel's eyes.

Halsey waited. Reifel's steady gaze hardened as the pause stretched out.

"It's none of your damned business what was between Iris and me," he said. The hand on the ankle tightened its grip.

Halsey pressed harder. "Were you in love with Mrs. Morland?"

"Don't be ridiculous." The response was instant, the words bitten off sharply.

"Were you surprised when Connor Tarlech's body was found with hers?"

An angry flush suffused Reifel's face.

"I was surprised when her body was found in such circumstances. It hardly mattered who was found with her," he parried.

Halsey watched the color darkening the other man's skin. Arnold Reifel had been no more successful than any of the others at escaping Iris Morland unscathed. That Iris should have returned to the arms of her previous lover while keeping Reifel on her string had dealt a humiliating blow to his self-esteem.

"Enid Regular says she sent this note to you," Halsey said, passing it over.

Reifel's lips tightened. "If she sent it, I never got it. Was she sober when you spoke to her?"

Halsey made no reply, and Reifel smiled knowingly.

"Her story's nonsense," he said briskly, handing the note back. "Enid's a drunk, and she frequently makes up fantastic stuff. This is just some poison pen thing she's had sitting on her computer for God knows how long."

"You're quite sure you haven't seen it before?"

"Quite sure," Reifel said, using his professional voice.

"Was Mr. Morland aware of your relationship with his wife?"

Reifel laughed. "Surely he's told you he caught us in a, shall we say, compromising position?"

"I'd like to hear your version," Halsey said, keeping his expression neutral.

"Probably the same as his, I imagine. Iris and I were making love in her living room when we discovered him lurking behind the sofa."

Halsey struggled to keep his eyebrows from climbing into his hairline. "What was his reaction?"

"He went to his office and locked the door."

"Did Mrs. Morland mention any subsequent reaction to you?"

"She said they were not intimate anymore, and that she planned to divorce him."

"How did you meet Mrs. Morland?"

"She was a guest on my show. She'd written a novel that drew an analogy between mothers with young children and vampires and their victims. In her novel, the children were the vampires, draining the mother of the vitality she needed for a life of her own."

"Was this the book where the mother abandons the children at a rest stop on the freeway?"

Reifel looked surprised. "Yes. I wouldn't have thought you one of Iris's readers, Chief." *Or even that you read at all,* his tone implied.

"Anyway," Reifel continued, seeing that Halsey was not to be drawn, "the book was a *cause célèbre* for a while, denounced by the family values militia and hailed by the feminist apparatchiks. I invited her on my show to debate with representatives from both sides. She slaughtered them all."

"Even the—what did you call them—feminist apparatchiks? Weren't they supportive of her book?"

Reifel gave an amused snort. "They thought she was writing about feminist issues—the lack of daycare facilities for working women, and so forth. Iris had absolutely no interest in such things. Her approach was always the impartial dissection and labeling of what she saw. One critic referred to her as 'the Great Vivisectionist.' "

"Did she take the same approach in life?"

Reifel paused for a moment.

"To a degree, I suppose." He shrugged. "Iris was a formidably bright woman, with a powerful personality that drew people to her. And she could focus her attention on you with an intensity that seemed flattering at first. Most people didn't realize how analytical her interest was: once she had figured you out, she discarded you."

"And do you think she'd figured you out?" Halsey asked.

"Evidently," Reifel said dryly.

"Were you planning to marry Mrs. Morland?"

Reifel gave him a patronizing smile. "You seem to forget I am already married to Marjorie."

It was time to puncture the man's haughty composure. Halsey let his gaze rest on Reifel.

"Doesn't seem to be an issue for you," he said.

The effect was galvanizing. Reifel's face darkened to the color of old brick, and his fists clenched. "You insulting bastard! Get out—from now on you can talk to my lawyer."

"When did you last see Mrs. Morland?"

"I said *get out*!"

The smooth professional skin that Reifel appeared to inhabit so effortlessly seemed to distort as though it were swelling to contain his wrath. Halsey almost expected the stage disguise to fly apart into its individual elements.

Halsey stayed put, staring into Reifel's face as it twisted through various stages of fury. By degrees, the urbane mask reassembled itself, as if it were reacting to a countdown prior to a camera being switched on. With one quick gesture, Reifel smoothed his hair, then leaned deliberately against the back of his chair.

"That was *very* good, Chief," Reifel said. "I suppose that's Chapter One of the *Police Procedural Manual*—provoke the suspect into losing his temper and he'll blurt out something incriminating. Sorry to disappoint you." His color was normal again, but the authoritative baritone was not quite as assured.

Halsey waited a moment before repeating his previous question.

"When did you last see Mrs. Morland?"

Reifel waited twice as long as Halsey had before answering.

"On the Friday before her party. We had dinner at an Italian restaurant in the West End."

"June fifth," Halsey observed, consulting his notes. "You're sure you didn't see her later than that?"

"I didn't see her after that, and I didn't kill her," Reifel said.

"No one said you did, Mr. Reifel," Halsey said. "What did you talk about?"

"What?" Reifel seemed startled by the question.

"Your conversation at the restaurant—presumably you talked of something. What?"

Reifel's eyes narrowed maliciously. "In fact, I do recall one part of our conversation. She mentioned Cecil Atkinson—called him a contemptible weasel."

Reifel smiled. Directing the beam of Iris's burning glass against someone else was obviously a relief for him.

"What made her speak of him?" Halsey asked.

"She'd seen him recently. She said he'd never have got anywhere if his wife hadn't slept with his faculty dean years ago. According to Iris, Peggy Atkinson got pregnant by the dean, and Atkinson used the situation to ensure he got tenure."

Halsey remembered Peggy Atkinson's remarks about having her children *after* Atkinson got tenure. If Iris had been correct, the child Peggy had conceived with the dean had not been born. Halsey remembered the note in her voice when she told him she was glad he'd never had to be responsible for someone's death. The reason for the Atkinsons' long stand-off with razors to each other's throats was suddenly clearer.

"How did Mrs. Morland know this?"

Reifel shook his head. "Atkinson told her. She could make you *need* to tell her stuff like that. It was the only way to hold her attention—continually revealing yourself."

"Did she make any further comments about him?"

Reifel considered for a moment. "I believe she mentioned he was way over budget on some building program he was committed to. She was on the board of directors of that tin-pot college he runs, you know."

Halsey studied Reifel thoughtfully. He'd apparently liked hearing his predecessor savaged, without suspecting the same treatment might lie ahead for him.

"Did it ever occur to you that someday Mrs. Morland might tell your secrets?" Halsey asked.

"No. Because I never told her any," Reifel said.
Maybe not, Halsey thought, but I'll bet she knew them.

CHAPTER 25

Pieter Rempel's spatial perceptions were hardly his strong point, Halsey thought, watching the man attempt to force a suitcase lid shut on a portable television set.

Rempel was a big man, with crew cut brown hair fading to gray at the temples and brown eyes magnified by thick-lensed glasses. He was packing to return to New York when he let Halsey into his suite at the Vancouver Hyatt.

"Present for the kids," Rempel said, hoisting the TV out of the welter of socks and underwear he'd been using for padding. "Damn thing won't fit in there," he muttered, frowning as though someone should have warned him.

"Won't it get broken during shipment?" Halsey asked.

"Not if it's packed right," Rempel said.

Precisely the point, Halsey thought, though he forbore comment.

"I'd like to ask you some questions," Halsey said, as Rempel flung items from the suitcase like a man tossing ballast from a boat taking on water.

"Yes, of course, go ahead," Rempel said absently.

He laid the television, screen down, in the center of the suitcase, rotating it in alternating half circles, as if he might be able to augur a deep enough hole for it.

"I published all of her books, even the first, which everybody said would never sell."

Rempel advanced the suitcase lid slowly on the protruding

back of the television set, as though hoping to take it by surprise before it had time to inflate itself beyond containment. The lid stopped a good four inches before touching the case.

"Nuts." He flipped the clasps up and down experimentally, but they failed to bridge the gap. "Of course it didn't."

It took a second before Halsey realized the last remark was a continuation of his comments about Iris's first novel, not a comment on the recalcitrance of his luggage.

"But the next one—*After a Long Illness*—did all right. That was the one about the woman who saw her children as vampires. And then there was *The Shapeshifter* and *Mrs. Forrester.*"

"*The Shapeshifter*—that was the one about the sex change?" Halsey asked.

"Mmmm. And her last one is pretty good." Rempel draped a trench coat experimentally over the television. "Maybe it'll go in the flight bag."

"*The Rest of Esther*?" Halsey rubbed his forehead. The disjointed conversation was confusing. It sounded as if he were asking whether the titular Esther's torso would fit in the flight bag. Rempel appeared to be having no difficulty following the thread, however.

"Yes, that's right," Rempel said, pleased. He abandoned his packing and sat on the bed. "It hasn't even been released yet and you've heard of it already—that's good, that's very good; the marketing department is finally on the ball. Maybe we'll make a respectable profit at last."

Halsey didn't tell him he'd heard the title from Peggy Atkinson, not through any advertising campaign.

"If her books don't make money, why do you publish them?" he asked.

"Well, they don't lose money either—we generally get our investment back. And Iris was beginning to be recognized internationally, so there's a certain amount of prestige in being her publisher." Rempel moved his hands up and down in a weighing motion. "It's like playing the stock market. You take on certain writers and hope their stock will go up."

"Did Iris have an agent?"

Rempel laughed. "Iris was the toughest negotiator on earth. She wouldn't have given the smallest fraction of control to anyone else. She didn't need to; she knew the business inside out, and she was very realistic about her work—she knew it would never make the money that came from mass-market sales."

"Ever hear of a writer called Amber St. Clare?" Halsey asked.

"Nope. Sounds like a pen-name on a bodice-ripper."

"A what?"

"The kind of novel where the hot-blooded young lord of the manor tries to seduce the virtuous governess."

Halsey described the similarity in their work Marjorie Reifel had noticed. "Do you think Iris might have known Amber St. Clare?"

"I doubt it. I hate to think how Iris would have reacted to any comparison of her work with that type of novel." Rempel paused for a moment. "Who noticed the similarity?"

"Marjorie Reifel."

"The shopping mall college," Rempel said instantly, obviously recalling the message Iris had broadcast at the publishing party. "So that's what that was all about."

"You were right about Mrs. Morland's reaction to comparisons she didn't like," Halsey said. He glanced at Rempel's face and decided to move to a different level of questioning.

"I understand that you and Mrs. Morland were personally involved at one time," Halsey said.

Rempel looked at him ruefully. "I was afraid you'd want to talk about that. It was at the beginning of her career. It didn't last long, and I don't think poor old Kenneth ever knew. At least, I hope not. My wife did though—she got an anonymous letter telling her about it. Took me years to realize that Iris sent it. And even after I did, I still thought for a long time that it was a desperate, if reprehensible, attempt to make our relationship permanent. Of course it was nothing of the kind, just another performance in the Theater of Cruelty Iris presided over."

"What did you do?" Halsey asked, surprised by a sudden surge of rage. An image of Vivien and The Actor laughing at him seemed to come out of nowhere.

"The first sensible thing I did since meeting Iris—told my wife the truth, promised it would never happen again, and begged her forgiveness. Fortunately she still wanted me, and I've never forgotten how lucky I am that she does."

"How did she feel about your working with Mrs. Morland?"

Rempel smiled. "She knew that once Iris was finished with you, you didn't exist anymore. Our relationship was strictly business, and my wife knew it."

"Was the business relationship amicable?" Halsey asked.

Rempel gave him a level look. "Not always. Iris threatened to sue me once when she felt Stanford Publishing hadn't provided a suitable publicity budget for *Mrs. Forrester*. And she was never happy with the physical appearance of her books—the binding, the cover art, the typeface—there was always something she didn't think measured up."

"A difficult client," Halsey observed.

"Not *that* difficult," Rempel replied, his meaning clear.

Halsey nodded and changed the subject.

"Can you tell me what the new book is about?"

"Same as all her other books—the exploration of lives in crisis."

Halsey recognized book-jacket blurb-speak. "Someone at the party apparently credited Kenneth Morland with inspiring the book. Does that seem likely?"

"You must be talking about that old fool Hubert Mandeville. The book is dedicated to Kenneth, and there are certain similarities between him and the husband in the novel."

"Like what?"

"The physical description of the husband is similar, and the character is an unhappily married journalist. His wife is having an affair." Rempel spread his hands. "You can see why people might have thought of Kenneth."

"What does the husband do?"

"He doesn't kill his wife, if that's what you're thinking. He begins an affair also, only to find he's involved with a woman who systematically strips him of everything that matters to him."

A real laugh riot, Halsey thought. "Do you think Kenneth Morland was having an affair?"

Rempel tilted his head from side to side. "Who knows? Even if he was, that doesn't mean Iris was writing about it. A novel is never a blueprint of the writer's personal life, no matter how many apparent linkages exist. Things get turned around, characters trade places, events don't unfold in the same way they actually did."

"What do you think she'd have done if he had been having an affair?" Halsey asked.

Rempel grinned. "In the book, the husband is eventually devoured by a crocodile. If Kenneth was the model for the husband, it's clear how Iris saw her role."

CHAPTER 26

Marjorie and Arnold were seated in their living room, she on the ivory linen sofa, he in the massive gray and black armchair to her right. As usual, he had a decanter on the glass table beside him and was gulping scotch from a Waterford tumbler while resting his feet on the engraved edge of the coffee table. Marjorie detested the way he used the table for a footstool, but since she refused to have such an object in her living room, she had to content herself with insisting that he at least remove his shoes before planting his heels on the face of Wotan, the Norse god of thunder.

Only one lamp was lit, and the firelight flickered invitingly on the hearth. Really, Marjorie thought, casting an appraising glance over the faux marble surround, now that Iris was dead, she was beginning to like the way the plastic stuff looked again, and people were bound to forget in time.

Marjorie finished perusing Lucy Mitchum's review of the local theater group's production of *A Doll's House*. ("Henry Gibson, the late Norwegian playwright, provided an evening rife with dramatic moments. . . .") She put the paper down deliberately and met her husband's aggressive glare.

"I don't think so, dear," she said.

Marjorie's tone of voice suggested she might have been responding to an enquiry about whether there was any more raisin bread for toast, or if it was likely the dog was savoring one of Arnold's slippers in its basement lair. The question, or rather statement, put to her, however, was laden with enough drama to have done justice to the late Norwegian playwright himself.

Arnold repeated it. "I'm divorcing you," he said.

His face was showing the flush it took on when he reached a certain point in his alcohol consumption. The color developed in stages, first outlining features where the skin lay close against the bone, as though his skull were beginning to radiate heat. As the level in the decanter dropped, it blossomed in the finely reticulated pouches beneath his eyes, surged up over his high pale forehead and swept across his scalp until his silver hair appeared to float on a bed of coals.

He was not, Marjorie knew, quite to the point where liquor made him incoherent and helpless, and she judged it wisest to avoid outright confrontation. Until the drink had done its work, he could be incredibly quick-witted, and arguing with him was impossible. It wasn't that he wouldn't let you speak, but he could prove you wrong, prove it without even trying, prove it so well that you were forced to admit even to yourself that you were wrong. She supposed he'd learned the knack from all the politicians he interviewed.

"I'm afraid I don't understand, dear," Marjorie said. She kept her voice even, in spite of her growing unease.

It wouldn't take too much more to put him out, but the glass had stopped its steady ascent to his lips, and was now being passed reflectively from hand to hand while he stared into the liquid it contained.

"I want my wife and daughter back," Arnold said.

Oh hell, Marjorie thought. *That old chestnut again. Back in the good old days when I was part of a happy family—boo-hoo, poor me, all alone and you don't love me.*

"Arnold, I *am* your wife," she said, maintaining the same patient tone.

"I know about you and Selby," he said.

Marjorie's lungs seemed to have completely emptied themselves of air. She really hadn't thought he'd guessed. While Iris was alive, he'd been too obsessed with her to notice anything else, and Marjorie had ended the affair with Selby shortly before Iris's death.

Marjorie realized he was watching her intently, raising the glass to his lips again as he gauged the effect of his bombshell. The idea of Arnold, of all people, playing the role of betrayed husband was infuriating. Marjorie steeled herself to remain calm, even managing a little smile as she forced herself to speak.

"And I know about Iris," she said.

She leaned toward him and patted the toe of one foot gently. She was delighted when he yanked his foot back as if he found it suddenly thrust into fire. The glass rose swiftly twice, and he twisted around to grab the decanter. She kept the smile in place while she watched him fill the glass again. It wasn't just the need for liquor that generated his actions, she suspected. He was engaging in this little flurry to cover his confusion also. In control of himself again, he returned to the attack.

"Nothing to know," Arnold said. "You're simply repeating some appalling gossip you've heard." He swallowed half the contents of the glass and glared at her.

"As you must be, linking me with that repulsive Selby creature," Marjorie replied, keeping her voice light. "I've never fancied apes."

"You were at that roach motel he runs—plenty of times." Arnold took another hefty swig. "You were seen there. Often."

Marjorie managed not to flinch, remaining outwardly composed while her mind raced. She hadn't been lying when she told Arnold that Selby didn't attract her. But he had been attracted to her, and that had been enough to bring her to acquiesce. She missed the delicious sense of power she experienced with a man who wanted her more than she wanted him, and once Arnold was no longer among that group, she'd found Selby's pursuit the only available consolation. And it made a diversion from watching Arnold orbit between Eleanor and Iris, like an object caught between the gravitational pull of opposing planets.

Iris had told him, of course. *Iris, the bitch.* But Iris was dead now, beyond contradicting anything Marjorie said from here on. This last thought calmed her again.

"Yes," Marjorie allowed, "I probably was seen there. I warned Iris that would happen in time." She smiled. "But of course, Iris never cared about anything like that. I think she enjoyed the risk, actually."

"What are you talking about?" Arnold's tone was skeptical, but his expression was less confident, and his voice slurred slightly.

He fumbled the decanter toward his glass and dumped the last of the scotch in. Marjorie watched him carefully. She mustn't make her move too soon, yet she had to play her hand while he was balanced on the edge, the moment just before the liquor took him completely. In that state he was highly suggestible, and Marjorie knew whatever she told him then he would have great difficulty resisting. He was very close to the point she needed him to reach, very close. She waited until he got another couple of swallows into him, then fired point-blank.

"Why, Iris and Selby, of course," she said in an amused tone. "She used to hide in my car while I drove her out there. I'd spend a couple of hours by the lake reading, and Iris . . ." She let her voice trail off. "But of course, that was probably before you and she became . . . friends."

The effect was all she could have hoped for.

"You're lying!" Arnold roared, revivified by rage. *"Lying, you're lying!"*

His thin lips drew back from his teeth in a snarl, and the

flush surged in his face until it appeared to stand out in bas-relief. For all his fury, it wasn't sufficient to generate the strength required to heave himself from his chair. He bellowed with rage and frustration, and a second later the glass swung in an arc toward her. Fortunately, his motor skills had deteriorated to the point where his missile-launching capacity worked only in slow motion. Marjorie remained immobile as the glass tumbled through the space between them. At precisely the correct moment, she reached up and plucked it from its trajectory like a conjurer pulling an object out of thin air and set it gently on the coffee table. Arnold watched this in utter befuddlement, sagging back in his chair open-mouthed.

Marjorie leaned forward again, staring deeply into Arnold's eyes. The fire was fading from their fierce glare; in a moment it was gone completely and they were lifeless as stones. Slowly, the planes of his face slackened, and his head fell forward. A flap of silvery hair dropped onto his forehead.

Marjorie rose and stood beside him.

"Arnold?" she said quietly. There was no response.

She ran her fingers lightly across his eyelids. He didn't stir. When she drew her hand away she felt a faint moisture on her fingertips. *Drops of liquor from the glass?* she wondered, absently raising her fingers to her lips.

No, not liquor, she decided, as her tongue explored the fluid. She stood looking down at him. Not liquor at all.

He had believed her.

CHAPTER 27

Hermione Hopkins floated contentedly in the meringue of white linen that frothed over the enormous double bed, luxuriating in the heat from the lights. Beside her, Raul de Castro, the actor playing Felipe, her Mexican lover, snored softly. Pierre Blondin and a camera operator were conducting a rapid-fire exchange in French just outside the brilliant cone of light that was baking Hermione into a delicious torpor.

Oh, this was lovely, she thought, utterly restful. Being paid to act while you were lying down. Not that it was the first time she'd had to act lying down. . . . Hermione giggled. She regarded Raul's shaggy, barrel-chested torso with fascination. Already the bristles had provoked a rash on her shoulders and neck as they did take after take of the love scene. Really, the man was hairy as a billy goat.

But he was a good actor, and a considerate one too. During the staircase scene, his casual acceptance of her nude body had made her as relaxed as possible, given the circumstances. God, even with a closed set, the moment she'd had to let her wrapper slide from her shoulders and allow herself to be picked up . . . Anyway, for better or worse, she'd done it. The hard part was over. Although the bedding was carefully arranged to make it appear they were both nude, Raul was wearing bathing trunks, and Hermione was clad in a strapless nightgown that fastened over her breasts. She was more concerned now with keeping her hot, itchy wig from slipping askew than worrying whether audiences would bolt from theaters in disgust at the sight of her ancient flesh.

A faint stir made Hermione look across to the other side of the studio and instantly put her good mood to flight. Chief Halsey was coming toward them, accompanied by that young boy who worked at the police station. The temperature seemed suddenly colder, and Hermione was forced to remember that she now inhabited a world in which Connor had not existed for more than two weeks. It was so unfair that they should show up here and deprive her of a few precious moments of forgetfulness. Hermione shut her eyes against the sight of them.

Notebook in hand, John Larsen sat opposite Pierre Blondin and Chief Halsey in the chairs someone had quickly dragged together after Blondin impatiently ratcheted out a couple of sentences in French. When Larsen shifted the focus of his gaze beyond them, he was staring at the brilliantly lit set and its inert occupants. In the rigging above the set he could see dozens of lights projecting beams of pale blue, pink, and yellow at a point about ten feet above the bed. At their intersection, a peculiar effect took place—the individual colors melded into a creamy white, as if a prism were working in reverse, and the resulting effulgence made the set beneath look as if it were carved from ivory. The light took custody of Larsen's eyes, overwhelming his perception until he felt he was being drawn into it.

He roused himself, feeling Halsey's glance on him. Had they said anything he should have written down?

"Yes, we have a brief *liaison*," Blondin was saying. "It is not unusual for her."

"When was this?" Halsey asked.

Larsen marveled at how coolly Halsey took Blondin's remark. From his manner, you'd think adultery were an everyday occurrence. That thought caused a memory from a few days earlier to flash through his mind, and he shifted uncomfortably. It wasn't the same thing, he told himself: neither of them was married.

Blondin sighed gustily and looked as if he were trying to recollect. He also seemed remarkably unembarrassed, Larsen thought. He hadn't even bothered to lower his voice when responding to Halsey's questions.

"Oh, about four or five months ago," Blondin said. "It was during the time we were negotiating the rights to *Mrs. Forrester.*"

"Was she involved with anyone else at the time?" Halsey asked, wondering if Blondin had known about Reifel.

"I don't know. Perhaps."

"Were you and Mrs. Morland still seeing each other prior to her death?"

"We did see each other quite often. She wished to stay informed about the film."

Blondin had obviously taken the meaning of "seeing" more literally than Halsey intended. He reworded the question.

"Did your *liaison* continue until her death?"

"No," Blondin said. "Such a thing could never be long with her."

"You attended her party," Halsey observed.

"Yes," Blondin said. "It is necessary to go to many parties when you are producing a film."

"Did you hope to talk her out of suing you?" Halsey's quiet tone belied the suddenness of his attack.

Blondin's face darkened. His eyes glittered as he leaned forward. "She would *not* sue me. She was getting a percentage of the film profits, and any harm she did to me would endanger the film."

"She was prepared to file suit against you, nonetheless," Halsey said. "Her lawyer had instructions to obtain an injunction against your completion of the film. She felt what you were doing would damage her reputation."

Blondin laughed derisively. "It is all fake," he said. "She is caring only for money. We make a certain agreement, she is satisfied, then she tries to get more. When I refuse, she threatens the lawyers are coming."

"Was this before or after the party you attended?"

"Before. I went there to make her understand I could not give her more money."

"And what was her reaction?"

"She says she is very sorry my film will not get made, after I have spent so much time on it."

"And now it will get made?"

Blondin smiled. "Yes, now it will get made."

Larsen's scalp prickled at the ruthlessness of Blondin's expression. It was not surprising that Blondin did not regret Mrs. Morland's death, but the fact that he made no attempt to disguise his satisfaction at her removal from his path was chilling. And he was speaking of a woman with whom he'd once had an intimate relationship.

Hermione was thankful she'd worn her hearing aid. She couldn't hear the whole of the conversation, but she did catch enough to comprehend Iris's plan to sue Blondin.

She had been right to suspect Iris might interfere with the film. Thank God that couldn't happen now. She supposed that Iris's estate would pass to Kenneth Morland, but she doubted he had any taste for litigation.

Of course, if Morland were found to have murdered his wife, it would mean he couldn't inherit. Who would her estate go to in that case? Would whoever it was feel obliged to carry out Iris's ostensible wish to stop the film's production? The idea made her frantic. Hermione knew this would likely be the last film she ever made, and she desperately wanted it to be a success.

Success would carry all before it, sweeping aside the condemnation certain to arise from some quarters for her participation in the film. Failure would result in the humiliation of being perceived as a confused old woman whose failing faculties had been unable to comprehend the degradation to which she was being subjected. Let people talk about her sad departure from her distinguished stage career, let them be scandalized, revolted, or angry; she could stand blame, even relish it, but she could not bear being found pathetic.

Hermione suppressed a shudder. She wanted to appear completely unconscious, lest her awareness inhibit further discussion. She matched her breathing to Raul's and remained motionless.

Larsen's eye was drawn back to the set. The stillness of the bed's occupants was eerie. On its far side, the dark bulk of the actor loomed, appearing oddly artificial, as if it were composed of canvas and paint. Against that backdrop, his companion's pale, skeletal shoulders and faintly saurian profile stood out in startling relief. She lay on her back as if pinned there by the light.

Larsen's grandmother, reminiscing about her youth, would speak of primitive cars with engines that had to be cranked by hand to start. His grandmother was an old, old woman of eighty, but he knew that Miss Hopkins was far older—perhaps from a time before there were cars at all. Larsen watched the sheet covering her chest closely, but could not detect any movement, and the utter immobility of her face never altered. A persistent unease gripped him. Was it possible . . . she was very old, and so completely motionless . . . what if, while they had been sitting there talking . . .

★ ★ ★ ★ ★

"I was visiting Mrs. Atkinson," Blondin was saying in response to a question from Halsey about his whereabouts on the night of the murder.

"Did you see Mr. Atkinson also?"

Blondin smiled. "No. He was not at home."

Clearly, Blondin's visit to a married woman late at night when her husband was absent had implications that were favorable neither to Mrs. Atkinson nor Blondin. Larsen noticed a faint alteration in Halsey's expression and wondered if, for all his dispassionate demeanor, he was finding Blondin as repellent as Larsen was.

"When did you leave?" Halsey asked.

"After midnight."

"Could it have been later than that?"

"Not much later—I was home before one. I remember it was just after that I was making the alarm to wake me for the next day's shooting." Blondin paused, and his face twisted sardonically.

"Not that kind of shooting," he added.

CHAPTER 28

Halsey turned slowly in the soft envelope of the sheets, drifting up from sleep, parting unwillingly from the erotic tendrils encircling his limbs. His dream partner's delicious yielding warmth clung to him as the light began to register on his closed eyelids.

"Peggy," he muttered, reaching for her, feeling the warm flesh slip from his grasp just as he awakened.

But the bed he occupied was neither Peggy's nor his own. It was empty except for him, however. Halsey sat up and swore under his breath. Had he said the name aloud? How did Peggy Atkinson get into his head like that anyway, and why didn't she get the hell out?

According to the clock beside the bed it was 7:00 A.M. He listened for sounds outside, then sat up and pulled on his shorts. A moment later, Lucy padded in wearing a pale green satin wrapper. She handed him a mug of tea, her expression unreadable. He was stunned by how beautiful she was: with her great mass of fiery hair and flawless skin, she reminded him of some exotic flower.

"Thanks," he said. He gulped a mouthful of tea. "Been up long?"

"Nope." She sat down beside him, which he took as a good sign. He slipped one arm over her shoulders, nudged the edge of her wrapper aside, and kissed the white curve of her breast. She didn't respond.

"Anything wrong?"

"Could be," she said.

"Look, I just want you to know that I think you're the best thing that's ever happened to me," Halsey said, hoping to head off whatever reproaches might be in store. She turned and shoved him backward, flattening him against the bed so suddenly he barely managed to keep from spilling the contents of the mug.

"Who's *Peggy*?" she growled menacingly, her beautiful hair tumbling in perfumed waves onto his face.

He groped blindly for some place to set the mug, gave up finally, and tossed it aside.

"A *nightmare*," he growled back, pulling her against him.

"Oh, good," she said. "Then you'll understand that sometimes in my nightmares, I call out *'Raoul, Raoul.'* "

"Call out anything you please," Halsey said, struggling for breath, "as long as I'm beside you."

An hour later he was making her breakfast in the kitchen, trying not to laugh as she searched helplessly for the most mundane cooking implements. He was cracking eggs into the skillet he'd discovered in the drawer beneath the stove, but she was still hunting for salt and pepper shakers, and vaguely eyeing the empty shelves in the cupboard hoping to spot the toaster. Fortunately, Halsey'd been able to pick up bacon and eggs and a box of doughnuts from a nearby convenience store; otherwise, as far as he could tell, they'd have been breakfasting on sour milk and a very old jar of maraschino cherries.

She'd flipped on the television set in the living room, and the Channel Five Tuesday morning news drifted in to them. She floated around the kitchen aimless as a butterfly, scattering doughnut crumbs, humming old Beach Boys songs, and caroling *bitch*! whenever Delia Bendel came on.

"I was just wondering . . ." Lucy snuggled under his arm, wheedling.

Halsey cut her off. "You know that while the case is under investigation I can't give you anything I don't give Bendel."

Lucy grinned. "I hope that doesn't mean you're giving her *everything* you give me."

Halsey shuddered. "No fear."

"How much longer do you think we'll have to sneak around?"

"I'm really sorry, Lucy." Halsey said, trying to keep the guilt out of his voice. "It's just that you're a competitor of Bendel's. If she found out we're involved, she'd say that's why I'm refusing her interviews." True enough, but Peggy Atkinson loomed like a wolf stalking prey. If she told Lucy what had almost happened . . .

"You don't understand—I like it." Lucy laughed. "It's so wonderfully clandestine. *Meet me under the Town Hall clock at five P.M.,*" she said out of the corner of her mouth. *"I'll be wearing a raincoat over black panties—"*

"Stop that," Halsey demanded.

"Why? Did you want to wear them?"

Halsey chased her around the kitchen for a while until the TV anchor's booming voice deepened dramatically.

"After three weeks, the murders continue to baffle the Honeymoon Falls police, but has our Delia Bendel solved the case? Stand by for a live report from the sleepy little town that's been living in fear ever since these grisly murders were discovered. Over to you, Delia."

"Thank you, Tom. This is Delia Bendel reporting live from Honeymoon Falls. According to my informants, the search for the murderer is over, and it's no thanks to William Halsey, the town's police chief, who's been attracting criticism for lack of progress since the case began. But one citizen is sure she knows the truth, and here she is to tell her story."

Halsey and Lucy raced into the living room. "Ah, hell," Halsey groaned.

"Now you're both members of the town council, aren't you?" Delia said.

"Yes, I am," Cora Delbrook said. Irene nodded agreement.

"And you've uncovered evidence that you believe proves the identity of the murderer?"

"That's correct. The murderer is right here in Honeymoon Falls," Cora said. "We've found the clue that links him to both murders."

Delia Bendel smiled pleasantly into Cora's wattles. "And by 'we' you mean . . . ?"

"Suzie and me." Irene burst in excitedly. "We found the link between the murders and the suspect."

Lucy screeched with laughter. "Oh God, I can't believe it. She's so fixated on smearing you, she hasn't done the slightest amount of checking. She's got no idea Irene dispensed with reality years ago."

Delia Bendel seemed a bit confused. "And what was your involvement?" she asked Cora, who'd started to look slightly uncomfortable at the mention of Suzie.

"The moment Irene informed me of the evidence she'd uncovered, I advised her to take it to the police. I felt it was our civic duty to assist them as much as possible, especially given the positions of responsibility with which the citizens of Honeymoon Falls have entrusted us." Cora repositioned one of her brooches and drew a deep breath preparatory to launching another flood of oratory, but Bendel cut her off and turned to Irene.

"Could you explain what the two of you have uncovered and how?"

"Well, I don't think I'm supposed to be talking to you, really. That nice young Officer Larsen asked me not to say anything until he'd had a chance to talk to Chief Halsey."

"Suzie, how about you?" Bendel said, turning to Cora, who stared at Delia at if she'd lost her mind. "Is Chief Halsey trying to silence you too?"

"Certainly not," Cora said. "I'd like to see him try. And furthermore, you don't seem to understand—"

"So Chief Halsey's department is trying to clamp a lid on the story, are they?" Delia said, turning back to the more co-operative Irene. "Is that why you and Suzie are reluctant to provide more details?"

"Look," Cora said, her eyes glinting ominously, "I am *not*—" She was interrupted by Irene's anxious intervention.

"It's just that I couldn't catch her this morning."

Lucy began to sob helplessly. Even Halsey started to laugh.

"Couldn't catch her?" Bendel looked at Cora, and the first signs of doubt appeared on her face. "Why couldn't she catch you?"

Cora exploded. *"You idiot!"* She turned and stomped out of camera range.

Irene turned to Bendel and smiled uneasily. "Suzie jumped out the upstairs window after I gave her the furball medicine this morning, and she won't come down off the roof."

Delia Bendel positively goggled. *"Are you talking about a cat?"* She snarled so savagely that Irene drew back in fright. "You told me earlier that Suzie was a longtime resident of Honeymoon Falls."

"Well, she was born here eight years ago," Irene said. "And she was the one who discovered the letter. Oh dear—I wasn't supposed to—I really think I'd better go." She turned and hurried down the street after Cora.

Delia Bendel turned to the camera, a series of tics animating her usually controlled expression. She drew a deep breath and forced a smile.

"It appears that this is just another crazy chapter in the comic opera being conducted around these vicious murders," Bendel said through gritted teeth. The picture wavered as if the cameraman was shaking with laughter. "As long as there's no professional police presence on this case, the citizens of Honeymoon Falls will continue to . . ." Her image vanished and the screen went black.

Lucy lay on the sofa, whimpering helplessly, wiping tears from her eyes. "Oh, there is a God," she said, steepling her hands. "And from now on I shall attend church every Sunday to give thanks."

Halsey had stopped laughing the minute Irene mentioned the discovery of a letter.

Lucy's eyes narrowed. "What's up?"

Halsey didn't answer, but he was thinking about the anonymous letter Enid Regular had written. The one Arnold Reifel denied receiving. Had it turned up at last?

CHAPTER 29

Halsey shifted uncomfortably in one of the sagging armchairs that populated Iola Collinson's living room. The room was dark, and thick with the smell of liniment underlaid with a faint chemical scent that drifted up from the basement. The roots of several large plants spilled over the sides of their containers, as if they were trying to crawl closer to Iola. The heat was oppressive, but Iola kept an afghan drawn up under her armpits. Deployed around her was a flotilla of small tables bearing pill bottles, old letters, a stuffed robin, tobacco cans, torn magazines, and bowls of dusty candies.

"She's not going to say a word to him," she muttered. "You're barking up the wrong tree there, mister."

They were watching *Love of Life* and Iola was riveted by the courtroom scene where Tiffany was clearly lying about the baby's paternity. Whenever Halsey asked where Herb was, she shushed him impatiently.

"Soon," was all she would say. "He'll be home soon."

None of the clocks in the room worked, and in the darkness, the program seemed to drag on with hypnotic slowness, uninterrupted even by commercials. Halsey was just beginning to wonder why Kirk couldn't see how obvious it was that Tiffany was lying to him when Collinson entered.

"Chief Halsey," he said.

Halsey stood. "Mr. Collinson, I need to ask you a few questions. Is there somewhere we can speak without disturbing your mother?"

"Right here's fine," Collinson said, taking another armchair across from Halsey. He glanced at his mother. "Nothing disturbs her unless you get in front of the TV."

Halsey studied him for a moment, trying to decide the best way to begin. Collinson's long face wore a shrewd expression that indicated he was no fool, in spite of the fact that the orange ruff encircling his bony skull gave him a slightly clownish aspect.

"It's about that TV interview with the Delbrooks, isn't it?" Collinson asked, sparing Halsey the decision about how to initiate the discussion.

"Yes," Halsey agreed. "Irene Delbrook says she was here visiting your mother yesterday evening. She says you were not at home."

"True. I never leave Mother alone in the evenings. I use the time Irene is here to run errands. I was at the supermarket, then I went to the mall for an hour. You can check of course."

"No need," Halsey said. He already had. "Did you see the interview with Delia Bendel today?"

"No. But several people told me about it."

"What was your reaction?"

"That Irene can't tell real life from soap opera any more than Mother can."

"You aren't angry with Irene?"

Collinson laughed. "At least she didn't say my name on TV, so I don't have to put up with being ribbed about it. And even if she had, the whole town knows that ever since she and Cora got on this detective kick, they've been finding murderers everywhere. Until today, they had Kenneth Morland pegged as the obvious suspect."

The music from the TV swelled dramatically, then subsided,

replaced with a commercial showing penguins cavorting on ice floes.

"I'm cold," Iola said.

"I'll turn the heat up, Mother," Collinson said, to Halsey's horror. However, Collinson remained seated.

Iola grunted happily. "Sshh," she said, as the program music swelled again.

"Irene told Officer Larsen that she found a letter in your basement," Halsey said.

"You mean she said her cat found it," Collinson corrected. "But she's already telling everyone the cat ran off with it, and all she could tell Officer Larsen was that it was about Tarlech." He leaned back in his chair. "She's got Tarlech on the brain now."

Halsey unbuttoned his pocket and removed the copy of the letter Enid Regular had said she sent to Reifel. Collinson's face tightened slightly, but his posture didn't alter.

"Irene said it looked like this," Halsey said, holding it out.

The other man made no move to take it. "Have you dusted it for fingerprints?" he asked.

"No," Halsey said. "This is a copy that came into my possession a while ago. According to Irene, the letter her cat retrieved from your basement was identical."

Halsey continued to offer the letter. Collinson waved it away with a contemptuous expression.

"Don't you even want to see what it says?" Halsey asked.

Collinson lifted a shoulder. "Read it to me," he said. His eyes glittered challengingly.

Halsey read.

She's making a fool of you. If you don't believe me, ask her what she's doing with Connor Tarlech at the mill.

209

Collinson's lips drew back from his teeth in a rictus intended for a smile. There was a faint whiff of preservative chemical coming off his clothes.

"Chief Halsey, are you accusing me of anything?" he said.

"*Was* somebody making a fool of you?" Halsey asked, ignoring the question.

"No," Collinson said, his face darkening.

"Have you seen this letter before?"

"No." But Collinson's glance wavered slightly this time when he answered.

"Why would anyone think you were being made a fool of?" Halsey persisted.

"Nobody thought *I* was a fool," Collinson exploded. "It was—"

"*Sssshhhh!*" Iola commanded, banging the table beside her. "I can't hear what they're saying."

The interruption gave Collinson time to regain his composure.

"Let me get this straight," he said contemptuously. "A woman everyone knows is batty says her cat found a letter in my basement. She can't produce the letter, but she's sure it was the same as a letter you showed her. And you think this is evidence of murder?"

"No," Halsey said, sensing the submerged fury rumbling in the other man. "But I do have to investigate all leads, no matter how tenuous."

"Well, now you have, so I suggest you leave."

"Just one more question," Halsey said, getting to his feet. Collinson rose too and stepped toward him. "Have you been up to the mill lately?"

"Yes, of course. About three weeks ago. There's plenty of game up there and I'm a taxidermist. Why wouldn't I go? But I wasn't there on the night of the murders, and I can prove it. I was giving a demonstration in the library on how to stuff small animals."

"When did your demonstration end?"

"Around ten. And then I went to Dairy Queen. The waitress there knows me; I talk to her all the time."

"Do you recall what time you got home?"

"Shortly after eleven. Mrs. Slater was here with Mother; she can vouch for me."

"And after that?"

"I went to bed."

Like all of the other suspects, Halsey thought. All said they were tucked peacefully in bed at the time of the murders, but at least one was lying. Halsey moved toward the door, Collinson's heavy tread right behind him. The bolt shot home behind him as he went down the steps.

Collinson was lying about the letter, Halsey decided. His refusal to touch the copy betrayed a caution that someone with no involvement wouldn't have had. And he'd been about to explain some part of its contents when his mother interrupted. That meant he had seen it, and also that he'd known Tarlech was back. In her drunken muddle, Enid must have accidentally sent the letter to him instead of Reifel.

The person who destroyed Tarlech's boat had never been caught, but Collinson's obsession with Selena Coyle was no secret even then, and Halsey had always suspected Collinson was the arsonist. Had his obsession with Selena made him determined to remove Tarlech from her life once and for all?

CHAPTER 30

Bailey read from the jackets of half a dozen paperbacks she'd spread across the table in the station office.

"*Mistress of Everleigh.* When Amanda accepts a position as handsome Lord Randall's private secretary, she soon finds herself swept into a passionate romance. But can her love triumph over the evil that faces her at Everleigh Castle?

"*Sweet Passionate Fury.* Caught up in a turbulent romance with dark, brooding Duncan Mauberley, Caitlin's love is threatened by the terrible secret in his past.

"And there's *In the Arms of a Stranger*—did Elizabeth Sloane really know the man she married?, *Savage Kisses*—Megan melted when hot-blooded Percy Hightower touched her, but she sensed danger coiled within him, and *The Flowers of Love*—a story of love beyond the grave."

Halsey struggled to keep a straight face. There was something irresistibly comic about Bailey's brisk, no-nonsense voice reading phrases like "Megan melted when hot-blooded Percy Hightower" etc., etc., and the way she thumped each book down on the table when she finished.

Bailey held up *The Flowers of Love*. "This is the one with the dessert that Marjorie Reifel noticed was similar to one described in Iris Morland's book. It was published about two years before *Mrs. Forrester.* Both mention a trifle shaped like a flower in a pot."

"What's a trifle?" Larsen asked.

"Sponge cake soaked in wine, topped with custard."

Larsen grimaced. "Sounds disgusting."

"Well, I'm sure it's not the equal of a Twinkie or a Ding Dong," Bailey said.

In spite of her jab at Larsen's penchant for packaged treats, her tone wasn't as cutting as usual, and Larsen only grinned in response. Things were looking up, Halsey thought.

Bailey had stopped talking, but she clearly had more information. She wanted to be asked for it, Halsey realized.

"So what's the explanation for the similarity?" Halsey obliged.

"Mrs. Morland wrote both books," Larsen guessed. "She and Amber St. Clare were the same person."

Bailey smiled and looked at Halsey, inviting him to speculate. The smile suited her. Her gray eyes lost their hooded look, and the curve of her lips animated her usually set expression.

Halsey doubted Iris had written anything like the St. Clare books; her sardonic style was incompatible with flights of romantic fancy. Nor could he picture her either deliberately or unconsciously lifting the idea from the other writer. Clearly her own creative powers were more than the equal of St. Clare's, and she was well able to generate her own ideas. Still, it was highly unlikely that two separate writers would invent such similar descriptions out of whole cloth. There seemed to be only one possible explanation.

"The trifle thing actually existed somewhere," Halsey said. "Both St. Clare and Morland saw it—maybe in a magazine. It stuck in their minds, and they incorporated it into their books. Morland wouldn't be familiar with St. Clare or her books, so she'd never know the other woman had already used the idea."

Bailey nodded approvingly. "Right—at least most of the way. It actually existed, and they both saw it. But not in a magazine. And Iris Morland was certainly familiar with St. Clare, if not a devoted reader of her work."

She paused again, regarding Larsen and Halsey with a pleased look, clearly enjoying their attention. This time Larsen provided the prompting.

"So who is Amber St. Clare?"

"That's what I asked the publisher in Vancouver this morning," Bailey said. "Took a while to get it out of him, but I finally succeeded."

"*Aaand—?*" Larsen urged.

"Amber St. Clare's real name is Enid Regular," Bailey said.

Larsen was disappointed. "Who's she?"

Halsey remembered the paperbacks trampled into the swamp on Enid's bedroom floor. Her own books, he realized now. He let Lydia explain to Larsen.

"She's Iris Morland's sister. She lives in Vancouver. I talked to her this morning too. She seemed to enjoy the idea that anyone who noticed the similarity between the books would suspect Iris of copying her. They don't appear to have been very close—I gather Iris was pretty contemptuous of her sister's books. Enid suspects Iris pressured Stanford Publishing not to take her on as a client. As a result, she had to sign with a much smaller publisher."

"So what's the story on the dessert? Where did they see it?" Larsen asked.

"A few years ago, according to Enid, at a dinner party given by Colin Ainsley, the president of the company that produces Arnold Reifel's TV show."

Bailey tossed a copy of some clippings across to Halsey. Photographs of Iris and Enid bookending Ainsley were prominently displayed. Arnold Reifel could be seen in the background of some of them.

"These are from a recent Ainsley clambake. I suppose Reifel got Iris and Enid invited."

Halsey was impressed with the amount of information Bailey

had dug up in such a short time. It looked straightforward enough when it was presented with all the connections made, but he knew it represented hours of cross-checking, investigation, and analysis to put together.

"Nice work, Lydia," he said, passing the clippings to Larsen.

"Oh, there's more," she said. "Enid says Iris was negotiating with Ainsley for a television program of her own. Apparently the deal was pretty close to completion before her death."

"What kind of show?" Larsen asked.

"That I couldn't discover. Something about books, I suppose. Enid didn't know, and I couldn't get anything out of Ainsley's office."

"Probably not important anyway," Larsen said. "The main thing is, you cleared up the plagiarism issue Marjorie Reifel was talking about."

Bailey's buoyant mood began to deflate. "None of it seems important, though," she said. "All we've learned is that both sisters were writers, and both were at Ainsley's party. So what? It doesn't bring us any closer to knowing who the murderer is."

"I wish we knew what kind of TV program Iris Morland was negotiating to do," Halsey said.

"Why? What difference could it make?" Bailey asked.

"I don't know," Halsey admitted.

A comment Pieter Rempel had made about Iris's last book kept running through his mind: *things get turned around, characters trade places.* Halsey reached for his notes.

An unhappily married journalist whose wife was having an affair was how Rempel had described the book's main character. He begins an affair with a woman who systematically strips him of everything that matters to him.

If Lucy was right about Marjorie's affair with Selby, the journalist described in the book could be seen as Arnold Reifel as easily as Kenneth Morland. There was the character's physical resemblance to Morland, of course, but that didn't necessarily mean anything. And as for stripping people of what mattered to them, Iris was certainly without peer there. According to Marjorie, Iris had been on Reifel's show a couple of times and had even filled in as host once. Had her appearances served as an audition? Was *Reifel Range* the program she was negotiating for?

Halsey remembered Rempel's remark that a novel was never a blueprint of the writer's life, but that didn't stop him from suspecting that Iris's book might well have incorporated her plans for her next victim. It was the kind of thing she'd find amusing, and she was confident enough to be sure her target would never recognize himself. But what if he had? Arnold Reifel hadn't attended Iris's party, Halsey recalled. He tossed his notebook back on the desk.

"What?" Bailey demanded, responding to his expression.

"What if Reifel's show was the one she was after?" Halsey replied.

"You think Reifel may have found out they were considering replacing him with Iris and decided not to let it happen?" Bailey asked.

"Just a theory." Halsey said. "Maybe too neat."

"Maybe not," Bailey said. "And if it wasn't him, then who does that leave us with? We're back to Morland again."

"What about Atkinson?" Larsen said. "That so-called director's fee of Iris's was nothing but blackmail. And he was going bankrupt."

Bailey frowned. "Why kill Iris after she helped him save his business by persuading council to give him the mill site?"

"Maybe she had another string on him she was yanking on," Larsen speculated.

An image flashed into Halsey's mind: Kenneth demonstrating the Castle game. Was the mill some kind of lever Iris was going to use against Atkinson? But why? She'd already had her fun with him and Peggy years ago. And without Atkinson there'd be no payoff, and she needed the money.

"Who else would benefit from her death?" Larsen said. "It popped into my head this morning when we were talking to Blondin. His benefit is obvious: Iris can't interfere with his film." He paused for a moment. "Do you know they're saying that old lady is actually naked in that thing? Not just looking like she might be undressed under the sheets, like we saw on the set, but actually bare naked—," he broke off.

Halsey and Bailey maintained neutral expressions while Larsen struggled to wrench his mind free of the spectacle mesmerizing it. Bailey finally took pity on him.

"I suppose Kenneth Morland would be the obvious beneficiary," she said. "Would her estate have amounted to much, I wonder?"

"According to her lawyer, she didn't have much in the way of tangible assets to leave: less than fifty thousand dollars and her share in the family home," Halsey said. "The royalties from her new book are potentially valuable though, and since her death there's been a lot of interest in reprinting her earlier books. A couple of her novels have been optioned for television, and there's Blondin's film. Over time, her heirs could eventually earn close to a million dollars from her estate."

"Her heirs?" Larsen asked, his composure regained. "Who else besides her husband would inherit?"

"Amber St. Clare herself," Halsey replied. "Except for Iris's share of the house, which goes to Morland, he and Iris's sister were to split the estate equally, unless Morland predeceased Iris—then her sister got it all."

"So Enid Regular stands to inherit half a million bucks," Larsen said.

"Or twice that, if Kenneth Morland is convicted of his wife's murder," Halsey said, unconsciously echoing Hermione Hopkins's thoughts.

"But only if the estate makes money," Bailey pointed out. "When Iris died, all Enid could have expected was a few thousand in cash."

"Don't forget Enid would be thoroughly familiar with the way the publishing world works," Halsey reminded her. "If anyone could assess the potential value of Iris's literary estate, it would be her. And if she believed her sister had sabotaged her own career, it could have been hatred, not money, that motivated her. Where was she the night of Iris's death?"

"She said she was at home. I asked if anyone could verify that, and she said her partner, Millicent Mountjoy, could. I called Mountjoy at her office—she's an optometrist—and according to her, she and Enid were at home all night following the party."

"Enid Regular is an optometrist as well as a writer?" Larsen inquired, amazed.

Neither Bailey nor Halsey could help sighing.

"*What?*" Larsen demanded, looking from Halsey to Bailey with an aggrieved expression. "You said she was an optometrist's partner."

"It's a personal partnership, not a business one," Bailey said.

Larsen flushed to the roots of his blonde thatch. "God, I'm so *stupid*!"

Halsey waited for Bailey to concur, but she just gave Larsen a good-natured grin.

"You were anything but stupid when you talked to Eddie Novak," she said comfortingly.

Halsey stepped in to complete the diversion. "How'd that go?"

"Well, I started out like you said, asking him about the theft of Edna Sigurdson's cash bag. He was pretty unfriendly at first—I guess he suspected I was going to ask him about the murders. So instead I started asking him about good places to go hunting. He used to hunt with Dad, so I figured he might be willing to talk about the best places to go around here."

Larsen's color had returned to normal, and he was speaking with his usual confidence. Halsey marveled at Bailey's expression as Larsen talked—it was receptive, even encouraging.

"Anyway," Larsen continued, "he started talking about hunting up near the north end of Bridegroom Bay. Lots of deer there, he said, just have to watch out for a few bears. Said he had to shoot one of them once to get back into his four-by-four."

Halsey frowned. "That area's all dense bush and straight up the mountain side. How'd he get a vehicle in there?"

"That's what I asked. According to Novak, there's an old logging trail that takes you right up above the end of the lake. Full of deadfalls, but still drivable if you're not fussy about what you do to your vehicle."

"That's less than a quarter of a mile from the mill," Halsey mused. "And high enough above it so you could see everyone coming and going in the mill yard."

"So the killer could have sat up there and watched until Iris Morland arrived, gone down and killed her, and then left by the same route." Bailey said.

"That could explain why Selena Coyle didn't meet anyone on her way home from the mill," Halsey agreed.

"You're both assuming the killer was after Mrs. Morland," Larsen said. "Novak's the one person we know for sure that knew about the spot, and he'd be gunning for Tarlech, not Mrs. Morland."

"He'd hardly be likely to tell you about the spot if he'd used it as a base for the killings," Bailey objected.

Larsen laughed. "He could have figured the baby-face fuzz

here was too dumb to pick up on it."

The man was developing the ability to laugh at himself, Halsey thought. Wonders would never cease.

"We're going to have to get up there and see what we can find," Halsey said.

"Uh—" Larsen mumbled. "I hope you don't mind, but—"

"You've already been," Halsey finished. "You realize this could be an important crime scene, and if you disturbed any evidence—"

"I didn't touch anything, I swear. I was real careful where I walked. I just looked, nothing more." Larsen's contrite expression struggled with the elation surfacing in his eyes.

"So what's up there?" Halsey said, trying to keep his tone stern.

"Paint," Larsen said. "Black automobile paint on the trunk of a fallen pine. And on a huge boulder on the same side of the road a few feet away. Right at fender height."

"You've checked the body shops for repairs to black vehicles, of course," Halsey said, dropping the disciplinary tone and allowing some approval to show.

"Yeah." Larsen was now grinning ear-to-ear, basking in Halsey's commendation.

"Nothing at Tom's Auto City, of course," Larsen said, naming the only body shop in Honeymoon Falls. "But I never really expected it would be that easy. I faxed most of the repair shops in Vancouver this morning. No luck at any of them. I was beginning to think whoever had the vehicle was just going to keep it hidden until the heat was off.

"Then Lydia pointed out it was unlikely someone would use their own vehicle on a drive like that, and it suddenly clicked that some of the rental agencies have their own repair facilities. So I faxed them."

"And got what?" Halsey said, content to play the prompter.

It had not escaped his attention that not only had Larsen and Bailey performed well independently, they'd also cooperated like professionals.

Larsen handed Halsey a page of fax paper with a Hertz logo at the top.

2013 Jeep, black. Rented Saturday, June 5, returned Monday, June 7. Total mileage: 246. Damaged right front fender. Client's explanation: hit and run. Client's name: Marjorie Reifel.

"Well, well, well," Halsey mused. "Maybe she wasn't willing to let Iris have the last laugh after all."

"The mileage is just slightly more than the distance from Vancouver to Honeymoon Falls and back," Larsen said, unable to keep the excitement out of his voice. "Of course, by now it's been cleaned and repaired, but I asked the rental company to hold the vehicle for inspection and comparison of paint chip samples."

"I'll call the lab in Vancouver and get them on it first thing tomorrow," Halsey promised.

"Still don't think it's a woman," Bailey said. "Too violent. And too weird—all that dressing-the-bodies-up stuff."

"Well, I thought it could be a woman all along," Larsen reminded her. "And I'd sure like to hear Marjorie Reifel's explanation for being up behind the mill on the night of the murders."

"You don't know she was up there the night of the murders," Bailey pointed out. "They took place on Sunday night, and she had the jeep from Saturday to Monday. *If* she was up there, it could have been before or after the murders. And even if the vehicle was up there Sunday night, that doesn't necessarily mean she was driving it."

"Who else would be driving a vehicle she rented—space aliens?" Larsen retorted.

"Well, if it was aliens, I'll bet it was the males that committed the murders," she said. Larsen rolled his eyes. "And speaking of aliens, you're forgetting about Herb Collinson—he knew Tarlech was back, and he was determined to keep him away from Selena. He might not have found it that big a jump from mounting animals on a parade float to mounting bodies on a parade float."

Halsey feared the unprecedented mood of amity that had existed for so long was about to disintegrate and changed the subject.

"What happened with Wendell Baker?"

"I braced Baker like you said," Larsen said. "He admitted straight off he took Edna's cash bag. He never had any intention of keeping the money—just wanted to get Edna's goat."

"What I don't understand is how you knew it was him who took it," Bailey said to Halsey.

Larsen had asked the same question when Halsey sent him off to see Baker. Out of Bailey's hearing, of course, just in case she'd figured it out and he hadn't.

"I saw him," Halsey said.

"Saw him?" Bailey blinked. "You mean you were there when he did it?"

"Nope. But when I was talking to Novak, I noticed the security cameras were showing far fewer people in the mall than I'd seen when I came in. Eventually I realized the picture wasn't live—he was running the tape the cameras recorded the day Edna's cash bag was stolen."

"I don't get it," Bailey said. "If you saw Baker take the cash bag, why wouldn't Novak? With Edna breathing down his neck, he probably went over that tape a hundred times."

"He did see him. He just didn't recognize what he was seeing. The camera angle is down the length of the mall lane, so you can't see directly into Edna's shop. The tape shows Edna and the rest of the group leaving the shop entrance, with Baker exiting last, a few steps behind the others."

"You figured he grabbed it off the counter, right?" Bailey said. "But the shop was unattended for several minutes while Edna was with the group at the door. Anyone could have come along during that time."

"But no one did," Halsey said. "The tape shows not one single person going near the shop until Edna reappears. She enters the shop, and a split-second later she comes flying out of there like a bat out of hell on her way to Novak."

"Isn't there a back entrance to the shop?" Bailey asked.

"It was locked, according to Edna. And there are cameras at the back too."

"So it had to be someone from the group in the shop," Larsen said.

Bailey nodded. "And the obvious culprit was Baker. Crazy old coot."

"There's one more thing, Will," Larsen said. "Baker said he mailed Edna's cash bag back to her anonymously. I checked with her, and she agrees she got it back a couple of days ago. Obviously she realized I knew who took it, but not only did she not ask the name of the thief, she wants to drop all charges. Go figure. I thought she'd demand the death penalty."

"Maybe there was something else in the bag she'd just as soon not talk about, now that she's got it back," Halsey said. "Did Baker mention anything else besides cash?"

"Just a letter from some financial advisor about shares she owns in a company called Venture Resources."

"Venture?" Bailey said. "Isn't that—"

"The company that owns MFR," Halsey finished.

Larsen's eyes widened. "Edna Sigurdson has shares in MFR?"

"The town savior trading with the enemy," Bailey marveled. "No wonder she was frantic to get the bag back, and why she wants the whole thing dropped now. That news could cost her big time in the next election."

"Venture owns other things besides MFR. Her shares could be in one of their other companies. Lydia, why don't you do a little research on that."

Bailey hesitated. "It's not illegal for her to own shares, even in MFR itself. What's the point?"

"MFR was the instrument that destroyed Connor Tarlech's business," Halsey reminded her. "Remember, Selena Coyle said he was looking for early council records with any information about the awarding of the timber licenses. She couldn't find any, and neither did I when I checked. Since Hannah Spofford's death, Edna Sigurdson is the only person left who might have been involved in the decision."

"Why would she destroy the town?" Larsen asked. "She must have known it would put an end to her own business."

"Unless MFR gave her enough shares to make it worthwhile," Bailey said. "She was on the verge of going under for years. A nice chunk of valuable stock could have been mighty tempting."

Larsen shook his head. "Doesn't make sense. She stayed here and revitalized the town with The Theme. Why wouldn't she just clear out once she got the money?"

"According to Selena Coyle, that's exactly what Edna was planning to do," Halsey said.

Bailey nodded. "I was working at Arlene Peterson's beauty salon then, and Edna was one of my customers. I remember she came in just after the mill closed, and Arlene asked her what she thought would happen to the town. Edna said she'd applied for a business license in Vancouver, and if Arlene had any sense she'd do the same." Bailey frowned. "You know, now that I think of it, Edna left a tip. She never left one before."

"Still doesn't explain why she went to so much trouble to try to save the town," Larsen said. "If she was going to leave, why would she care?"

"She wasn't the savior a lot of people think," Bailey said. "All she did was talk about how Niagara Falls pulled in the tourists. It was Selena Coyle who got everybody all fired up, and arm-twisted the money men until she made it happen. Once Edna realized the town was going to survive, and she was getting most of the credit, it didn't take her long to figure out how to capitalize on it.

"And that's another thing," Bailey said, after a pause. "Edna going to Niagara Falls, I mean. She never went anywhere for years—she had to keep that shop of hers open six days a week to stay afloat. Suddenly she shuts it down and takes off. Where'd the money for that come from, I wonder?"

"Good question," Halsey said. "Think you can get an answer?"

"Oh, yeah," Bailey said.

"John, I think you and I will go chat with Marjorie Reifel about the damage to her rental vehicle."

Halsey glanced at Bailey to see how she was taking this, since he was obviously allowing Larsen in on an important lead. Her expression remained calm. For his part, Larsen seemed determined to avoid all outward signs of satisfaction, responding to Halsey's statement with a businesslike nod.

"I think that's enough for today—*officers*," Halsey said.

CHAPTER 31

But the next morning, it was Kenneth Morland's house, not Marjorie Reifel's, that Halsey found himself entering.

Helen Stewart had taken the call. There was deafening music pouring out of Morland's house, and even if it *was* Wagner, Morland's neighbors were not in the mood for it at 7:00 A.M.

Helen was standing on the back steps of the Morland house when Halsey arrived. She was clearly disappointed at Halsey's appearance, suspecting rightly that, given the location, he was going to take over.

"There's nobody here, and no sign of forced entry. The back door was ajar when I arrived. I've left everything the way it was, except for turning the stereo off," she said.

"Did the caller identify himself?" Halsey asked.

"Herself. A Mrs. Slater. She lives next door."

"Reverend Slater's mother. Anything obvious missing?"

"Hard to tell. Looks like somebody was hunting for something in Morland's study. It's been ransacked, but the rest of the house doesn't appear to have been touched."

Halsey let Helen lead the way into the house. She pointed out the stereo in the living room.

"It's plugged into a timer, along with several of the lamps. Once the timer kicked in, all the lights went on and the walls started to shake."

Halsey looked at the set-up doubtfully. "Why didn't the burglar just yank the plug out of the wall?"

"Depends on where he was when the timer kicked in, I suppose," Helen said. "If he was upstairs ransacking the study, it'd be too late to do anything but run. By the time he got down here, the racket would already have awakened everyone on the block."

"Still doesn't make sense," Halsey said. "Even if Morland had the stereo programmed to come on, he'd never have turned it up that high."

"Maybe the burglar fiddled with the controls, trying to shut it off," Helen suggested.

Halsey shook his head. "Something fishy is going on here."

"Okay, I give up," Helen said. "Want to see upstairs?"

The scene in Morland's study resembled the aftermath of a tornado. Books flung from their shelves lay in a heap in the center of the floor. All of the desk drawers had been yanked out and upended, their contents strewn over the desk, on which a precariously perched gooseneck lamp still burned. Sheets of notepaper littered the floor, and a gray filing cabinet lay on its side with its innards exploded like a mortally wounded soldier.

A small white envelope lay atop the rubble toward one end of Morland's desk. It was addressed to *Mr. Connor Tarlech, Avenida Liberdade, 681, Rio de Janeiro, Brazil.* Halsey recognized the cursive script—it matched the writing on the guest list for Iris's party. He picked the envelope up carefully by its edges and tilted the contents onto the desk. A single sheet of paper fluttered out. The message was brief:

Most of the pieces are in place—all you have to do is assemble them to regain the mill. Now, my dear, do be sensible and come back right away. As for Kenneth, that's all over with. You are, and always have been, the only one who matters to me.

Halsey could not help flinching at the last sentence. Regardless of how suspect its sincerity was, given Iris's character, he could imagine the damage it had inflicted on Morland when he read it, especially the dagger thrust provided by the *always have been* phrase. Not only was Morland past history as far as Iris had been concerned, he'd never mattered at all. How many times had he read the letter, and how much had it nourished his hatred of his wife and her lover?

How had Morland come by the letter, Halsey wondered—the envelope bore a stamp showing receipt in Brazil over a month ago. What "pieces" had Iris been talking about assembling, and which had been the greater enticement for Tarlech to return—his property or his mistress?

"You're sure there's no sign of forced entry?" he asked Helen.

She nodded. "They've got deadbolts everywhere. Whoever did this got in with a key."

"I wonder who else besides Morland has one."

"Mrs. Slater." Helen said. "She told me she puts it out for the cleaning lady when the Morlands are away."

"Did she say when the cleaning woman was here last?"

"Yesterday afternoon."

Halsey inhaled slowly. "Did you get her name?"

Helen consulted her notebook. "Shirley Novak." She was astonished at the reaction the name produced.

Halsey swore fiercely, grinding his teeth. The wife of one suspect had had unlimited access to another suspect's house. If that didn't muddy the waters, nothing would. The chances of discovering what the intruder sought had been slim, but now, even if they figured it out, there was no way of knowing whether it had been taken by the intruder, or by Shirley Novak—a woman who might have very good reasons for concealing evidence.

Shortly after 9:00 A.M., he was knocking on Shirley's door.

"So I took a disc from the garbage. Big deal." Shirley gave Halsey a truculent stare through the screen door. "Morland saying I stole something? He better not be—there's a lotta people saying he done worse."

Disc? From Morland's house? Halsey kept his expression neutral. This was going to take some careful maneuvering, if the disc was what he thought it might be.

"He's not accusing you of anything, but I'm wondering what you were doing at the Morland house yesterday," Halsey said. "Bertha Slater said it wasn't the day you usually worked for them."

"Yesterday?" Shirley scowled. "What're you talking about?"

"Mrs. Slater said you called and told her Mr. Morland asked you to clean yesterday afternoon, a day you knew was her regular volunteer day at the hospital. You asked her to leave the key in a planter in the back yard. The Morland place was ransacked the same day."

"You're crazy," Shirley said. "I never phoned Mrs. Slater. And I wasn't at Morland's place yesterday, either. The last time I was there was a couple days after the murders. Don't you try pulling anything on me."

"Mrs. Slater says she's spoken to you before, and she recognized your voice."

"I don't care what the old bat says. It wasn't me. Hey—I can prove it," she said suddenly, pleased. "I was at the mall all day yesterday. Eddie got me a chance to work a shift clearing tables in the Food Fair. One of the regular girls called in sick."

It seemed unlikely she'd lie about something so easily checked. Mrs. Slater was elderly, and it was possible she'd been suckered by one of the tabloid leeches who'd known enough to spin a plausible yarn. Still, she'd insisted she recognized Shirley's voice. Could Shirley have made the call to set up the invasion of Morland's house by someone else? Halsey wondered if Eddie Novak had been at the mall all day.

"I'll need to see the disc you found," Halsey said, getting to the real reason he was still there.

"Why?" she snapped. "It's only a lousy CD I found in the garbage. It couldn't cost more than a couple of bucks."

"It's part of a murder investigation," Halsey said.

Shirley scowled through the screen, stubby fingers plucking at her cheap cotton shift. Her hair, which Halsey remembered as blonde and lacquered into a shiny structure folded firmly together in back and puffed up on top like a soufflé, was now a lank, grayish mop. Her dull brown eyes reminded him of a dog's; confusion and defeat jostled with some other, darker emotion in their depths.

"I gave it to my daughter," she said. "I don't know what she did with it. And she's gone shopping with her girlfriend in Vancouver, so I can't ask her."

"Would you check her room?" Halsey asked.

Shirley's face set. "Eddie says you need a warrant to search someone's place. You got a warrant?"

"I can get one," Halsey said, although he doubted it. Convincing a judge that a forced search of the Novak home was justified to obtain an item Shirley had committed no crime in taking, and which Halsey could not prove was crucial to the investigation, would be uphill work.

"Yeah, well, why don't you get one then?" Shirley challenged.

"Right now, I'm not searching, I'm asking for your co-operation," Halsey said. "I won't be asking if I have to get a warrant."

"We got nothing to hide!" Shirley erupted. "I'm gonna call Eddie. He'll settle your hash in a hurry." She backed away from the screen and grabbed the handle of the inner door.

Halsey knew he had to hold her, or lose his chance altogether.

"Mrs. Novak," he said urgently, "I have to have that disc. Refusing to hand it over could hurt Eddie."

Shirley halted. "Hurt Eddie? How?"

"When the mill closed, Eddie threatened Connor Tarlech in front of witnesses. Eddie's a suspect."

"Hah!" Shirley said. "Everybody knows Eddie was just blowing off steam, and you know it too." She kept her hand on the door handle.

"Eddie knew Tarlech was at the mill the night of the murders," Halsey said. "Selena Coyle phoned to tell him. You remember the call, I'm sure."

"What if I do? I can swear he came straight back to bed afterward."

"Funny, Eddie told me you went right back to sleep as soon as he got up."

"Well, I didn't," Shirley said, but her eyes shifted away from his.

"Refusing to provide a disc you took from a murdered woman's house makes it look like you're hiding something," Halsey persisted. "That's not going to help Eddie."

Halsey waited while she considered this. Finally, directing a look of pure loathing at him, she pushed the screen door open and allowed him in.

Pearl's room was across from her parents' on the upper floor of the house. Halsey had expected typical teenage decor—pictures of rock stars, animal figurines, a jumble of hair ornaments and dime store jewelry. The reality was a small, striking room, whose drawbacks—one poky window and the awkward slope of its ceiling—had been converted into assets by the use of green and violet striped draperies to suggest a luxurious Arabian Nights type of tent. The bed continued the theme, a low, narrow platform over which was flung a magenta satin throw. If the overall effect was like something from a magazine layout, it was still expressive of a certain flair, and the will to erect a determinedly personal vision on unpromising foundations.

"She did it all herself," Shirley said. "I helped her sew the material, but she picked it out and said how she wanted it."

"It's remarkable," Halsey said. "Especially for a young girl."

"She's going to be a designer," Shirley said. She looked around and sighed. "Good thing she got this stuff before Eddie lost his job at the mill."

She trudged over to the foot of the bed and lifted the padded lid of a chest. She rummaged for a moment, then stood back, leaving the lid ajar.

"Not in here," she said, beckoning Halsey to see for himself.

A miniature recorder Halsey recognized as a type used for surveillance sat on a heap of fashion magazines. Halsey pressed the *eject* button but there was nothing inside. He gestured to a shoe box at one end of the chest, careful to leave the opening of it to Shirley. As long as she voluntarily gave him access, he didn't have to worry about anything he discovered being tossed out of court later on the grounds of unlawful search or seizure. She flipped the lid off to reveal a neat array of CDs and dismissed them quickly.

"There was no picture on the one I found." She jumped as a faint rattle echoed up the stairway and hurried to the window.

"Just the mailman," she said, turning back to him. An embarrassed expression crossed her face. "For a minute I thought it was Pearl. She'd explode if she caught us going through her stuff like this. She's a hot-tempered girl. Like her father that way."

They found nothing in the small dressing table, and Halsey recognized growing resistance in Shirley's expression.

"Just a quick look in there," Halsey said, nodding at the closet.

It yielded nothing either, although Shirley went through the pockets in all the girl's clothes. She shut the closet door with a bang.

"For all I know she's given it to someone else," Shirley said.

"What's the point in looking when we aren't even sure it's here? You'd better go now. I'll ask her about it when she gets home."

Fat chance, Halsey thought. Either Shirley wouldn't mention it at all for fear of her daughter's wrath, or if the disc was found, any relevant information on it would be destroyed before Halsey got it. He'd have to try for a search warrant after all, and come back and tear the place apart when the daughter returned. He could imagine the uproar that would result; the Novaks no doubt giving interviews to Delia Bendel on the front porch while the search went on.

Shirley marched determinedly to the door, jerking her thumb pointedly toward it. Halsey started forward, then paused. There was still one place they hadn't looked.

"What about under the bed?"

"Under the bed?" Shirley looked baffled. "There is no 'under the bed'—it's a platform bed. Sits right on the floor."

"The wooden frame does. There's usually a few inches of clearance between the mattress and the floor." Halsey knelt at the side of the platform. "I'll lift it and you look under."

"Then you go," Shirley insisted.

"Then I go," Halsey agreed.

Shirley came and knelt facing him. He lifted the bed frame, which was surprisingly light, and Shirley leaned forward and looked.

"Letters," she said.

Shirley swept the letters into view and Halsey lowered the bed. There were about a dozen, all addressed to Pearl care of a Vancouver post office box number. No doubt the real purpose of today's visit to Vancouver was to collect the latest in the series, Halsey thought.

He frowned, disappointed. All kids had hiding places for stuff they wanted kept concealed from their parents. His instincts had been right about Pearl's, but he had no interest in her love letters, and he foresaw trouble for the girl in their discovery. His foreboding increased when he recognized the box number in the return address—it was for the Provincial Correctional Center, although the institution's name was discreetly absent.

Shirley was eyeing the letters as if they were a hornets' nest she'd poked loose with a stick. Clearly, she wasn't about to touch them.

"Can't we put them back?" she asked, as though she hoped to stuff them and the trouble they brought back into containment under the bed. "We don't have to look at them, do we?"

Halsey stirred them gently, and the contents of one spilled onto the floor. Even without Shirley's despairing groan, Halsey knew the object before them was the missing disc.

"Yes, I'm afraid we do," he said.

CHAPTER 32

Uh, well, I can't think of too much more to say. Thanks for everything—the message and checking out the mechanic's course, I mean.

Back at the station, Halsey sat in the office, letting the disc play on the desk behind him while he wrote up his notes on his interview with Shirley Novak. Whatever had originally been on the disc, it seemed pretty much useless now. The first ten minutes of it contained nothing but Gary Rasmussen's response to Pearl Novak's message.

I don't know about the mechanic thing . . . I've been talking to one of the guys who's getting out of here in a couple of months, and he's got this idea for a, uh . . . import-export business . . . There could be some real big bucks involved. I'll tell you more when I see you.

Halsey shook his head. God, the kid was stupid. He'd be the mark smuggling the drugs across the border while his partner sat back and collected the profits. Eventually, Rasmussen would take the fall, and this time he'd be doing serious prison time.

After a couple of awkward messages for his mother, Gary's voice trailed off. This was followed by a few seconds of door-banging and Gary singing along with a song blaring from a radio. After that, only a faint low-level hum emerged from the machine's speaker.

Halsey stared meditatively into the computer screen before him, mentally reviewing his and Larsen's interviews with

Marjorie and Arnold Reifel. Marjorie had unhesitatingly confirmed renting the jeep from Saturday until Monday while her own car was being repaired. She swore she'd never driven up behind the mill, and if paint from the vehicle had been discovered there, it must mean that instead of being damaged in a hit-and-run, as she'd assumed, the jeep had been stolen late Sunday night and returned before Monday morning when she discovered the damage.

The stolen vehicle scenario was more than a little implausible. Still, it was not only the Reifels who couldn't prove their whereabouts on the night in question: none of the prominent characters in the case—Kenneth Morland, Blondin, the Atkinsons, Novak—had alibis either. Had any of them taken the vehicle? And if they had, why return it later?

Morland had stood in his ransacked study, reading his wife's letter to Tarlech while the skin tightened over his foxy face until his nose and jaw bone seemed about to slit the pale tissue covering them. Finally, he tossed the note back to Halsey and said he'd never seen it before. He had every reason to hate Tarlech, and Arnold Reifel—what better way to revenge himself on both by killing Tarlech while using a vehicle he probably assumed was Reifel's?

The theatricality of the murders might point to Blondin. If Iris had been a serious threat to his film, Halsey had no doubt Blondin was capable of murder. He was already giving interviews about the tragic end of the great writer who'd created the characters in his film.

"So ironic," he murmured to Delia Bendel during one televised interview. "She died just as I was giving life to her book for the whole world. But now, with my film, she will live forever."

Bailey made gagging noises during that comment, and even Bendel looked as if she'd had about all she could take.

They were all lying in one way or another, Halsey thought. The trouble was that sifting through the lies was a maddeningly imprecise activity, each assessment only opening up new contradictions to be resolved. The council was growing increasingly restive over the lack of progress in naming a suspect, and Delia Bendel was now referring to him as "a small-town Sherlock, in over his head."

Halsey sighed and reached for the binder in which the station's faxes were filed. He flipped the binder open and stopped abruptly. Instead of a fax, the first page was a pen-and-ink sketch of the wedding cake parade float, showing Iris Morland's and Connor Tarlech's bodies on top. The next few pages were cartoons of Halsey and Bailey, mostly depicting Bailey as a walrus-like creature bellowing with such force that filing cabinets teetered before her while a desperate-looking Halsey crammed his fingers in his ears.

Halsey couldn't help laughing. The caricature of himself with his eyeballs contracted to the size of pinheads, fingers thrust up to the second knuckle in each ear, captured the way he felt when Bailey started ranting so perfectly that it was clear he hadn't always been able to maintain the detached expression he'd striven for during her outbursts.

Halsey checked the spine of the binder. It was labeled *FAX*, all right. Larsen presumably used it as a blind when he was working alone at the station, so he could put the drawings out of sight if someone came in unexpectedly. Given all the extra excitement going on, he must have absent-mindedly filed it on the reference shelf instead of putting it back in his locker. God help them all if Bailey had found it.

Halsey turned a few more pages, coming across head-and-shoulders portraits of Larsen's mother and sisters, and another of Edna Sigurdson. Halsey marveled at the skill Larsen displayed in depicting her. The hard, good-humored face was fully realized, the likeness neither flattering nor unkind. Yet there was also, in the forward thrust of the head and the veiled look of the deep-set eyes, an unsettling counterpoint to the uncomplicated bluffness of the expression.

A series of nudes began on the following pages, some consisting only of a few rapid lines capturing the curve of a shoulder or buttock; others intimate, detailed evocations: nymphs dancing, black hair swirling in wild clouds about them; a woman singing to her baby; two girls swimming, their bodies glimpsed through the slightly distorting lens of clear river water. Halsey recalled Bailey sneering about Larsen's locker full of smut, and realized she'd taken his collection of art magazines for something else.

The final nude in the series was a sensual drawing of a woman lying on her back, right arm flung overhead, fingers twined in her hair. Her legs were very slightly turned toward the viewer, and her other hand cradled one breast, as though offering it. Beneath her, bed sheets fell away in luxurious folds.

Unlike the idealized bodies in the other sketches, this picture conveyed the sense of a real woman. The body was compact, legs slightly too short to be in proportion to the rest of her, waist only a little narrower than the rib cage, the arms and hands strong rather than graceful. The woman's eyes had a fey, impish expression, set in a youthful face somehow at odds with the fullness of the body. Halsey's mind presented him with a quick flash of Nicole Bailey's inviting glances. The girl wasn't even eighteen yet. If Larsen was involved with her and Bailey found out, his life was over.

Halsey shook his head impatiently. Larsen could have drawn any face, real or imagined, to complete the drawing. Halsey'd already noticed the face didn't seem to go with the body—it was entirely possible Larsen created the face without noticing the likeness himself. Still, Halsey had been a lot happier before he saw the drawing than he was now. He pondered his next move. Ask Larsen straight out if he was involved with Nicole? And if he was, what then?

Halsey was debating how to return the binder to Larsen's custody when Bailey entered suddenly.

"Oh, you've got it," she said, holding a hand out for the binder.

"Uh—no, no—this is—another binder," Halsey mumbled. He cursed inwardly, struggling to close the binder, which obstinately refused to obey.

"That's the Fax binder," Bailey said, taking hold of one corner and beginning to draw it toward her.

"It's—an *old* one," Halsey said, attempting to draw it back while his mind searched frantically for an explanation, which he knew was aboard a train of thought that was going to arrive at the station far too late to help. Bailey frowned and twisted the binder spine up.

"No, it's not," she said impatiently. "Look, the spine tag is yellow—that means current year."

The next moment the binder rings snapped open and the drawings spun out around them.

"Oh, hell," Halsey said, as naked women spiraled through the air.

Bailey bent slowly to gather them up. She grimaced as she saw the cartoons of her bellowing at Halsey, and he heard her quick intake of breath as she discovered the nude on the bed. She stacked the drawings deliberately, carefully aligning the holes punched in the margins. When she finished, the nude on the bed was on top of the pile. She turned back to him, her color heightening as she held the bundle out to him. Halsey reached to take it, waiting in agonized silence for the storm to break. Just when he thought things couldn't possibly get worse, they did.

"Oh, here you are," Larsen said, coming through the door. "Have you seen the Fax bind—" He stopped cold as he realized what was being transferred from Bailey's hands to Halsey's. His eyes flicked rapidly from the drawing topping the pile to Halsey's face, which Halsey could feel settling into rock-like sternness.

"Uhhhh . . ." Larsen said. His own face was glowing like a lantern. "It's not what you think—"

"Oh, God, of course it is," Bailey said. "There's no point in pretending it isn't."

There was something *off* about her reaction, Halsey thought. He'd expected volcanic rage, but she looked more embarrassed than angry. Had he overestimated her disapproval of a relationship between Larsen and her daughter? Or was she upset because he'd stumbled into a situation that she already knew about and was dealing with?

"No, you don't understand," Larsen protested. "He thinks—he thinks—"

Halsey was by now so confused that he waited with real interest to hear what it was he thought, since he was no longer able to decide for himself.

"He thinks Nicole and me . . . you know," Larsen said.

"*Nicole?* Why would he think that?" Bailey asked.

Why wouldn't I think that? Halsey wondered.

"He saw us talking while I was waiting for you, and when he saw the sketchbook, well she looks a lot like you, and I guess he just assumed—"

At the mention of the sketchbook, Bailey's color deepened precipitously.

"Why on *earth* did you leave it lying around?" She buried her face in her palms. "Oh, God."

"I'm so sorry, honey," Larsen said.

Honey? *Honey?* Halsey felt like someone who comes in at the middle of a movie and has to work out the plot on the fly, but a few things were becoming clear. The drawing was not of Nicole Bailey; it was of her mother. And Larsen's involvement was with the senior member of the family, not the junior.

"John—please go now," Bailey pleaded. She forced her hands away from her face.

"We need to straighten this out," Larsen protested. He took a step toward her, but she retreated.

"Later," she said. "I promise," she added when he showed no sign of yielding. "Please, John."

Larsen's slow tread down the hall was so reluctant, they were not sure he'd actually leave until they heard his car drive out of the lane behind the station. Bailey let her breath out in a long sigh and looked ruefully at Halsey, her cheekbones still tinged pink.

"I think we'd better get some java," she said, crossing to the coffee machine.

"Look, this is none of my business," Halsey said as she plucked cups from the shelf above. "You don't owe me any explanations."

"Oh, I think I do," Bailey said.

She sat down across from him and slid one of the mugs and cream and sugar over to him. She stared into her cup for a moment and drew a deep breath.

"You're wondering how I got into this situation, aren't you?"

Halsey considered for a moment. "I'm a little surprised," he allowed, which qualified as the understatement of the century as far as he was concerned. "But like I said, it's none of my—"

"Oh, hell," Bailey said. "Of course it is. We have to work together, and unless we get the explanations out of the way now, we're going to feel awkward forever. So let me explain. Please."

"Okay," Halsey said.

"The day I made a fool of myself at Marjorie Reifel's—I was feeling pretty low after that. Like I could never be a real police officer. John invited me for a beer after work. I don't know why I agreed—he still irritated the hell out of me. But I could see he was trying to be nice, and I figured if he could make the effort, so could I." Bailey turned her mug in small circles and sighed. "Turned out we actually had fun once we stopped going for each other's throats. I invited him to my place for supper, and, well, Nicole was staying with a friend overnight, and he was really sweet and—" She raised her hands helplessly. "I don't know," she said with an exasperated expression. "Next thing I knew, it was like the movies.

"He's twenty-five, I'm forty—you know the fatal phrase that springs to mind. Old-enough-to-be etc., etc. I can't understand how it happened, but it did. He's an artist." She blushed. "I guess you know that. But I mean, a really good one. A couple of galleries in Vancouver are interested in him."

Halsey took a swallow from his mug. Bailey's eyes had a look he didn't ever recall seeing in them before—happiness, perhaps. Her next statement almost caused the coffee to go down the wrong way.

"He wants me to marry him." She smiled at his expression. "That's not going to happen, of course. It's ridiculous—two weeks ago we couldn't stand each other. I know it's not going to last, but he won't listen when I try to tell him that. He never listened before when I tried to tell him anything, and that hasn't changed."

"If you're happy together, surely that's all that matters?"

"No, it isn't all that matters, Will. We don't fit into each other's lives. There's Nicole. And John's mother. Neither would ever accept it. There'll come a time when we'll just . . . go on without each other, I guess. He doesn't realize that—he hasn't lived yet."

"Isn't that what he's doing now?" Halsey asked.

Bailey smiled. "I guess. Thanks for being so understanding, Will. I guarantee there'll be no complications on the job over this."

"You've taken leave of your senses," Iris said behind them.

Halsey leapt to his feet and whirled toward the answering machine. Bailey said something, but he raised his hand in a peremptory silencing gesture.

"No, I've finally come to them. You aren't going to do any more damage."

There was a tremendous blasting sound, followed by a clattering noise.

"What the hell are you doing here? Where's—*Oh, God!*" Connor Tarlech's voice.

Another blast. Tarlech's voice shouting in pain. The final shot, exploding before the reverberations of the previous one, had completely faded.

Halsey stood riveted, staring at the machine's plexiglass window. Bailey stood beside him, gripping his arm. The faint hissing noise signifying an empty disc resumed. Halsey felt as if he'd been standing in the shadows at the mill, watching the murders take place, unable to move or do anything to prevent them. The air seemed to shrink around them. The tiny speaker vibrated and began to produce sound again.

"What the hell am I going to do now . . . ?"

A noise behind them made Halsey turn to the doorway. Larsen had returned, his determined expression giving way to confusion as he saw the two of them transfixed, staring at the answering machine.

He looked at them curiously.

"You two okay?"

Halsey nodded, still stupefied by what he'd just heard. Bailey's hand had begun to tremble on his sleeve.

"Wasn't that Art Selby's voice I heard when I came in?" Larsen asked.

"Yes," Halsey said. "It was."

CHAPTER 33

"I didn't kill 'em, I didn't kill 'em," Selby muttered, stroking his knuckles.

He stared at the answering machine as if it were a rattler coiling toward him across the polished expanse of the council chambers table. Halsey and Bailey sat opposite, watching him silently. Selby's fingers drummed on the dark wood, then dropped from sight. Halsey leaned forward and switched the machine off.

"I've got no motive," Selby said. "There was no reason for me to kill either of them."

"What were you doing there then?" Halsey asked.

"I didn't kill them," Selby repeated.

"What are the sounds on the disc after you spoke?" Halsey demanded. "What were you doing?"

Selby drummed his fingers on the table again.

"Look, I don't have to answer any of these questions," he said. "The rest of the council will be here soon. I've got a right to my privacy."

"So you do," Halsey said. "Would you prefer we take you to the station for this? You'd be the only one in the cell there."

Selby's face flushed.

"Listen, you two-bit security guard, you'd better keep in mind who pays your—"

Halsey leaned forward and pressed the *Play* key on the answering machine, and once again Selby's voice rose into the air between them.

"Oh my God! Oh, God. What the hell am I going to do now . . . ?" The sounds of heavy objects being dragged, hoarse breathing, rumbling of wheels, frantic footsteps.

Selby jerked forward as if touched by an electric current, fumbling for the *Off* switch. The machine skidded away from him, rotating on the smooth surface as though turning its back on him in order to keep on testifying. More dragging noises, and a sound that might have been something like a sob.

"Shut it off!" Selby yelled, throwing himself back into his seat.

Halsey watched impassively, not moving. The disc finally concluded with the sound of slamming doors.

"What were you doing?" Halsey repeated.

Selby leaned forward, burying his face in his hands. His shoulders slumped. The fight had gone out of him.

"I didn't kill them," Selby muttered through his hands.

"What were you doing!" Halsey said, slamming his hand down on the table. "Can the crap and spit it out, or by God, you'll sit in jail until you do."

Bailey and Selby both jumped involuntarily when he yelled. *Haven't lost your touch, Will,* he congratulated himself.

"I was . . . arranging them," Selby said.

"*Arranging* them?" Bailey queried, clearly startled by the floral associations of the word.

"Yes, yes," Selby said impatiently. "Putting them into the wedding clothes. Getting them propped up on the float."

"But why?" Bailey asked. "You say you didn't kill them—"

"I didn't kill them!" Selby leaned forward with a fierce expression. "How many times do I have to—"

"Then why would you treat their bodies in such a sick, twisted—"

"Because it was the only way left, you stupid cow!" Selby shouted.

Bailey's face began to assume the lip-tightening, chin-jutting expression that signaled trouble, and Halsey felt it was time to intervene.

"The only way left for what?" he said, resting his hand lightly on Bailey's arm. He could feel her bristling, but she remained silent.

"To throw suspicion onto Kenneth Morland. It's obvious he killed them anyway. Everybody knew his wife screwed around with Tarlech before."

"How did you know Tarlech was at the mill again?" Halsey asked.

Selby snickered. "The honeymooners go up there to screw in the forest when they want a change from the beds in the lodge." His face assumed a repellent goatishness. "Sometimes I follow them up there; it's like a private video, you know? Anyway, I was trailing this hot Swedish broad and her stud up there and I saw Iris and Tarlech."

Selby exhaled deeply, and Halsey knew they were approaching the center of the story, as far as Selby's involvement was concerned.

"Why did you want Morland to be suspected?" Halsey asked, keeping his voice conversational.

"He found out something about Edna and me, and he was going to publish a story that would've ruined me. I knew Iris was the only one who could shut him up, so I waited for her to show up at the mill that night."

"In the jeep you stole from Marjorie Reifel," Halsey said, playing a hunch.

"Stole? I didn't steal anything. I told her I needed to check out some fishing areas around the lodge and she gave me the keys. It was darker than hell on the old logging road above the mill, and I bashed the jeep up a little.

"She knew Reifel would wonder about the damage, so she

247

cooked up a hit-and-run story." Selby's mouth stretched into a satisfied grin. "There's a lot Marjorie wouldn't care to explain to Reifel about her and me."

Bailey made a sound of disgust and Selby's smirk widened.

"And how did you figure you could get Mrs. Morland to stop her husband from publishing his story?" Halsey asked.

"I was going to threaten to tell Morland about her affair with Tarlech unless she got Morland to drop the story. When I found them both dead, that plan was out the window. The only chance then to stop Morland was if he were arrested for the murders. I thought if you were drawn a blueprint"—he glanced contemptuously at Halsey and Bailey—"you might eventually figure it out."

Halsey marveled at Selby's ignorance in thinking he could have threatened Iris. For all his bluster, Selby had been a rabbit trying to menace a python.

Bailey stirred beside him. She'd fixed on one of Selby's first remarks.

"Edna and you?" Bailey asked.

"I used to work for MFR when she and Hannah Spofford were the only two town councilors. The three of us came to an arrangement about the awarding of the timber license. They prepared a report saying Tarlech was violating some of the cutting restrictions laid down in his license."

Which explained Selena Coyle's comments that all Tarlech had been interested in were council documents around the time of the mill closure, Halsey thought. Selena had been sure Iris concocted the story about the council's chicanery to lure Tarlech back, but it now seemed likely she'd learned the truth from her husband.

"And was he violating the license restrictions?" Bailey demanded, sounding disappointed to find the relationship between Selby and Edna had been criminal rather than concupiscent.

"MFR wasn't paying me to be a boy scout," Selby said. "They wanted that license, and I had to figure some way of getting it for them. Based on Hannah and Edna's report, the Forestry Department pulled Tarlech's license and awarded it to MFR."

"That was it?" Halsey said. "They were willing to shut down a whole town without any further investigation?"

"Why not? The report came from the town's two elected representatives. And MFR had friends in official positions who were prepared to accept the report without looking too closely."

"What did Hannah and Edna get for their cooperation?" Halsey asked.

"Same as I did—ten thousand MFR shares."

"Worth nearly half a million bucks in total!" Bailey's eyes were wide. "MFR must've wanted that license bad."

"The timber's worth twenty times that," Selby said. "They got a gold mine, we got less than two hundred thousand each. MFR didn't want me around after they got the license, so I was out of a job. Buying the lodge took most of what I got, and Edna was so deep in debt her share barely helped her avoid bankruptcy."

"Do you know what Hannah Spofford did with her share?" Halsey asked.

Selby sneered. "Her will left it all to the mill workers' benevolent fund. The old bag's conscience must have got the better of her."

"Not a problem you had, obviously," Halsey said.

Selby's eyes hardened. "That doesn't change the fact that I didn't kill Morland or Tarlech."

"Oh, we know *that*," Halsey said.

Selby stared incredulously.

"Then why the hell did you keep saying I did?"

"I never said you killed anyone," Halsey said. "Lydia, did you hear me say Mr. Selby killed anyone?"

Bailey shook her head. "Nope. Don't believe I did."

"In fact, we know you didn't kill Mrs. Morland or Mr. Tarlech."

Selby looked incredulous. "I suppose next you'll tell me you know who did."

"Matter of fact, we do know," Halsey said.

"Then what the hell are you doing here questioning me?" Selby exploded. "Why aren't you arresting the murderer?"

"We're about to," Halsey said, as the door to the council chambers opened behind them.

CHAPTER 34

"Didn't expect to see you two here," Cecil Atkinson said, nodding affably at Bailey and Halsey.

Atkinson began unpacking a projector and slide trays from a box he'd carried in. He unwound the power cord from its reel and scanned the room for an outlet. After a moment he noticed the answering machine sitting in front of Halsey.

"Catching up on your messages?" he asked. "Or are you going to share some of the leads coming in with council?"

"Actually, I think you'll be interested in one of them," Halsey said.

Atkinson's expression tightened slightly, but there was no alarm showing. Selby's eyes flicked between Atkinson and Halsey.

"Really?" Atkinson's tone was casually polite. He found an outlet, plugged the projector in, and loaded the slide carousel.

"I'm just going to step out for a moment," Selby said to Halsey, making it a question, rather than a statement. Halsey nodded at Bailey, and she rose and escorted Selby to the door.

"I think I saw that young officer of yours out there," Atkinson said, halting Selby in his tracks. "Are all three of you going to be addressing council tonight?"

"Remains to be seen," Halsey said.

Bailey clamped a hand on Selby's biceps and drew him forward. Before the door closed, Halsey saw Larsen march Selby away. Bailey was back a moment later.

"Don't mind if I turn the lights out for a minute, do you?" Atkinson said, punching the wall switches behind him. The room dimmed into a quasi-twilight. He flipped the projector switch, and the end wall lit up with an architect's drawing. He gestured mock-dramatically at it.

"Ladies and gentlemen, I give you our town's newest seat of learning—the Honeymoon Falls campus of Pacific Western College. That is, if I can persuade council that having college students walking the streets will not irreparably damage the unique ambience that we so rightfully cherish."

He laughed and sat down in the chair Selby had vacated, directly opposite Halsey. The projector, situated a couple of feet to Halsey's right, poured its funnel-shaped beam of white light between them, rendering Atkinson's dark face pale as a stone idol's touched by moonlight. The slides continued to advance automatically, punctuating the silence with whirs and clicks, flooding the wall with images. Atkinson's ghostly face turned again to the answering machine.

"And what is so interesting about your messages?" he asked, the faintest hint of challenge in his voice now.

"They're not my messages," Halsey replied. "They're Kenneth Morland's."

The lines in Atkinson's face receded faintly. "Morland's messages? Why bring them here?"

"They're from Iris on the night she died," Halsey said.

The end of the room blossomed in a montage of landscaping details. Atkinson leaned forward into the light.

"I presume you intend to startle us all with amazing revelations," he said. "What can it be? New details of Iris's affairs? Her commentary on Marjorie Reifel's legendary performance vis-à-vis the infamous shopping mall incident? Or one of Iris's grotesque flayings of poor Kenneth? I'm sure it will be—"

He broke off as Halsey pressed the *play* key, and the voices on the disc rose through the motes dancing in the projector beam.

"You've taken leave of your senses," Iris said.

"No, I've finally come to them," Atkinson said. "You aren't going to do any more damage."

"Not do any more damage? That sounds like a threat, Cecil. But we both know you haven't the guts to do anything."

"You bitch. It never seems to have occurred to you that someday your turn to roast on the spit would come."

"My, my, a gun." Iris's mockery had the force of a whiplash, even when heard through the tiny speaker. "You really have gone all out with your silly melodrama. But you aren't going to do anything, and I'll tell you why—"

"Keep your hands in sight. You thought you'd finished me for good this time, didn't you? Pretending you cared about me again, demanding money when I was desperate, and promising to help me get the mill site for the College. And all along you were using my money to put Tarlech in my place."

"*Your* money? *Your* place? It's Connor's place. And all of your money comes from private investors and those cozy share-the-wealth arrangements you've got with government officials. And when the police find out what you've been up to with them, your *place* will be in jail."

"Maybe." Atkinson's voice was choked with rage. "But one thing's certain. Neither you nor Tarlech will be around to see any of it."

"I'll tell you what's certain—the whole town will laugh when they find out what a fool you've been. And they will find out, Cecil," Iris said. "Everything you've said—"

The first shot rang out, followed by Iris's gasp of pain and astonishment.

"You *fool!*" she cried.

There was a crash as her body fell. A moment later, two

more shots bracketed the sound of Tarlech's voice roaring in anger and pain, followed by the sound of footsteps moving rapidly away. Finally, there was silence.

Atkinson's face twisted into a corpse-like rictus.

"How did she do this?"

"Why were you telling her to keep her hands in sight?" Halsey asked. "What was Iris reaching for?"

"I don't know—nothing. She was groping behind her for something. She was just trying to distract me."

"She was going to show you her phone," Halsey said.

Atkinson shook his head determinedly.

"She didn't have any phone!" His fists clenched convulsively on the table.

"Oh, but she did," Halsey said. "She'd set it down on the table behind her. When her body fell backward against the table, the phone fell to the floor behind it. You'd have found it if you'd searched the area."

"She had no chance to call anyone. I never took my eyes off her."

"She made sure she positioned herself so you couldn't see the phone. All she had to do when you entered was hit the *re-dial* button. That reconnected her with the last number she'd called, which happened to be Kenneth Morland's," Halsey said. "The connection remained in place until the battery failed, nearly an hour and a half later."

"Why would she do that? She didn't know I meant to kill her—I didn't even let her see the gun until just before I shot her."

"You're right—she didn't know you were going to kill her. She did know you'd make a scene, and nothing could have appealed to her more than recording it—a companion piece for Marjorie Reifel's ravings. Once she realized your intent, she knew the only way to stop you was to show you she'd recorded your whole conversation on a disc you couldn't get at. Unfortunately for her, for once Iris misjudged her victim—you killed her before she could tell you."

"A viper to the end," Atkinson said. "Why didn't Morland give you the disc? It obviously clears him."

"He didn't realize there were more than two messages on it. Selena Coyle called as soon as she arrived home to alert him to Iris's whereabouts. Then Iris called with her alibi. Her message was followed by a lengthy silence—Iris presumably forgot to terminate the call, so about a half hour went by until she remembered and switched off. When she hit *redial*, the connection was reestablished, and your conversation began recording. The connection was still in place when Selby showed up to put the bodies on the float."

"*He* put the bodies on the float? I thought it was Morland in a fit of jealous rage. Christ, that really was sick!"

"Almost as sick as killing people," Halsey said.

"She was going to ruin me," Atkinson said. "She was like a disease you can't get rid of any other way."

The slide carousel jerked the last slide down before its beam and flashed an image up on the wall: a close-up of Cecil Atkinson, smiling broadly, the words *President, Pacific Western College* appearing at the bottom of the picture. The president's piercing eyes looked confidently back toward their originator, whose face was curiously white and blank, as though the original had been robbed of its features to create the image on the wall.

Atkinson seemed to be crumpling, folding in on himself. Halsey was marveling at Iris Morland's labyrinthine scheme.

"The woman wasn't human," Bailey said, unconsciously echoing his thoughts. "What kind of person would screw so many people just for the fun of it?"

"Iris was just playing the Castle game," Atkinson said. His voice was hollow now, the confident baritone vanquished.

"The what?" Bailey asked.

"She had a game called the Castle. You put the castle together; she pulled a lever and everything you'd built collapsed. But that was only a toy. She played the game for real with people's lives. She let me think I'd be king of the castle, but Tarlech was the lever she was going to use to bring the whole structure down on top of all of us."

"King of the castle, for God's sake," Bailey said.

"I might have known she'd win in the end." Atkinson muttered. "She always did." He glanced at the answering machine between them. "That damned machine was her own personal torture device."

"It is amazing," Halsey agreed. "She used it to torment so many people—you, your wife, Marjorie Reifel—and even to trap her killer."

"At least none of us will ever have to listen to her poisonous recordings again," Atkinson said.

"I'm afraid you will," Halsey said.

Atkinson looked at him blankly.

"In court," Halsey explained. "During your murder trial."

CHAPTER 35

Bailey's and Larsen's relationship was apparently back on track to the point where they completed each other's sentences. Right now, they were sketching the sequence of events that had led to the biggest, most scandalous series of arrests in the history of Honeymoon Falls.

"So, let's see now," Bailey mused. "Edna Sigurdson and Art Selby conspire to get Connor Tarlech's timber license in return for MFR shares, Iris finds out about it from Kenneth—"

"Iris tells Tarlech, he returns to reclaim his property—" Larsen put in.

"Selby gets word of Morland's investigation, decides to blackmail Iris to pressure Morland—"

"Meanwhile, Atkinson finds out Iris is double-crossing him with Tarlech and decides to shut her up permanently."

"He didn't plan to kill Tarlech at first, though—it was only Iris he was after," Bailey said. "He'd been following her for days, hoping to catch her alone. He probably couldn't believe his luck when he realized she was heading for the mill—a nice, isolated spot where he could settle her hash at his leisure. Then Selena Coyle drove up and he had to hide."

Larsen picked up the thread. "The minute he saw Tarlech go off with Selena, the set-up was perfect—he'd be able to finish Iris off, and his former rival would be the likely suspect. What he didn't count on was Tarlech's early return and having to kill him too."

"Leaving Selby to show up later to play bridesmaid to Iris and Tarlech in the hope of derailing Kenneth Morland's exposé—"

"Whose house is burgled for mysterious reasons . . . hmm, over to you, Officer Bailey."

Bailey inclined her head graciously. "Why, thank you, Officer Larsen. I could speculate that Selby broke in hoping to find what info Morland might have had on him. However, I believe I'll defer that issue to Chief Halsey."

"Very kind of you," Halsey said, going along with the game. "However, Morland's house wasn't burgled. In fact, the opposite of a burglary took place."

"The opposite of a burglary?" Larsen blinked doubtfully. "What's that? Someone breaks in and—"

"And *leaves* something," he finished in unison with Bailey.

"Excellent, excellent," Halsey commended. He sniffed mock-pompously. "You two are becoming quite . . . adequate."

"Leaves *what*?" Bailey demanded.

"The letter from Iris where she tells Tarlech to come back and reclaim the mill. Even before Morland denied ever seeing it, I thought it was just a little too convenient when we found that letter in his study—how could he have got hold of a letter mailed to Tarlech in Brazil? Not to mention the fact the stereo system was programmed to come on at seven A.M. and turned up to blasting level."

"You think someone planted the letter and set the stereo to draw us there?" Larsen asked. "Who would benefit from that?"

"Someone who wanted to make Morland's motive for the killings look stronger," Bailey said. "The Delbrooks were convinced Collinson was the murderer by that point, and anyway, they'd never plant evidence. But Selby admitted trying to cast suspicion on him."

"Wasn't Selby," Halsey said.

"You know who it was, don't you?" Larsen said immediately.

"Yep," Halsey said.

"Atkinson," Bailey guessed.

"Nope." Halsey leaned back with his hands behind his head.

"Tell us!" Bailey demanded.

Halsey laughed. "Mrs. Slater said she received a call from Shirley Novak asking that Morland's key be left out for her. But Shirley was working at the mall when the break-in occurred. Now Shirley could have called from the mall and asked for the key to set up a break-in for her husband, or someone else. But that didn't seem too likely. She would have known that Mrs. Slater would reveal her involvement."

"So . . . ?" Larsen prompted.

"So, at first I wondered if one of those tabloid sharks had managed to fool the old lady into thinking she was talking to Shirley. But that didn't seem logical either. Whoever impersonated Shirley had to know too many details: that Mrs. Slater had a key in the first place, when she'd be volunteering at the hospital so the caller wouldn't have to meet her, and where to ask her to leave the key. Also, they'd have to have the skill to imitate Shirley's voice well enough to fool someone who'd heard it often before. That meant it was someone local, someone acquainted with the Morlands."

"Shelagh Tarlech," Bailey said. "She believed all along Kenneth killed her son."

"And she used to be an actress who specialized in impersonations," Halsey agreed. "She found the letter among some papers Tarlech had given her for safekeeping when he returned."

"What about the break-in?" Larsen asked. "Will Morland press charges against her?"

"Not a chance. He asked me to give the letter back to her and forget about it. There's enough publicity for him to deal with as it is."

"I'll say," Bailey agreed. "Half the town is under arrest—Atkinson for two murders, plus financial diddling at the college; and Edna and Selby for corruption. I hear Peggy Atkinson filed for divorce before she left."

"Left?" Halsey asked. "To go where?"

"Apparently she got a job in Vancouver as some kind of PR director for a hotel chain. I guess now the college has gone under, she needs the money."

Halsey would have been happier to hear she'd moved to the other side of the earth, but at least she wasn't in Honeymoon Falls anymore, and he could stop dreading the moment those cold wolf eyes tracked him and Lucy for the first time.

"Thank God the trials will be held in Vancouver," Bailey said. "That should keep Delia Bendel off our doorstep, at least."

" 'Fraid not," Larsen said. "She called three times today alone. She says if Will gives her an exclusive on the story, she and Channel Five can make him a celebrity."

"Yeah, sure," Bailey said. "Now that she wants something, she's changed her tune."

"Well, looks like I've missed my chance to be a celebrity," Halsey said.

"What do you mean?" Larsen asked.

"I mean I just finished giving Lucy Mitchum an interview for All News Network explaining how the three of us solved the case," Halsey said.

Actually, Lucy had conducted quite a lengthy personal interview with him prior to the one for *ANN*, and she'd seemed highly satisfied with the responses she elicited from both. Halsey didn't know what being a celebrity was like, but he was pretty sure it didn't get any better than what he'd already experienced.

Bailey and Larsen high-fived while Halsey grinned.

"Come on, we'll celebrate. I'll buy you coffee at the Doughnut Hut," Halsey said.

"Sugared, glazed, or cream-filled?" the counter clerk asked when he stood before the glass-fronted display case in the Hut. Halsey thought of Lucy, who was all three and then some. "Just coffee," he said.

ACKNOWLEDGMENTS

I want to express my sincere thanks to Mary Daheim, Alice Duncan, Kate Kingsbury, Tamar Myers, and Liz Zelvin for making time in their busy schedules to read and comment on *Death of a Bride and Groom*. Their generosity and graciousness are unequaled and their advice invaluable. If you haven't yet had the pleasure of reading their books, don't wait any longer— you have hours of enjoyment ahead.

INVITATION TO READERS

I hope you enjoyed *Death of a Bride and Groom*, and I'm happy you chose to read my book out of all the others you might have selected. I'm at work on the next Honeymoon Falls book, which will feature the return of many in the cast of this one, along with new characters, surprises, and another unusual murder.

I'd love to hear your thoughts about the story and characters in *Death of a Bride and Groom*. Was there something that you particularly liked? Something that didn't work for you? A question you'd like answered? Visit my blog at www.allanjemerson .com and let me know.

As you probably know, there's nothing that contributes more to a book's success than a recommendation from a reader. If you liked *Death of a Bride and Groom*, please consider mentioning it to friends, your local library, and bookstore. Reviews on Amazon, Goodreads, or anywhere that features book reviews, are helpful, too.

I'm always happy to talk to groups about the Honeymoon Falls series, and writing in general, so any place books are available is welcome to contact me for appearances, either virtual or actual, depending on location.

I look forward to hearing from you, and I hope you'll want to return to Honeymoon Falls often.

Best,
Allan

ABOUT THE AUTHOR

Allan J. Emerson is a Canadian writer who was born and brought up in small towns in Saskatchewan and British Columbia. He has lived in Australia and New Zealand and, as his mother could tell you, has been making up stories since he was a little kid. He and his wife live on the west coast of Canada. Although the town of Honeymoon Falls and all its inhabitants are purely fictional, the idea of marriage and murder in close proximity came to him when he was visiting a slightly more famous honeymoon destination, Niagara Falls, and wondered about the daily lives of the permanent residents. Visit Allan at *www.allanjemerson.com.*